THE GAME OF MURDER

K. LEE BROWN

First addition published © 2022 ISBN 9798364507228

10 9 8 7 6 5 4 3 2
Paperback ISBN: 978-1-0689559-2-1
Ebook ISBN: 978-1-0689559-1-4

For my family

1

Last-ditch effort
Friday

PICKLED EGGS AND gasoline!

It was enough to bully me from the sweet dreams of Death By Chocolate and plunge me into a more pungent reality.

When I readjusted in my seat, I spotted a vintage orange Tupperware container. An educated guess led me to assume that it was *indeed* the culprit for my sudden nausea. The container rested precariously on the dashboard; the lid, however—which had no business existing apart from said container—had been forsaken in the middle of the driver's seat. I shifted toward the mysterious smell and, with reluctance, picked up the bowl. As I peered into the depths of some culinary nightmare, an odor so foul hit me in the face like a ton of bricks and had me screaming, "Whoa!" And for the second time today, I swallowed my breakfast.

I tossed the bowl back on its perch, then fell into my seat, eyes shut and nose scrunched, attempting to recover from the noxious assault. My senses were now fully awake, which made me realize I must not have been sleeping for long. When I peered through the back window and saw Quinn pumping gas into the Kia Soul, it wasn't hard to put two and two together: a menacing cloud of vapor swirling around her head like smoke, the quick puffs of air she blew into her clenched fists, the enthusiastic bouncing on the balls of her feet. It meant one thing.

It was cold.

So much for the chinook lasting throughout the weekend, I thought to myself.

I debated whether or not it was too cold to open the door for some fresh air, but I needed *something* to combat that stench. I pushed the door open and inhaled deeply, the air hitting my lungs like sandpaper. Cold and dry. Pretty typical for southern Alberta. One minute, you're basking in the warmth of a fleeting chinook wind. The next, you're kicking off your flip-flops and digging out the parkas. Although the summer-like conditions only lasted a few days, I embraced the reprieve from the harshness of the cold, long winters.

I took one last breath before shutting the door, knowing I'd be cooped up with the stench for the entire trip. Quinn opened the door a minute later and slid her petite self into the driver's seat. Her eyes widened as she retrieved the Tupperware lid from underneath her bottom. "You're awake!"

"I am," I said snidely. "Because something in that container either died a horrible death, or it's a lunch experiment gone terribly wrong. I'm guessing you meant to throw that out weeks ago but forgot?" I held my nose and pointed to the offender.

"Oh!" she said with way too much enthusiasm. "You want some? It's comfort food." Before scooping up a spoonful, she began spouting off words like they were succulent ingredients dripping off the tip of her tongue. "There's eggs, celery, cucumber, onions, black olives, mustard, hot sauce, and, last but not least, a dash of pickle juice."

I held my hand over my mouth, encouraging my breakfast to stay put. "Disgusting! Comfort food? I think not; a dish like that would be more corporal punishment if you ask me. How can you eat that stuff? Especially this early in the morning. You're not pregnant again, are you?"

"Gosh, I hope not!"

She covered the container and put it on the floor in the back of the car, fondly referred to as her organized muddle. She deemed herself an authority on all things whimsy, straddling the line between collector and pack rat but never admitting she was a hoarder. Of course, she insisted the necessary stockpile, which seemed to grow with each passing day, was pertinent to her art. And I had to admit, forming a striking sculpture using only mosaic tiles and parts from a classic Cadillac was pretty impressive. But still, so much junk. Everything from boxes of old clothes to overdo library books, not to mention blankets, sweaters, and enough water to put out a small forest fire. I knew one thing: If we ever found ourselves in an apocalyptic event, I would hope to be in the vicinity of Quinn's car.

"You dozed off fast. Haven't even made it out of Mahogany Falls."

Despite the limited space, I awkwardly stretched my long, lanky arms above my head, scraping the backs of my hands against the felt like a gorilla. "I'm not surprised. I've been so tired lately, but I just can't seem to stay asleep. I fall asleep within seconds, but my eyes pop open sometime after three. I spend the next few hours counting sheep, hoping the monotony will knock me out. Unfortunately, I'm usually wide awake to see the sunrise peeking through my window."

Tired was an understatement. Downright exhausted was more like it. Sleep eluded me for the past few nights. Tossing and turning and dwelling on the fact I couldn't come up with a suitable ending for my latest novel. Six months of smooth sailing then, boom! The proverbial wall.

I was blocked before, but this time was different. Being this unproductive for so long had me fearing my creativity had shriveled up like a raisin. Not to toot my own horn or anything, but the first twelve books were a huge success. They even became best sellers, and I would be well on my way to a thirteenth, too, if I could just nail down the ending. It was infuriating.

This trip was a last-ditch effort to inspire something resembling a literary work of art (well, in my eyes, at least). Quinn figured a girl's weekend in the mountains might be the nudge I needed to get my mind out of the clouds and back on my keyboard. What could I say? There was no better place for inspiration than a weekend of murder in a secluded lodge in Kananaskis country.

Quinn took her cell phone from the dashboard mount and began to scroll. She reached back into the hodgepodge of no return and pulled out a multicolored afghan. "Here," she said, tossing it over to me. "I picked a classical playlist 'cause I know it's your favorite. Bundle up and try to get some sleep. I'll let you know when we get there."

I wrapped the blanket over my lap and tucked it under my legs and feet. "Thanks, but I doubt I'll be able to get any sleep, but maybe I'll try writing for a bit."

"That's why you're here, right…to come up with an ending to your book?"

"Let's hope so."

"I have faith, Scarlet. I know you'll have the *inspiration*, that's for sure. By the way," she said, blatantly clearing her throat, "they don't allow cell phones."

"You're kidding?"

"Yeah, apparently, it takes away from having an authentic experience…or so I've been told."

"Authentic experience? What about my laptop?"

"Oh! I'm sure that's fine. It's not like you're going to be walking around with it. It's probably just the phones."

"How much writing will I actually get done anyway? Maybe the drive through the mountains might get me in the mood, and with any luck, I'll have a conclusion before we even get there."

Now, where was I?

2

Chase Ridgeway

Like a rudder in a speed boat, Chase Ridgeway dug his ice axe into the snow, glissading down the mountain in pursuit of his nemesis. Pushing his feet through the white powder like a plow, he lifted the axe to increase speed.

Would this be the moment? The moment he could finally put the past behind him? Ten years was long enough to watch a killer roam free.

"There's no place to run, Wells!" he shouted as he closed in on him.

He drifted down the sun-baked path with accuracy and speed, maneuvering his body over the ice and snow like he'd done it a thousand times before. Trees thrashed against his body, clawing at his flesh as if forbidding him to complete his mission. He could feel the surge of adrenalin building up with each passing second; soon, he'd be within his reach. "Almost there," he grunted, feeling the snow spray from Richard's axe.

Just a little further...

Darn, that blinking cursor, I thought as I mulled over possible reasons why I was at a standstill. Was it that Chase Ridgeway was on the verge of ending an ugly vendetta that had been a part of him for a decade? Or was it the fact that I was about to wrap up his story for good?

Was that it?

Deep down, I knew it was, and maybe that's why I was so unfocused. How was I supposed to end something that's been a part of me for so long?

I loved the fact that Chase was a charmer, a no-nonsense investigator. Millions of readers around the world loved him just as much as I did. Who was I to put a stop to it? The protagonist I created was everything I wasn't. Best-selling author or not, hiding behind the anonymity of my pen name, Harper Redstone, was where I felt safe. It comforted me that only three people knew my true identity. The rest of my small-town world only knew me as the shy, introverted housewife working part-time at The Happy Bean in Mahogany Falls.

It's not that I didn't want to be more like Chase, someone who commanded attention just by walking into a room. If I had, I might have been more inclined to reveal myself. Instead, I was the queen of unwanted captivation—usually from toppling trays of coffee mugs onto the floor. It wasn't the kind of attention I embraced; heavens, no! But definitely one I was used to. Writing about my drama was much more comfortable than starring in it.

My love for writing began in middle school, but only after an embarrassing rendition of the school play, *The Wizard of Oz*. Not only did my acting debut come to a screeching halt the moment I walked onto the stage, but Leena Hensley had to jump to my rescue after an uncomfortable bout of stage fright while portraying the character of the Cowardly Lion. Ironic, I know. One minute, I'm looking out over an audience of proud parents, enthusiastically snapping pictures with their Nikon film cameras; the next moment, I'm looking up at the ceiling, pondering why I had lost all feeling in my extremities. It was at that moment I realized the stage was not for me.

One night, while I journaled about the most embarrassing day of my life, a thought came to me. Instead of hyperfocusing on the dreadful occurrences of my day, why not write as though I were a character in a story? And just like that, a passion was born. A compelling discovery that allowed me to escape the awkward stages of adolescence by immersing myself in the intriguing conflicts I wrote about on paper. Vicariously living through these characters, I created a welcomed diversion from the day-to-day struggles of being the "weird kid."

However, when Quinn suggested I submit one of my manuscripts years later, I immediately responded, 'No.' I didn't have the stomach for that kind of rejection. Writing was for me. My stories were private, not for thousands of anonymous critics to pick apart in the privacy of their own homes. *No, thank you!*

But of course, Quinn would eventually talk me into making the call (a skill she excelled in). Before I knew it, I was having a face-to-face with Joan Rossi, sipping a Venti Americano, while introducing her to Chase Ridgeway.

"I'm convinced," said Joan, pushing her purple cat-eye glasses up the bridge of her nose, "This sounds like a great idea for a series. And if you agree to work with me, I promise I'll make it worthwhile."

While the flattery was dreadfully uncomfortable, I never thought my writing could be good enough to put out in the world. And I still believed Joan was blowing more smoke than she needed to.

"You have to do it," Quinn said. "You have to let her work with you. You never know. You could be the next big thing."

"That's what I'm afraid of," I said.

"I've never met anyone who oozes so much talent yet lacks the confidence and true grit required to be a best-selling author. You should start taking cues from your characters."

I knew Quinn was right; she usually was. It was apparent I needed to possess some of the pluck Chase exuded. Still, I also lived in the real world, where bouts of bravery consisted of serving piping hot coffee without scalding the regulars.

Although stepping out on the ledge (figuratively speaking) scared me half to death, I knew I had to try. Fortunately, per Joan's promise, I got my first book published ten years ago, selling ten thousand copies in the first month and another thirty thousand the following month, putting Harper Redstone on the New York Times Best Seller's list.

With the sudden success of my book, being thrust into the limelight was the last thing I wanted. And for this anonymity thing to work, my best friend, husband, and editor/publicist needed to keep my secret.

For the next ten years, I lived a double life. Scarlet Lane—the introverted barista of Mahogany Falls, who collected generous tips from the locals because they tended to feel sorry for her. And Harper Redstone—the mysterious, best-selling author whose novels sold more than twenty million copies worldwide and who didn't have to work another day in her life.

I was getting nowhere, staring at the blinking cursor. I removed my headphones, closed my laptop, and turned to the backseat to find something to drink.

"Whatcha looking for?" asked Quinn.

"Just thirsty. I know there's water back here somewhere—oh, wait a minute, I found it."

The case of bottled water was buried under a stack of art books, and I had to stretch out my fingers to pluck one from its plastic casing, but they were out of reach. I unbuckled my seatbelt and leaned over the heap, trying hard not to trigger an avalanche. "You want one?"

"No, I'm good," said Quinn, "I'm still nursing this coffee Brian made for me this morning."

I secured a bottle without incident and flopped back in my seat. I nearly downed half of it in one gulp.

"Guess you *were* thirsty," said Quinn, tilting her head back to drink the last bit of coffee from her thermos. But as she set her eyes back on the snow-covered road, and before I had a chance to buckle myself back into my seat, an enormous thud hit the front of the car, forcing the Inferno Red Soul into a spiral, like one of those spinning strawberries at the Calgary Stampede.

Before I knew it, the bottle flew from my hand, rotating through the air like a sprinkler. Water sprayed everywhere. I tried to move, but the force of the spin had me plastered up against the passenger side window, squishing my face into the glass like a suckerfish. I pushed myself off the door with all my strength, trying desperately to resist the pull. I grabbed the center console for dear life, hoping it would act as my lifeline.

The world spun in a hypnotic rhythm of green and white blobs: trees, snow, trees, snow. My entire life flashed on the glass like a movie playing out before me. My childhood. Friendships. My marriage. Regrets. Everything swirling in the serenity of the cyclone.

Quinn tried to get control of the car, frantically twisting the steering wheel to the left and then to the right.

"Turn into it!" I yelled.

"I'm trying," she shouted, "but the car won't stop spinning. I think we're going to crash!"

I grabbed the back of Quinn's seat with one hand and pushed against the door with the other, bracing for whatever was coming next. It was all happening so fast, but yet in slow motion. The sound I heard from the organized muddle was like a scene out of *Twister,* and the look of sheer panic splayed across Quinn's face didn't inspire confidence we'd make it out alive.

Finally, the car struck the side of the road, jolting us from its vortex and plunging us toward the ditch. Turbulent bumps battered us from side to side like we were driving through giant potholes.

"Quinn…look out for those trees!"

Barreling through the rocks and snow at a speed not recommended for the shoulder of the road, we headed straight into the darkness of the forest. I closed my eyes and prayed harder than I had ever prayed before.

"Hold on, Scarlet!"

Oh, I held on. I held on until I couldn't hold on any longer.

3

Leaping moose and buffalo plaid

IT WAS QUIET.

Limbs quivered through the towering pine trees above us, agitating the snow like crystals in a snow globe. Even the birds seemed to pause, marveling at the chaotic misfortune that careened through their peaceful habitat.

I moaned and gazed through the window, unsure where I was.

"Scarlet, you okay? Scarlet?"

I gently hoisted my head from the dashboard, gazing at the inescapable terrain. Trees surrounded the car, and we were nowhere close to the road.

I recoiled. Not because it hurt when I touched my head (although that was excruciating). But because I had just been made aware of the most unfortunate sensation running down my legs. To my dismay, not only was the bottle resting on my lap, spilling the remaining water all over my jeans, but

Quinn's disgusting egg salad container ditched its lid again and proceeded to find its way to my thighs. Needless to say, marinating in hot sauce and pickle juice was a tad unsettling.

My head hurt. My clothes reeked. And my laptop was nowhere to be found. Throbbing with every breath, I caressed the protruding lump on my head and turned to face Quinn. She was removing collateral from her body that forced its way to the front of the car.

"Besides the goose egg I have growing on the side of my head," I said, "and the fact that I feel like I've bathed in a swamp, I think I'm okay. You alright?"

She glanced at herself in the mirror, brushing debris from her shoulders. "Just a little shaken up. What was that?"

"No idea."

As if my nerves weren't frazzled enough, a tap on the driver's side window nearly rallied me into another spiral.

A brown, bushy beard and a sea of black and red plaid pressed against the driver's side window. The man frantically tapping his fingers on the glass appeared to be a lumberjack who had possibly misplaced his axe. I hoped that wasn't the case. I wasn't mentally prepared for an encounter like that in the middle of nowhere.

Quinn rolled down the window enough to hear what the man with the beard was trying to say.

"You alright, ma'am?" he repeated.

"I think so," she said, looking to me for confirmation.

"I witnessed the whole thing," said the man. "You are two lucky ladies. Did you see the size of that thing?"

No!" said Quinn. "What did we hit?"

"A moose! But you only got a bit of 'em. I've never seen anything like it. He seemed to leap right over the car as if it was nothing. Don't think you'd be talking to me right now if you'd hit 'em straight on, that's for sure. He was a big son-of-a-gun."

"Is he okay?" Quinn asked. She turned as if expecting to see the moose waiting in the trees for an apology.

"Well, he took off into those woods back there. No doubt you scared 'em. But the question is, are you guys alright? Is anybody hurt?" The man made eye contact with me.

"I'm okay. Might have a headache for the next few days, but I'm alive."

"I'm Henry, by the way," he said, focusing on the front of the car. "It doesn't look like too much damage, just a little dent. As I said before, you ladies are fortunate to be alive. I got a winch in the back of my truck. I'll have you two back on the road in no time. Where ya headed, anyway?"

"Mystery Ridge Lodge." Quinn turned to me and smiled. She'd been looking forward to this trip and had difficulty restraining her excitement.

Henry stood up straight and stroked his chin. He was big and tall and looked like a grizzly bear. His small, dark eyes were hard to find in the shagginess of his beard—which took up most of his face. And his long brown hair fell below his earlobes, which added nicely to his unkempt appearance.

His voice, however, was soft and gentle. "Oh," he said, shoving his hands deep into his pockets.

"Something we should know?" I asked.

"Not at all," he said. "It's just that...are you aware of the storm they're calling for this weekend? They say we could be gettin' close to forty centimeters by mornin', and with the strong winds they're predicting, well, we could see drifts of more than that. Can't see you gettin' too far on the roads in this little thing."

"Hopefully, it'll clear up by Sunday," Quinn said. "We're spending the next three days up there for a murder mystery."

"Oh, I'm well aware of what goes on up there," he said, looking up toward the mountains. "Well, enough yappin'. Let me get you back on your way."

"That's a pretty big truck you got there," I said, looking back at the giant black monstrosity. "I'm glad you were nearby."

"Sure is. Can usually get this bad boy to tackle any road— no matter what the weather throws at it." Henry stomped back to the truck, then turned and shouted, "Sit tight, be back in a minute."

BY THE TIME HENRY PULLED us out of the ditch and back onto the road, it was almost nine o'clock. I had hoped to get to the lodge early before anyone else could check in. If we hurried, we could still have had plenty of time to register and unpack before the game started.

Quinn looked relatively tranquil for having survived a near-death experience involving a moose, and her spirits hadn't dulled one bit.

"Good thing he showed up, eh?"

"What?"

"Henry. It's a good thing he showed up with that big truck."

"I guess," I said. "Interesting, though, how he got to us so quick, don't you think?"

"What do you mean?"

"I mean, I didn't see anyone following us before we started to spin. Where did he even come from? And how did he get to us so fast?"

"Maybe he came from one of those side roads back there or something, not sure…but I know one thing: if he hadn't been following us, we'd still be stuck in that ditch."

"Didn't you find his reaction strange when you told him we were spending the weekend at the lodge?"

"Oh, Scarlet, you and your cynical mind. Henry's a Good Samaritan, that's all. He happened to be driving behind us. For once, take the win without reading too much into it. I'm sure he was just in the right place at the right time."

I looked out the back window. Henry had already turned the truck around and was heading in the opposite direction. The tires alone were almost bigger than Quinn's car. Henry seemed nice enough, and I shouldn't have been suspicious of someone who had just pulled us out of a snow bank.

"You're right, Quinn," I said. "Henry was just in the right place at the right time."

4

There's something strange about the butler

NINETY MINUTES LATER, we began our descent into a wintry Shangri-La. After Quinn parked the car, I got out and slowly opened the back door, hoping the fury of clutter in the back seat wouldn't attack me. I was surprised when it didn't and even more surprised to see my suitcase impressively balancing on one of Quinn's art pieces. "How does she come up with this stuff?"

I scanned the backseat for my laptop and spotted it on the other side of the car. It landed on the floor between a stack of sweaters and the case of bottled water. I quickly assessed the laptop from top to bottom, concluding it survived unscathed.

As I began the trek up the cobblestone path, my small, red valise wobbling alongside me, I relished every charming detail nature had to offer. It was breathtaking. The freshly fallen snow couldn't have been more magical—like a sea of crystals shimmering in the sunlight. I stopped to see if Quinn was behind me, but she was still rummaging through the mess in the back seat. More than likely, deciding which items were essential for the next few days.

I yawned and stretched my arms above my head. It was good to stand, and the *crack, crack, crack* was satisfying, even though my head felt like a kick drum.

"Everything okay back there?" I said, shielding my eyes from the sun glaring off the snow.

"I'm coming."

She sprinted up the shoveled pathway, tufts of blonde hair blowing through the holes in her bright pink toque. Although we both turned forty a couple of months ago, I was amazed at how much younger Quinn seemed; she was like a college student ready to take on the world. I, on the other hand, barely had enough energy to bend down and tie my shoes.

"It's so gorgeous here!" said Quinn.

"Isn't it? I can't wait to see the inside of this place."

We scuffled along the walkway and took in the majestic surroundings. From the outside, the lodge was magnificent, an impressive dwelling of natural wood and stone resting beneath the shadows of the Rocky Mountains. It was like something out of a magazine. Scanning the property from left to right, I let myself soak in the spectacular views. "This must be awesome in the summer as well," I said, peering out over the cracks in the frozen lake, which were like ghostly webs knitted together beneath a turquoise prison.

I gazed into the myriad of trees surrounding the property. There was a chill. It swept through the dense forest, inspiring a dubious breeze to rustle the limbs of the trees as though they were saying hello. Something in the air made my skin crawl; I couldn't be sure if it was the weather or something more ominous.

We stood in awe for a minute before Quinn let out a squeal. "You excited?"

"Well, I don't know if I'm as excited as you are, but I am looking forward to some inspiration sprinkled with a little relaxation." I tugged at the side of my jeans. "But mostly, I'm anxious to get out of these clothes. I smell like a rotten pickle."

Quinn scrunched her nose in agreement. "Maybe you can forget about your book this weekend and...have a little fun?"

The question was delicate. I was up against a deadline, and Quinn knew I was a little on edge. Finishing my book was my only priority. But I couldn't fault her for attempting to get me to relax. "I'll try," I said begrudgingly.

I rummaged through my purse, trying to locate my phone. "I should probably text Dominic to tell him we made it safe and sound. I won't tell him about the accident until we get back home. Don't need him worrying about me the whole time we're away."

OUR LUGGAGE CLUNKED BEHIND US as we climbed the stairs leading to the lodge. We had to stop once we reached the landing to gaze at the impressive ten-foot doors. Carved with a skillful array of nature and most likely made of solid oak, the entrance had me wondering if the rest of the lodge would be as welcoming.

I reached for the knotted branch handle as though I were about to shake hands with a mighty oak tree when a tall, handsome man dressed like a resident from *Downton Abby* pushed the door open wide.

"Welcome to Mystery Ridge Lodge," he said.

I didn't *want* to be pulled in by his handsomeness. However, to my chagrin, I failed miserably. I looked into his eyes (like melted pools of chocolate, by the way), wondering why a man of such beauty would be working in a place like this. He was more than qualified to portray some hot doctor role on one of those ridiculous TV shows.

What was it about this man? I wondered. While my eyes drifted toward his licorice-coiled hair, I realized I hadn't acknowledged his greeting.

"Oh! Ah...hi." I was annoyed those were the only three words that managed to fall out of my mouth.

"You alright?" Quinn whispered.

"I'm fine," I said through gritted teeth.

"I'm Caffrey. I'll be your butler this weekend. If you have any questions, please don't hesitate to ask." He reached for our luggage and walked inside before we could respond. He was a no-nonsense butler. No chit-chatting for this guy, I thought to myself.

"Well," said Quinn, "I do have one—"

"The manager is this way," said Caffrey rather abruptly. "Hope you've come prepared for a storm. Looks like the weather's about to change."

"Oh, we're prepared, alright, and if we need anything, I'm sure we can find it in Quinn's car."

She gave me a quick elbow to the ribs. "You can laugh, Scarlet, but I'm sure you'll be glad I packed a few extra sweaters once the temperature plummets."

Caffrey stood there. Expressionless. I thought about how difficult it would be to break him from the deadpan character he so expertly perfected. The guards at Buckingham Palace came to mind.

He nodded toward the reception desk. "Follow me," he said, leading the way.

"He certainly is tall," I whispered.

"Not to mention extremely gorgeous. Did you notice the butler's eyes?"

Of course, I noticed his eyes.

And then I suddenly felt guilty for noticing the butler's eyes. "I did. But don't forget, you are a married woman?"

"I know…and so are you."

"And happily at that," I said. "If you ask me, I found him a little frigid."

"I'm sure it's his character. It is a murder mystery weekend, after all."

"Right, a murder mystery." I had to keep reminding myself that I was participating in an interactive weekend to help me recover from my creative standstill.

Joan still didn't know I'd taken a few days off to regroup and probably wouldn't be thrilled, considering the release date was a mere month away. But Joan would have to deal with it. I needed this; my book *required* this. Besides, I sensed the ignition of creative juices revving through my brain the instant we drove onto the property.

While Caffrey stepped aside, allowing us to register, I glanced down at my jeans before checking in. I had hoped the pickled mess that drenched them earlier had at least dried to an acceptable shade of green. I couldn't wait to jump into a hot shower and rid myself of the funk.

"Welcome," said the short little man behind an exquisite antique desk. "Welcome to Mystery Ridge Lodge."

The English burr that rumbled out of the man took me by surprise. A strange dichotomy between a sultry, baritone voice and a short, bulbous stature was somewhat perplexing, like Danny de Vito lip-syncing to a British James Earl Jones.

Before speaking again, a devious smile spilled over his face, thrusting his florid cheeks upward, nearly burying his already narrow eyes into slits. "I'm the lodge manager, Harrison Hightower." He closed his eyes and placed his fingers on his temples, implying, for some reason, he had psychic abilities. "Let's see." He paused dramatically. "Scarlet Lane and Quinn Monroe?"

"Impressive," Quinn said sarcastically.

He smiled. "Well, since you are the only two ladies registering together this weekend, I decided to venture a guess." He chuckled.

He fiddled with the knot in his houndstooth bow tie that seemed visibly uncomfortable. It was most likely made of wool, like the rest of his ensemble—brown, itchy wool.

He reached for a piece of brightly colored paper and slid it across the desk. "Here is the itinerary for this weekend's festivities. But first things first,"—he peered over his wire-rimmed glasses—"I must ask you to hand over your cell phones. I'm sure you've been informed of our little rule here at Mystery Ridge?"

"Yes, we have," said Quinn. "But do you have to take away our phones? Can't we leave them in our rooms?"

"We tried that. Unfortunately, no matter how often we stress our no phones policy, someone always pulls one out, desperately needing to inquire about something of utmost importance. Like the weather, the score of the hockey game, or the number of likes on a plate of waffles posted minutes prior. However, since we've decided to store the phones in the safe, guests tend to participate without added distraction. And if truth be told, the separation can be quite liberating."

"What about my laptop?" I asked, "I would love to get some work done if there's any free time this weekend. Is it alright if I keep it with me in my room?"

"You are more than welcome to take your laptop with you. However, you may feel more comfortable leaving it with your phone in the safe." He waved his hand toward a red metal box on the floor. "Unfortunately, there are no safes in the rooms."

I thought about how much writing I would get done. The point of the trip was to clear my mind and soak up as much inspiration as possible. "Well, I guess it might be a good idea to keep it in the safe. My whole life is on this thing." I hesitated before handing it to him. "I can always come down and get it if I need to, right?"

"Certainly, Mrs. Lane."

Harrison took the phones and laptop, placed them in the safe, and shut the door. He stuck two fingers inside his vest pocket and pulled out a small key. After locking the safe, he returned the key to his pocket and tapped his chest as though it were the safest place in the world.

I glanced at Quinn to see if she was experiencing the same uneasy feeling. I was all for authenticity, but this was the twenty-first century. There were much better ways to store valuables, and a key in the pocket of a short little man didn't sound all that secure to me. Joan would have my head if anything were to happen to that laptop.

Quinn gave me a nudge and smiled. "It'll be fine."

"Right, then," said Harrison, "you're free to change into your costumes. I assumed you've both read up on your characters?"

"We have," said Quinn. "We're really excited."

"Right. Once you've finished getting ready and unpacked, you can come to the den, where coffee and strudel will be served. Some of the guests have already arrived." He craned his head around us. "I'm sure they will be down shortly."

I was happy that we weren't the last to arrive. I hated being late for things. "I don't suppose you know when the murder will occur?" Patience was not my virtue.

"Now, Mrs. Lane, that would take all the fun out of the mystery."

"Just trying to get an idea of what to expect." I was a natural planner who liked to know what was around every corner—always prepared and never one to improvise. I would plan my own surprise parties if I could.

"You'll be pleased to know that Sébastien, our chef, is providing a wonderful three-course meal for our dinner this evening. He is a world-renowned French chef who joined our Mystery Ridge family several years back. I'm sure you'll enjoy whatever he has prepared. Rebecca, his junior chef, will be assisting him."

He paused to wipe his brow. Beads of sweat trickled down his temple, leaving trails of orange streaks. I figured it was from the stage makeup. I could see how he'd be warm. He had to be toasty, between the head-to-toe wool he was sporting and the fire burning in the other room.

Harrison tapped a bell on the desk to summon back the butler, even though he was standing right behind us. "But for now, Caffrey will show you to your room, where you can slip into your costumes. We ask that you stay in character until the mystery is solved. Here are your room keys," he said, sliding two skeleton keys across the desk.

"Wow!" said Quinn. She held the key in her palm, bouncing it up and down. "No chance of me losing this bad boy."

"Well, if you do, the maid always keeps a spare key to each room. These will open the yellow door, as you can see by the yellow tassel at the end of your keys."

"Interesting," Quinn said, swinging her purse over her shoulder. "Guess we've gone back in time."

"Have a pleasant stay and…happy solving."

Caffrey grabbed the luggage and headed to the stairs. As we followed him down the hallway to our room, taking in the sights and smells of the cozy, out-of-the-way lodge, I was convinced I could have an ending to my book by the end of the weekend, with or without my laptop.

5

Gretchen

GRETCHEN BURKE GRABBED the large Gucci bag from the seat beside her and placed it on her lap. After combing through too many age-reducing cosmetics, she pulled out her favorite lipstick. She kept one eye on the mirror and one on the road (she wasn't planning on driving herself into a ditch today) and applied a generous coat of apple-red wax to her Botox-infused lips. Not that lipstick would seal the deal, but it did help in bringing a look together.

She glanced in the rearview mirror and sighed at the fifty-year-old woman looking back at her. It was all but impossible not to acknowledge the early signs of aging. She brushed a lock of bottled blonde hair away from her face, attempting to ignore the newly discovered pleats beneath her eyes. It was infuriating; just as she'd remedy one wrinkle, another would pop up someplace else. She had come to grips with the fact that aging with grace was not in the cards, but it didn't mean she'd have to accept it wholeheartedly. It translated into more of a labor of love: a new wrinkle here, a chin hair there, coloring pesky grey hair every six weeks. Inject. Pluck. Dye. Repeat.

She had been driving for the past hour on snow-covered roads with nothing but trees on either side, and it was beginning to feel like she would never see civilization again. Everything was white. But moments later, she spotted a sign that promised some hope. "Finally," she said, slowing down to make the turn.

Mystery Ridge Lodge 30 km.

She huffed and settled in for another stretch of driving. "How much more out-of-the-way can this place be?" she said, unwrapping a stick of gum.

As she continued down the colorless road, her mind began to wonder. The future seemed surprisingly bright now that she was single again. Not something she anticipated so soon after she said, "I do." But what did she expect, jumping into a marriage after only a few short months of dating? Did they even know each other? It takes months, or even years, to really know someone, she said convincingly to herself. Of course, she felt terrible for the way she left things. But what was she supposed to do? Live in a fun-less marriage? She was still young and had plenty of life to live. He must have realized that it wasn't working out. He *must* have known.

Gretchen caught a glance of herself in the mirror. She wished her reflection didn't look so tormented, but she did what she had to do, and no amount of second-guessing herself would change anything. She hoped that Thomas understood why she had to go, and maybe someday she'd be able to forgive herself for leaving.

The past was the past, and she was determined not to let the old life keep her from the new.

She spotted another sign up ahead and was grateful that her journey had finally ended. The white wilderness that had surrounded her (for what seemed like an eternity) had opened up to an idyllic hideaway, which was the perfect backdrop for murder.

It was time to get into character.

After finding the best parking space, Gretchen tightened her scarf and checked the mirror for one last touch-up. "Perfect." She opened the back door to a very large, very pink Louis Vuitton suitcase. It was a gift to herself—something to ease the pain from the recent separation. Of course, Louis could never take the place of Thomas. She smiled.

But it does help alleviate the anguish a little.

She placed a pair of Versace sunglasses over her icy blue eyes and proceeded down the path. But before heading up the stairs, she paused. Just how challenging would this be? she thought. She mentally calculated how daintily she could drag the pink baggage up the steps while remaining fabulous.

"May I help you with your luggage, ma'am?"

The voice came from a handsome stranger at the top of the stairs. But certainly, he couldn't be speaking to her. "Ma'am?" she said under her breath.

"Do you need any help down there, ma'am?" he repeated. He began walking down the stairs to greet her.

"It's Gretchen, Gretchen Burke." She involuntarily flared her nostrils.

"Of course," he said. He stood tall and folded his hands behind his back.

"I'm guessing you're the butler?"

"Yes, my name is Caffrey," he said, attempting to reach for her luggage."

She quickly swatted his hand away like a pesky fly. "I can manage." After all, she wasn't some feeble damsel in distress who needed help from a man, no matter how handsome he was.

"My apologies. I'm sure you're quite capable." The butler's eyes fell away like a child scolded for stealing a cookie before dinner. *Obviously*, he was intimidated by her appearance. In her opinion, beauty was as much a curse as a blessing.

Caffrey stepped aside, allowing Gretchen to haul her suitcase up the stairs. As clumsy as her ascent was, she arrived at the top in one piece. Steadying herself, she reached for the handle, but the butler beat her to it. "Allow me to get that for you, ma'am—ah, Mrs. Burke."

"It's Ms.," she said, pushing past him. She sashayed into the lobby, surveying the rustic retreat she'd spend the next three days in. Vintage furniture, vaulted ceilings, intriguing characters, it was as though she had stepped through the pages of an Agatha Christie novel.

The lobby was bright and open, and she couldn't help but appreciate the staircase leading to the second floor. A bit battered for her taste, but quite a centerpiece, nonetheless.

Outside the lobby was a cozy-looking room with floor-to-ceiling windows and a wood-burning fireplace. "Hmm," she said, catching sight of two women sitting expectantly on a rich burgundy sofa. They were already primped and looking eager to get started.

Once checked in, she started up the stairs. However, the warmth was too much to ignore, and she was immediately summoned back down. At the very least, she should make an entrance.

She was immediately drawn to the fireplace. Encased in a kaleidoscope of river rocks of varying shapes and colors, it greeted her with the fervidness that only a well-kept fire could. She stretched out her hands, careful not to get too close, and allowed the warmth to embrace her. She closed her eyes and thought of Thomas. Did she make a mistake in leaving? Had she hoped for a different outcome? Of course, but she had to believe it was for the best.

She rubbed the itch from her eyes as she gained her composure. She had to forget about Thomas for now. This weekend was about her: a new life, a fresh challenge, and a thrilling adventure in the mountains.

She turned around and quickly discovered that she'd been daydreaming in front of the two ladies on the sofa. They looked eager to meet her, but she needed to change first if she expected them to experience the complete authenticity of her character.

They would have to wait.

Gretchen turned without a glance and strutted out of the den and up the stairs.

6

Elenor

ELENOR WALLACE PULLED back the heavy, velvet curtains to a breathtaking panorama below as she waited for Sam to put the luggage on the bed. She peered at the bruised sky in the distance and gently massaged her knuckles. Between the billowing grey clouds choking out the azure sky over the mountains and the pain creeping through her joints, a storm was inevitable. But for now, she enjoyed the sun's brilliance, which continued to beam a warm, welcoming glow across the hardwood floor.

"We should probably get dressed, don't you think, hun?" she said, attempting to break Sam from a trance.

"Ugh!"

She wasn't surprised that Sam was so pooped. Ever since his retirement a few years back, they'd been on one excursion after another. Whatever exciting adventure he could think up, they would do. Last year was a cruise across the Atlantic. The year before that was a wine-tasting tour in the Tuscany vineyards of Italy. Sure, she loved traveling to different worlds —learning foreign languages, experiencing new foods, and meeting new people. Still, she found it harder and harder to recover from the frequent flying, cruising, and driving that Sam insisted on taking every few months.

Retirement was exhausting.

They decided to begin their winter vacation with a suggestion from Maurine, Elenor's closest and dearest friend.

"You have to go," Maurine said. "You and Sam will love it. Frank and I have done it twice now, and it's a new experience each time we go. The food is divine. You'll meet so many interesting people and leave there making enough memories to keep you scrapbooking for months."

"How do you know who will be murdered?" The question sounded absurd when Elenor spoke it out loud.

"Oh, they have all that worked out before you get there, dear. Once registered, they'll send you an information packet. You'll know who your character is and if you're the murderer or the victim. Of course, you can't tell Sam. He might be the killer." She laughed. "There are also great suggestions on what to wear for a costume. It's an absolute hoot."

Years of hearing Maurine blather on and on about how much fun she and Frank had participating in that murder mystery finally convinced Elenor she at least had to go see what all the hubbub was about. Sam had a brother who lived an hour outside of Revelstoke whom he hadn't seen in years, and he figured they could stop and do the murder mystery before heading out to see him: two birds, one stone.

Sam picked up the stethoscope from his suitcase and placed it around his neck. He wobbled over to the mirror above an antique desk and chair. "How do I look?" he said, examining himself.

"Well, well," Elenor swooned. "Maybe you should consider a career in medicine."

"A little late for that. Can't see any universities jumping at the chance to enroll a sixty-seven-year-old retired cop wanting a career change." He climbed into a long white coat and raked his fingers through the remaining white strands loitering on his head. He rested his glasses on the bridge of his nose (which was as thick and crooked as the burls on a maple tree) and returned his gaze to the man in the mirror. "How did I get so old?"

Elenor toddled up behind him, taking his hand in hers; they were sprinkled in just as many liver spots as her own. She spoke to his reflection. "You are not old, my dear. You are classic and seasoned, rooted in experience and wisdom like no one I know. Your charm, albeit an acquired taste, is what I love the most about you—a gruff exterior with a soft gooey center." She nudged her finger gently against his belly.

He pulled her toward him, squeezing her tight. She fit perfectly under his chin. "I love you," he said.

"Love you, too. This weekend should be a lot of fun."

"Well, you better get dressed, Mrs. Wallace, so we can get this party started. I think you'll make a wonderful lounge singer."

She laughed. "It's too bad I can't carry a tune."

"Let's hope they don't ask you to try."

7

The facade

I OPENED MY jewelry case and pulled out a long strand of pearls my mother had given me before she died. She'd always said that my wardrobe needed a bit of class. And although my wardrobe had no business consorting with the likes of pearls, they held sentimental value. However, I never felt there was an appropriate occasion to wear them—until now. I slipped the pearls over my head, letting them fall over a silky cream blouse I'd chosen for my costume. It added a perfect touch of class.

As I studied myself in the bathroom mirror, a reflection of my mother looked back at me. My unruly, red hair—the pivotal basis for my insecure adolescence—was something I had inherited from my mother. And it was the first thing people noticed—red hair.

While my mother's fiery disposition usually got the best of her, I didn't usually lose my temper. I couldn't bear the thought of living up to that cliché. My fits of rage were reserved for Flames games and lost shipments of coffee at The Happy Bean.

I grabbed the brush from the side of the sink and arranged my mane into a stylish updo, indicative of the era in which the game took place. The lipstick (I vowed I'd never be caught dead in) was still in a bag wrapped in plastic. It's all part of the ruse, I told myself. I slathered the color onto my thin, pale lips, changing them from ashen pink to blood red, and after blotting out the intensity with a tissue, my thoughts turned to Dominic.

Why didn't he pick up? Was he ignoring me? Maybe I shouldn't have left without saying goodbye.

"Whoa!" said Quinn, pulling me back to the present. "Now those are some red lips."

"Too much?"

"No! Not at all. It's nice to see you with a little color on your face. It looks great."

"You think so? I feel like my hair isn't the only thing on fire."

"Nonsense! Embrace it. You are not Scarlet Lane, the barista, this weekend. You are Mrs. Lane, the heiress to Preston Lane, the billionaire. You never know. You might find this new side of you exhilarating and want to try it out back home."

"Well, I doubt that, but I must admit I feel like someone else has taken over my body."

"You're distracted…what's going on?"

I could never hide anything from Quinn, even if I wanted to. "It's nothing. I wasn't able to get a hold of Dominic."

"I'm sure he's fine."

"Oh, I have no doubt he is. We had a fight last night, and I feel guilty for leaving without saying goodbye. I regretted it as soon as I left the house. But my pride got the best of me like it usually does, and I guess I just wanted to stay angry."

"You could always try him again?"

Quinn skirted around her bed and picked up the rotary phone I hadn't seen since I was a kid. Oh, the aggravation of talking on a phone with a cord long enough to stretch down our street. Every ten minutes, someone yells, "Get off the phone, it's my turn!"

But I digress.

"Here," said Quinn.

I took the phone and began dialing numbers. "Maybe he's already called my cell." I sat on the bed and listened to four rings go in before leaving another message. "Hi, it's me... again. I wanted to let you know you probably won't be able to reach Quinn or me on our cells. If you need us, you can always call the lodge. I've left the number on the fridge. Okay, then, love you."

"Still no answer?"

"No. I'm guessing he's still angry."

"Or maybe he's at work and can't answer his phone. I'm sure everything's fine."

"You're right."

"You about ready to go down? I can smell the coffee from here. I know *I* could use another pick-me-up after that tumultuous ride in."

I smiled in agreement, finally noticing her costume. "Nerd alert!"

"What? You don't think I look like a sexy reporter?"

"Oh, was *that* the look you were going for?"

"Alright, Miss Hoity-toity, let's go mingle."

QUINN NODDED TOWARD the lobby. "Get a load of her."

I uncrossed my legs and leaned forward to get a better look. The woman was well put together: dark sunglasses, leather knee-high boots, and a long cashmere coat adorned with a fur collar. I couldn't tell if it was *real* fur. Still, I assumed it was to coordinate with her extravagant accessories.

As I stared at her boots, surmising whether or not they were designer or store-bought, she suddenly looked my way. I quickly slumped back in my seat.

With amusing theatrics, the woman struggled to get her luggage up the stairs. Then, she abruptly stopped. I hoped it wasn't because she caught me staring again (that would have been embarrassing), but I couldn't help but admire her outfit. It was expensive. From what I could gather, the luggage alone was more than my monthly salary at The Happy Bean. Not that I couldn't afford something like that; I most definitely could. Just not that pink.

When *Miss Glamor* (the name I decided to use until formally introduced) backtracked down the stairs, I thought her humongous suitcase might run her over. But after a few quick strides, she managed to avoid a collision and continued into the den. She planted herself at the fireplace, stretching out her arms like she was waiting for a hug. And after dallying for a few minutes, she turned around, and that's when I noticed her eyes. They were red and puffy. *Was she crying?* She gazed up to the ceiling and let out a dramatic sigh like she was rehearsing a scene for our benefit. To top things off, she left without saying a word. Not even a smile. She was in her own little world, and we were her audience. I admit I was envious of her confidence but irritated that she left without an introduction. Who does that?

"That was weird," said Quinn.

"Yep. And a little mysterious, too. I wonder who she's supposed to be."

"Someone with an attitude problem would be my guess. I could picture a movie star or a jilted lover."

"Maybe she recently inherited a large sum of money."

"Ooh," said Quinn, "Guess we'll find out soon enough. But whoever she's playing, I don't think I'll like her much."

"She does seem to have the snobbery persona down. Perhaps she's already in character."

"Or maybe she's not acting at all."

I turned toward the window and held up my finger. "Do you hear that?"

"What?"

"Don't you hear that yelling?" I got up and pulled back the curtain to see two people arguing. The woman was petite, with long, dark hair, and young; she seemed to be doing most of the shouting. Her opponent was huge and built like a linebacker. He was well over six feet, and from the silver splinters shimmering throughout the stubble in his beard, he appeared much older, too.

Quinn peeked through the curtain on the other side of the window. "It's getting heated out there."

"Agreed. If he dies, we'll know who to question first."

8

Jason

MADELINE PARRISH SLAMMED the door as hard as she could, nearly trapping her long-knitted scarf inside. "You don't even care what I think, do you? The fact that you sprung this on me—while driving up here I might add—proves you don't! How could you possibly think I'd be okay with a murder mystery weekend, freezing my butt off in the middle of nowhere? We should be on our way to Hawaii like we planned!"

Jason continued to let her ramble on, knowing it was hopeless to think he'd be able to calm her down any time soon. This was not the reaction he was expecting when he decided to surprise her with a romantic weekend in the mountains. Was she hoping to go to Hawaii for their fifth anniversary? Sure. And maybe he neglected to think things through before accepting the job and allowing her to believe they were driving to the airport to board a seven-hour flight to paradise. His mistake. He realized that now. The car ride up affirmed as much.

"And another thing," she continued. "What am I supposed to wear while I'm here? I packed for plus thirty degrees, not minus thirty. Do you realize I bought three new bikinis, hoping I'd be sprawled out on the beach tomorrow? No, you didn't!"

Jason opened up the back door and grabbed a huge black duffle bag. He smiled at the thought of fitting all his stuff and Madeline's things into one big bag. He shut the door and walked around the SUV, grabbing his wife by the hand and nudging her up the path while she blathered on.

"You must have known how much I was looking forward to Hawaii. I've only been talking about it for the past three months. What were you thinking?"

"Listen, hun"—he entwined his fingers with hers—"I'm sorry I deceived you. But to my credit, I was trying to be spontaneous like you've always wanted me to be. I had hoped you'd be surprised." He chuckled. "And I think I achieved that."

"Jason—"

"Madeline, can you please try and have a good time? I promise I will make it up to you. Maybe we can even take our trip to Hawaii in a few months."

"Really?"

Oh, here we go, he thought to himself. Madeline's full raspberry pout was not at all endearing. He'd become accustomed to her manipulation; the pout was the latest tool. Frankly, he didn't know how much more of her immaturity he could take. Something he didn't consider when marrying someone eighteen years his junior.

"It depends on how long the Whitmore job is…then maybe. But I can't make any promises."

"I'm getting pretty sick and tired of Mr. Whitmore, whom I've yet to meet, by the way." She yanked her hand away and folded her arms. She had the nerve to emphasize her sulk by stomping her foot. "And what am I supposed to do while you're out babysitting some billionaire?"

"Is that what you think I do?"

"No—it's just that—"

"You know *he's* the one footing the bill for this weekend, don't you?"

"Oh, that's who I gotta thank for this Siberian retreat!"

"I wish you'd show a little gratitude once in a while, Mads. Mr. Whitmore was kind enough to invite us to a weekend in the mountains. So what if it's a murder mystery? He seemed to think we'd enjoy ourselves. Sorry if you don't feel the same way."

"I'm sorry—"

"Let's go inside and get registered. We'll talk about this later."

She grabbed the waist of his coat as he walked away from her. "Jason…I'm sorry."

"I said we'll talk about it later!" He yanked his jacket away, nearly breaking one of her perfectly manicured nails. He was beginning to think it might have been a mistake to bring her along, especially since he had work to do.

"YOU MUST BE Jason and Madeline Parrish," Harrison said, clearly sensing their tension.

"We are," said Jason. "Nice place you got here."

"Thank you." Harrison grinned. "It's been around for many years. A few renovations here and there to make sure it's up to code, and a few upgrades, of course, but for the most part, it's as it was in the early nineteen hundreds."

"I can't seem to get my phone to work," Madeline said, disregarding Harrison's history lesson, her arms crossed in defiance.

Unfortunately, Jason had just realized he'd forgotten to inform his millennial wife that she'd have to give up her phone for the next three days. What was she going to do with herself now? Every few minutes, it seemed, she was posting something on Instagram: the heart made from foam in her latte, a selfie with the pink shirt, a selfie with the coat over top of the pink shirt, not to mention the umpteen shots of the mountains on the way up here.

He knew this wasn't going to be fun.

"Uh, hun?" He placed an arm around her waist and spoke to her as gently as possible, as though talking her off a ledge. "It's going to be okay, but they don't allow cell phones during the weekend mysteries."

She glared at him, eyebrows raised in defiance. "What do you mean no cell phones? How are we supposed to survive with no means of communication? What is this, the twentieth century?

"Why yes," Harrison interjected. "You'll notice the decor we've chosen here at the lodge depicts that era. Of course, it would be rather foolish if we were to permit the use of electronic devices now, wouldn't it? We feel it's part of the charm. However, there are landlines in each room, one here and one in the library if you need to make a phone call."

Jason wasn't sure why he was so surprised at the way Madeline was acting. He had seen it so often that he just grew accustomed to it. But this was embarrassing. "I'm sure we'll survive," he said, forcing his face to smile.

"The cell reception isn't that great, as it turns out," said Harrison. "You tend to have to walk up the mountain a bit, past the Paper Birch trees. Caffrey will show you where when he takes you on the tour."

"A tour?" said Madeline, exaggerating an eye roll. "Great."

Jason grabbed her hand and squeezed. She was like an unruly child in church.

While overlooking her childish behavior, Harrison tugged at the chain of his antique pocket watch; he flipped it open to check the time. "Which should be within the hour." He tucked the timepiece back into his vest pocket. "We're waiting on one last guest to arrive. Once everyone is in costume, Caffrey will begin the tour."

"It smells good in here," Jason said. "I've been up since five and still haven't eaten a thing."

"Ah, yes. After you've settled in, you can join the other guests in the den for strudel and coffee."

"Sounds good to me." Jason wrapped his arm around Madeline and nudged her to the stairs.

9

Truman

TRUMAN GLADSTONE FLAILED his phone about his head as though bees were on the attack.

"Great! No bars!"

He shoved the phone into his pocket and slammed the car door, nearly falling flat on his face. "Whoa!" he said, grabbing the roof for support. He looked down at his feet and realized it was his own fault for wearing dress shoes in icy conditions. Not the wisest decision he'd made today. He opened the trunk, grabbed a pair of winter boots and a small suitcase and garment bag, checked his phone for the last time, and headed up the path.

He wasn't sure what to expect, booking the trip at the last minute. Usually, his assignments came with a full itinerary. But this one was different. Details were light. And he knew the job would take a little finessing if it were to be done right.

He zipped his coat up to his chin and proceeded toward the stairs, grateful he was spending time indoors, hopefully by a fire.

After a quick introduction, Truman frantically waved his phone in Caffrey's face. "Is it true you must take my phone for the entire weekend?"

"It's a couple of days," said the butler. "There's a phone in your room if you insist on contacting anyone while you're here. I'm sure you've left instructions in case someone needs to reach you?"

"I have, but I'd rather keep my phone with me. I've grown accustomed to having it at arm's length."

"Think of it as freedom. By tomorrow, you won't even miss it."

"Somehow, I doubt that."

"May I take your luggage to your room?"

"Nah, I think I can manage."

"Enjoy your stay, Mr. Gladstone."

"I'm sure I will."

TRUMAN'S SHOES CLACKED on the weathered hardwood as he approached his room. He jiggled the skeleton key into the lock and entered through a muddy brown door.

If memory served him correctly, the lodge had been the setting for murder mysteries for almost twenty-five years. The plot wasn't the only puzzle Truman was here to solve. For years, the owner of Mystery Ridge Lodge had succeeded in keeping a low profile, living life as an affluent recluse. It was unheard of. To leave such an obscure imprint in the world where he conducted his business—not even a blurb in the local newspaper. How could a man prosper abundantly by scooping up some of North America's most impressive real estate properties and be so unknown?

After hanging his garment bag in the closet, he spotted the rotary phone on the nightstand and plopped down on the bed. He pulled a piece of paper from his wallet, picked up the handset, and dialed.

"Hmm," he said, "no answer."

Maybe he dialed the wrong number. He wasn't used to entering the entire phone number. At least with his iPhone, all he had to do was touch the screen or, better yet, use his voice.

He studied the number again and redialed. Again, no answer.

He slammed the phone down as hard as he could— something he had remembered doing many moons ago and missed the action immensely. For some reason, pushing the screen on a smartphone didn't deliver the same satisfaction.

He was about to pull himself up from the bed when the phone startled him with a loud ring.

"Hello?"

"Yes, sir. Harrison speaking. I'm informing you that the rest of the guests are waiting in the den. If you could please join us at your earliest convenience."

"Sure thing, be down in a minute."

He unzipped the garment bag and quickly changed into his costume: brown pants, red sweater vest, jacket, and bow tie. He walked over to the mirror, placed a pair of round, wire-rimmed glasses on his face, and couldn't help but be pleased for picking out a costume with such short notice.

After locking up, he bounced down the stairs, not as Truman but as Professor Gladstone, the alter ego randomly chosen for him. And for the remainder of the weekend, he was determined to play the part—mainly if it aided his cover. He had a job to do, and if it meant playing dress-up, then so be it.

But before joining the others in the den, it was imperative to scope out the place. A little snooping before getting to know the other players was a must.

The library will be an excellent place to start.

AFTER COMPLETING HIS tour, Truman joined the others in the den. He perused the motley crew of characters, which resembled the cast of a Humphrey Bogart movie. A doctor, lounge singer, mob boss—

Well, hello!

His gaze fell on a woman lingering by the fireplace. A stark, black dress danced over the tops of her feet, popping against her smooth, milky skin. He had always been a sucker for blondes, and she was no exception. He admired how she swept her long hair over one shoulder, exposing her bare, lissome back. She was mesmerizing.

He waited until she made eye contact before strolling over to introduce himself. "Good morning," he said, bowing his head slightly. However, after a closer look, the woman seemed a lot less desirable than she did from across the room. She didn't answer him; instead, she looked him up and down as though scoping out a car to test drive. It was uncomfortable. "I didn't catch your name."

"That's because I didn't give you one," she said.

He smiled wryly and waited her out.

"My name is Gretchen Burke. I'm an art dealer out of New York. I'm here on business." She ran her hand down her silky curls. "And you are…?"

"Professor Gladstone," he said, hand to his heart. "That sounds like an intriguing occupation. But aren't you a little overdressed for a business trip, Miss Burke?"

"Well, Professor, a girl doesn't need an excuse to look her best now, does she?" She continued to run her hands down the side of her dress. "Do you not like the dress, Professor?"

He cleared his throat and could feel his cheeks flush. "On the contrary, Miss Burke. You—you look ravishing."

"Why thank you, Professor. And it's Ms. Burke."

"Pardon me, Ms. Burke. It's very nice to meet you."

She sauntered toward him, brushed against his arm, and leaned in. "I'm sure it is." She continued her flirty swagger across the room and perched beside an older man wearing a doctor's coat.

Truman, again, cleared his throat, trying to pull himself together. The game was starting out to be more captivating than he anticipated.

"Professor Gladstone, I presume?"

He turned to see a tall, leggy redhead hugging a mug of coffee as though for moral support. "Yes?"

"My name is Scarlet Lane." She timidly held out her hand. "It's nice to meet you."

"Have we met before?" He squinted his eyes as if trying to place her.

"It's possible, but I overheard you introduce yourself."

"Ah, of course. What brings you to the lodge?"

"I'm here doing business on behalf of my father, Preston Lane. You may have heard of him?"

"I have indeed. May I ask what business you're attending to?"

"I'm looking to buy a painting. My father unexpectedly came down with a bad case of the flu. As a result, he's unable to travel. He has expressed interest in this particular piece and now has the chance to acquire it. I'm here to make sure that happens."

"Fascinating."

"What about you, Professor Gladstone...what exactly is your specialty?"

"I'm a chemistry professor, but I'm here on vacation."

"It's certainly a lovely place for peace and quiet," she said.

"Indeed."

After some uncomfortable silence, Scarlet raised her mug as if proposing a toast. "Have a wonderful vacation, Professor. I'm sure we'll run into each other again.

"I'm sure we will."

Truman looked around the room and spotted the tray of strudels on the table. He debated whether or not he should indulge, considering he wouldn't be hitting the gym for the next three days. His physique was slight, but he prided himself in his ability to run laps around the muscle heads. Pumping iron and blowing blood vessels was not his idea of staying in shape.

The aroma was too enticing to ignore; he picked up a pastry, poured himself a coffee, and sat next to a man who could easily bench-press him if given a chance. His arms were twice the size of his own, and his thick, bulky legs looked like they'd endured a few thousand squats.

Muscle head.

Truman placed his mug on the end table and held out his hand. "Professor Gladstone."

"How ya doin'?" said the muscle head in a New York accent. "Mr. Parrish."

His grip was tight enough to snap Truman's fingers like a twig.

"And this is my girl, Madeline, Mads for short." He leaned back and placed his arm around her shoulders.

"Hey," she said without breaking eye contact from her pastry.

"What brings you two to the mountains…vacation?"

"Gosh, no! If I were on vacation somewhere, it would be a lot warmer than this place."

If looks could kill, Mr. Parrish would be dead.

"What Mads means is that, yeah, we're on vacation."

"Not sure how good of a vacation this will be, just waiting around for someone to be murdered."

Mr. Parrish nudged Madeline's arm. "We're not supposed to know about that yet. Stay in character."

"Sorry," she said sarcastically.

"Either way," said Truman, "it should be a memorable weekend."

Madeline sighed. "If you say so."

The Parrish's were an intriguing couple, thought Truman. A couple worth checking out. But they'd have to wait. He was not there for them.

10

Let's rendezvous at two

"THEY'RE DELICIOUS, aren't they?"

I pushed myself away from the strudel, delighted to see a plump, white-haired lady adorned in a long, sequined dress and a blue feather boa wrapped snugly around her neck. "Oh," I said, with a mouthful of pastry. "I can't seem to stay away from them."

"Elenor," she said, eagerly offering her hand. "I'm the lounge singer here at Mystery Ridge Lodge."

I held her frail, wrinkled hand—which I imagined had a lifetime of stories—and gently squeezed. "It's nice to meet you, Elenor. I'm Mrs. Lane, but you can call me Scarlet."

"What a pretty name. Are you here for the show?"

"Show?"

"Yes, I'm singing tonight in the lounge. I hear it's a sold-out crowd."

"Well, I certainly wouldn't want to miss that. But first, I need to find someone. Gretchen Burke. Have you heard of her?"

Elenor glanced over her shoulder. "Oh, you must mean that one over there. She's been causing quite a stir with the gentlemen—if you know what I mean. In the last half hour, she's made her rounds to every man in the room. If you ask me, she's somewhat of a floozie." She held her hand to her face and whispered, "Not very lady-like, is she, dear?

I couldn't help but agree when I spotted Gretchen sitting on the arm of the loveseat, nearly falling into Harrison's lap.

"I can see that," I said, wiping strudel crumbs from my chin. "Maybe I should go introduce myself."

"It was nice meeting you, Scarlet."

"You, too. I look forward to hearing you sing."

Elenor giggled. "You might be sorry you said that."

I liked her. I immediately thought of my grandmother—sweet, soft-spoken, endearing. It would be a shame if she were the killer, I thought. A charming old lady committing murder was a hard thing to wrap my head around.

As I moved through the crowd, I noticed Quinn and the professor engaging in what seemed to be some very earnest dialog. And by the looks of it, she had settled into her character effortlessly. At the very least, she looked like a nerdy reporter; her glasses kept falling off her nose when she spoke. She smiled as I walked past, giving me a subtle nod without skipping a beat.

"Excuse me, Gretchen Burke?"

The puffiness in her eyes that plagued her earlier had disappeared; she no longer looked like she'd been crying. "Yes, that's me."

"I'm Scarlet Lane and I—"

"Ahh, you're Lane. I was expecting someone a little more…"

"Older?"

"Well, I was going to say…cultured."

"Sorry to disappoint you," I said, taking the insult to heart. "My father had to cancel at the last minute and asked me to come instead. I can assure you he's left this transaction in capable hands."

Gretchen picked up her mug and took a sip. "I'm sure he has."

"Do you have the painting here?"

"I do. I'd be happy to show it to you, but first, I have some other business to attend to. How about we meet in the library, say around two?"

"Fine. I'll meet you there."

Quinn was right; Gretchen was hard to like, not to mention downright intimidating. She commanded the room like she'd been playing the role all her life—*she was icy*. I thought about how advantageous it would be to capture some of that boldness to take home with me. And with only a fraction of that boldness, I might even be willing to reveal myself to Mahogany Falls.

After engaging in a few intriguing conversations, I sat on a leather chair closest to the fire. I gazed into the flames, lost in the hypnotic orange and red ribbons. The ache in my head had intensified, and I twinged at the slightest touch. Not only was I reeling from a narrow escape involving a moose, but the nagging guilt from my fight with Dominic was relentless. I knew he was feeling neglected. With all my time spent at the coffee shop or on my laptop, we hardly had time for ourselves.

I had never left the house before without saying goodbye. *What was I thinking?* Especially since I was going to be gone for the entire weekend.

I could have been killed!

The last moment we shared would have been arguing over how much time we spent together. Now, along with my pulsating headache and a knot pulling tighter in my stomach, I had also developed a kink in the back of my neck.

As usual, Quinn was right. I needed to get out of my head and forget about the fight—at least for now. My mission was to concentrate on the game and potential suspects.

HARRISON HOBBLED TO the center of the room like an Emperor penguin. One hand held a sleek wooden walking stick; the other shoved deep into the pocket of his woolen trousers. "Could I please have your attention? I hope the coffee and strudel were satisfactory. Caffrey will now take you on a tour of the grounds outside. Grab your coats and bundle up tight. I do believe a storm is imminent."

The crowd quickly energized, invigorated by the healthy dose of caffeine coursing through their veins. A sight I knew all too well from working at a coffee shop. Day in and day out, weary patrons stumble in, waiting patiently for a pre-work-day fix. Some order coffee to go, while others sit and savor their drinks one sip at a time (often with an order of carbs). It's what I loved most about my job—an acceptable stimulant providing a temporary remedy for the sleep-deprived. What could be better?

"You okay?" said Quinn, placing her hand on my shoulder.

More than likely, she noticed the discomfort manifesting throughout my entire body.

"Yeah, it's my head…can't seem to shake this headache. I'm sure I'll be fine."

"Maybe you should stay here. You *did* hit your head pretty hard. You might even have a concussion."

"I think it's a mixture of the accident, the weather, too much sugar, the fight I had with Dominic last night. I'll be okay. I need to get my mind off things for a while, that's all."

"Fine, but you'll tell me if you feel worse, right?"

"I promise."

We left the den and followed everyone upstairs to gather a few extra layers. On our way up, I noticed Caffrey and the maid huddled in the corner, talking in a low whisper. He sipped from a large thermos, nodding occasionally, while the maid continued to do most of the talking.

"Shhh," I said, trying to make out what she was saying.

"What is it?"

"Not sure, but something."

"Maybe it's part of the game."

I backed down a few steps to worm my way into better earshot.

"What are they saying?"

"I don't know, but she sounds intense."

Before I could take one step closer, the butler and his darn dreamy eyes made contact with mine. "Crap!"

"Can I help you with something, Mrs. Lane?"

"Oh, sorry." I could feel my face beginning to flush. "We're heading up to get dressed for the weather.

"Well," he said, "we'll be leaving shortly."

When I looked at the maid, she smiled and walked away.

Quinn grabbed my arm, and we continued our way to the room. "Weird. I wonder what that was all about?"

"Maybe she's tired of doing all the cleaning around here."

Quinn laughed. "Seems about right."

The first thing I needed when we got to our room was water. I hoped it would impede the infuriating vice grip from squeezing my head any tighter. Nothing worse than a pesky headache when you have things to do. However, I had hoped the drugs would have kicked in by now.

I opened the closet and reached for my boots and an extra sweater to throw over my flimsy blouse. Living in western Canada for the better part of my life, I realized that the more layers, the better. Don't get me wrong; I loved my winters. Skating on the lake with Rocky Mountain View's. Taking long strolls with Dominic through the scenic trails of Mahogany Falls. Staying up late to admire the northern lights while sipping on a mug of hot chocolate. Or basking in the beauty of the hoar frost, adorning naked branches outside my window. But as soon as the temperature dips enough to meld my nose hairs together, I settle for jigsaw puzzles and Netflix.

But now, here we were, about to take a scenic tour with a bunch of strangers in minus twenty-nine-degree weather (minus thirty-seven with the wind chill), which I would gladly exchange for a writing session by the fire.

"Alright," said Quinn, "do you think I'll be warm enough with all this padding?"

I laughed at the sight of her. She stood there like a statue, waiting for my response. Her arms fell by her side stiff as a board, and her hands were barely visible as the sleeves of the oversized white parka seemed to swallow her up. And with the white floppy hat and matching scarf shrouding most of her face, she looked like the Michelin Man. The bright purple leg warmers that stretched over her wide-leg trousers and climbed to the top of her thighs were the only things that didn't coordinate. I think I owned a pair of those myself in the early eighties. Who knew those things still existed?

"How can you even breathe under all that?"

The fluff of the scarf muffled Quinn's laugh. "I can't, actually. So we better head downstairs before I drop like a rock." She wobbled to the door.

"Yes," I said, closing the door behind us, "it would be ironic if you were to die of heat exhaustion in the middle of a cold snap."

11

A frosty tour

A FEW PEOPLE were already lingering around the large oak desk, sporting heavy winter coats and a smidgen of impatience. Caffrey was a bit agitated, too, sipping from his thermos that accompanied him everywhere he went.

I thought of myself as quite the connoisseur when it came to coffee. But after spending the morning mingling with the guests at the lodge, I realized that a few of them could give me a run for my money. It was lovely. Being in the company of habitual coffee drinkers made me feel at home—they were my people.

I looked at Quinn. *She could go down at any moment.* "I don't think he'll keep us out there too long," I said.

"At this point," she said, tugging her scarf away from her mouth, "I hope I can make it outside."

Eventually, the remainder of the guests arrived, dressed like participants in a scavenger hunt at the North Pole.

"Are we ready?" asked Caffrey.

He focused on me for answers like I was the team captain or something. But seeing that we were all about ready to melt, I figured it was safe to answer for the group. "We're ready."

I couldn't put my finger on it, but there was something a little off with Caffrey. He appeared to be in a fog—staring into space, staggering about, looking over his shoulder. Was he bored? Can you imagine how tedious it would be to portray the same character every weekend? Something was eating at him. But what?

Confirming his coat was securely fastened, Caffrey attempted the door. But it wouldn't budge. He dug in his heels, urging it to move like a stubborn mule. Finally, it surrendered and opened to a blustery scene. A sudden wind swept through the lobby, biting our skin mercilessly. And for a brief moment, I thought Caffrey had second thoughts about leading us into the cold. But to my dismay, he didn't.

"Follow me," he said.

And we did.

While I linked arms with Quinn, everyone else huddled in groups of two. The weather had changed drastically since we walked up the path earlier, admiring the scenic views. Once boasting in a cerulean blue, the sky was now a leaden ceiling, allowing a blink of light to escape through a few sporadic cracks. And the gentle breeze that once danced through the trees evolved into a boisterous north wind.

"It's freezing out here," said Madeline. She grabbed Jason's arm and buried herself in his sleeve.

"We'll make a quick run of the property before heading back," Caffrey said. "I'm sure you'll appreciate another cup of coffee once we return to the warmth."

"Why are we even out here?" whined Madeline. "Isn't this whole mystery thing happening inside the lodge?"

"Yes," said Caffrey, holding his scarf to his nose. "But in the past, some of our guests thought it would be a good idea to head out to do some sightseeing on their own, which resulted in them getting lost...and worse."

"What do you mean, *worse*? What's worse than getting lost in the middle of nowhere?" said Sam, pulling Elenor close.

Caffrey gulped his coffee while staring into the dismal forest, seeming to zone out. "Do you see that up there... through the trees?"

I wasn't exactly sure what I was looking at as I squinted through the wind and blowing trees. "What is it?"

"It's a giant boulder. A couple of years ago, one of the guests decided to go hiking. Alone. We warned her against it. It's easy to lose all sense of direction out here. Unfortunately, she thought she had enough hiking experience to find her way back alone. When she still hadn't returned later that night, we sent out a search party but had to turn back because of the sudden change in weather. It was dark. Couldn't see a thing." Caffrey stopped talking and continued to sip his coffee.

"Don't keep us in suspense, Caffrey," said Gretchen. "What happened?"

Caffrey turned away from the forest and stared at us intently. "The next day, we were told that her body had been found a half kilometer from the lodge. She froze to death."

"That's terrible!" Elenor said.

"So," he continued, "I'm sure I don't need to emphasize how important it is to stay together. The rock is a sober reminder to never stray too far from the lodge—especially alone."

"I wouldn't mind going up there and taking a look," said Truman.

"Let's stay together...alright, Professor? Probably not the best time to go exploring."

Quinn nudged my arm. "Do you think someone died up there?"

It was hard to take her seriously, looking the way she did. Quinn was quirky and had been since the very first day we met.

It was the first day of grade eight, and my name was not on the attendance sheet. I went to the office to find out why, and as luck would have it, Quinn was waiting alongside me. She was shorter than me, only came up to my chin, and I was immediately captivated by her sense of style. Dark denim jeans, red suspenders, hair dyed pink and gelled into spikes. It wasn't apparent at first which clique she fit into, but it didn't take long to realize she was in a whole other class of her own. It's what drew us together. Our differences. She was offbeat and outgoing and would attempt anything once. On the contrary, I excelled in the art of solitude, cringing at the thought of *anything* new.

"Who knows," I said. "Maybe Caffrey tells a story to set the mood. Or maybe someone *did* die out there."

"Truman's right, though. Don't you think we would have heard something about it? Oh, wait! I get it. It's strategic. Like a drawing card to pull people into their murder mystery weekend."

"You're channeling your inner reporter, aren't you? Maybe you should do some digging. Perhaps you'll stumble onto something juicy."

Quinn flashed her hands over her head. "I could see it now:

"SMALL TOWN REPORTER UNCOVERS SECRETS IN MYSTERY RIDGE LODGE"

I laughed. "I could see that too. But right now, I'm a bit envious of those leg warmers. Come on, let's catch up! It's freezing out here!"

"Over here is the lake," continued Caffrey. "However, right now, it's our skating rink. Feel free to skate here at any time. On the other side of the lake is a shed where you can warm up and lace up your skates. Keep the door shut; animals like finding their way there."

"What kind of animals are we talking about?" asked Sam.

"Deer, elk, moose. We've even had a bobcat or two skulking their way into the shelter. It's a great place for them to escape the wind, so please keep the door closed."

By now, the thick clouds had engulfed the sun, and a few flurries had already begun to swirl around our heads. My nose felt like it was going to fall off. I couldn't see anyone wanting to go for a skate—especially if the weather was only going to get worse. All I could think about was returning to the lodge and grabbing the closest seat next to the fire.

The group was led down the path to a fire pit, where several trees had been cut down to stumps and arranged in a circle. For some reason, Caffrey didn't appear as cold as the rest of us. But when he began reciting his spiel, as though he had done it a thousand times before, his words had a slight slur, and I wondered if maybe the cold was getting to him after all.

"Usually," said Caffrey, "when the sun goes down and everyone is full from eating one of Chef Sébastien's gourmet meals, he likes to come out here and start a big bonfire. We bring along a bag of jumbo m-marshmallows and—and we make s'mores and gaze at the s-stars while listening to the roar of the fire. Unfortunately, if the wind per-persists, we may have to put a pin in that plan until tomorrow."

"What's over there?" Sam pointed to the other side of the lodge.

"Nothing of relevance," said Caffrey. "The guests usually stay on this side of the lodge."

"Sounds good to me," Gretchen said. "Would you say the tour is over? I want to get inside before I lose all feeling in my toes."

"I second that," said Madeline, who was already in a slow jog up the path.

"By all m-means," Caffrey said. "There were a couple of other things I wanted to point out, but we can...we can do that later. We'll finish the tour inside before you all head to the dining room for lunch."

"Now that's music to my ears," said Jason. "I'm starving."

I had to agree with Jason; I was hungry, too. The strudel and coffee were delicious, but I needed something more substantial to warm my innards.

Soup. I could use some soup.

12

Victoria

AFTER GRADUATING FROM the University of Alberta with a Bachelor of Arts degree, Victoria Hale accepted a temporary gig at Mystery Ridge Lodge on the sole basis of living near the mountains. Hoping to break into the acting world, she figured it was a great place to get her feet wet. But playing the role of a maid in a murder mystery every weekend was not her dream job; however, it *was* smack-dab in the middle of the mountains. There was that, at least

But as life would have it, the temporary gig turned into something more permanent, and twelve years later, she found herself calling Mystery Ridge Lodge home.

Victoria picked up her feather duster and lethargically moved from one surface to the next, spying out the window to see the guests around the fire pit. She almost felt sorry for them as they tried to keep warm while putting up with Caffrey's dreary blah blah blah. It wasn't that she didn't appreciate Caffrey's contribution to the butler role. She did. But lately, his heart wasn't into it as much as usual and tended to ramble on and on without much enthusiasm, like he'd lost his spark.

That didn't matter now because while everyone was preoccupied with Caffrey outside, there was a small window of opportunity to scope out the rooms before the guests returned for lunch. She dashed down the hall and through the door, gaining access to the room with her key. First, the closet, then to the bedroom, and finally, a quick sweep of the bathroom and out the door before anyone was the wiser. The chances of someone returning unexpectedly were unlikely. If, by chance, they did return, they'd understand why she was there; she *was* the maid, after all.

Victoria peered through the window that overlooked the fire pit, realizing she probably had enough time to check one last room. Once again, she pulled the ring of keys from her pocket, finding the one that corresponded with the door.

Now, this room has promise. Immediately, a bright pink suitcase caught her eye. It sat in the middle of the bed, begging to be opened. This was the best part, the moment right before the big reveal. What would be inside? Would it shock her? Would it betray the secrets of a stranger she had yet to meet? The color alone was telling. Someone who was not afraid of being the center of attention.

She ran one finger along its sleek, pink leather, imagining what kind of person would possess such lavish luggage. The most extravagant thing she owned was a pair of diamond stud earrings gifted to her by her last boyfriend.

Her hand reached the gold lock that dangled from the zipper, but she hesitated. Of course, she realized what she was doing was wrong, an invasion of privacy that she herself fell victim to as a teenager while living with an overbearing mother.

But should that stop her?

Slowly, she pulled the zipper toward her, imagining a case full of valuables. *A diamond necklace? Sheepskin slippers? Or, better yet, a cashmere scarf?* She paused and took a deep breath before lifting the lid to reveal its contents. However, the knot in her stomach began to unravel when she discovered what was inside.

Nothing.

"Hmm." She walked around the room, mindlessly moving her duster from one object to the next. As she waltzed to the bathroom, an intense fragrance pushed through the air, nearly dropping her to her knees. It was like someone had let the air out of a balloon filled with Viktor and Rolf's Flowerbomb.

"Whoa, that's intense!"

Waving her hand in front of her face, she gazed upon the excessive amount of beauty supplies on the counter, leaving only enough space for a toothbrush on the side of the sink.

"Who needs this much stuff?" She picked up a jar of night cream to read the ingredients. There must have been twenty-five jars, tubes, and bottles promising to make you more beautiful. Was she planning on staying the month?

Victoria didn't see the need for all that primping. Her upbringing was more plain Jane than Lady Gaga; she never fell victim to the pressures of what society thought was beautiful. As long as her shampoo smelled good and her skin was hydrated with whatever lotion was on sale, she didn't have time for all that other goop.

She popped her head out of the bathroom when she suddenly heard voices wafting from the lobby.

"Shoot!"

She quickly scanned the room to see if everything was how she had found it. The sound of bulky boots barreled up the stairs, making her question whether she had enough time to hightail it out of the room unseen.

She waited until whoever it was got to their room, then she figured she could make a beeline across the hall before anyone could confront her. It sounded like a good plan. *Right?* She listened and could feel her heart thrash against her chest, not sure if it was fear or excitement.

The cumbersome footsteps galloped past the room. Victoria sighed and waited a full thirty seconds before hearing the slam down the hall. Confident the coast was clear, she opened the door, peeked both ways, and rolled out with the stealth-like moves of a secret agent.

That's enough snooping for today.

13

I think he's been lovestruck!

JUST AS WE returned to the lodge, thick snow descended on us like a weighted blanket. I whipped my head away from another gust of wind, only to see the snow had already obscured our footprints.

"Oh my!" Elenor said, slipping on a patch of ice.

My reflexes kicked in, and I grabbed onto her arm before she could fall. "Are you alright, Mrs. Wallace?

"Oh, I'm fine, dear. Thank you for saving me from an embarrassing tumble."

"You're welcome."

"How could something so light and fluffy be so deadly?"

"Exactly," I said. "I know all too well how detrimental ice and snow can be. I fell and broke my wrist last winter trying to pick up my keys I dropped in the snow. One minute, I think how beautiful the day is, and the next, I'm flat on my back with my arm under my bottom."

"Oh, heavens! Thank goodness it was your wrist."

"Yes, I'm more cautious in the winter—no matter how beautiful and innocent those flurries appear." I placed my hand over the top of hers and gave it a tap. "Hold on to my arm, Mrs. Wallace. We're almost at the door."

"Oh, please! Call me Elenor."

Caffrey reached the door first and held it open. I barely made it inside when I nearly got pushed to the floor.

"Excuse me!" I shouted.

"Sam!" said Elenor. "Your manners."

"Oh, my apologies, Scarlet." Sam tore at his coat as though he were on fire. "Just need to make a quick trip upstairs."

"Not sure what has gotten into that man. He's usually not so rude."

"Not to worry, Elenor. At least I didn't fall and break my arm."

"If I were to make a wager, I'd bet my dentures those strudels had a bit of a disagreement with his irritable bowel."

Thankfully, Jason stomped the snow from his boots so loudly that it alleviated the need to respond to Elenor's comment.

"Whoa! I think winter's upon us," Jason said.

"You think?" Madeline rolled her eyes and flung her coat over her shoulder.

I finally freed myself from my boots and branched off from the huddle. The warmth from the den was calling my name, but unfortunately, it would have to wait; Caffrey insisted on finishing the tour.

"I promise to make this quick. I'm sure you're hungry and perhaps even bored to death, but it will be over soon enough. Follow me, we'll start in the library."

My toes had just begun to thaw as I skimmed my feet across the hardwood to the opposite side of the lodge.

We arrived at the library, which was even more inviting than the den. Mood lighting, cozy atmosphere, and a fireplace complete with a nook. It was a perfect place to read a book—or, in my case, write one.

"What?" said Jason. "No TV?"

"I'm afraid not, Mr. Parrish."

Madeline scoffed. "Well, it *is* the twentieth century, after all."

Just then, Sam ran into the library like he had missed the last flight out of Antarctica. "What'd I miss?"

"Ah, Dr. Wallace," said Caffrey. "Nice of you to join us."

"The butler has informed us that there's no TV," said Jason.

"I guess it's not the end of the world," said Sam.

Elenor moved to the center of the room. She sat down, nearly disappearing into the plush leather as the sofa seemed to swallow her up. "We're not going to have time to watch TV," she said, trying to readjust.

"Are you performing tonight, Elenor?" Sam stood behind her, ruffling the feathers on her boa.

"I certainly am," she said. "I assume you secured yourself a ticket, Doctor?"

"Oh, I'll be there," said Sam, giving Eleanor a wink.

"If you come this way, you'll notice the exquisite pool table carved from rich mahogany, acting as the focal point for the room."

Caffrey was spouting things for memory again. I wondered if he was reciting word for word.

"And along with a large selection of books, you'll find a chess board and an assortment of other board games if you feel up to some friendly competition."

"I've been known to be somewhat of a pool shark," said Sam, reaching for a pool cue.

"Is that so, Doctor?" Truman said.

"Why yes, Professor. Are you up for a game?"

"That sounds like a challenge."

"Indeed it is, Professor."

Truman shook Sam's hand. "Then I accept. Meet here after lunch?"

"You can count on it. And don't forget to bring your wallet."

"Um, Doctor?" Elenor placed her hand on Sam's shoulder. "Are you sure that's such a good idea?"

"It's all in good fun, my dear. A harmless game between friends. Isn't that right, Professor Gladstone?"

"If you say so, Doc."

Quinn nudged my elbow. "Do you think Elenor's objection was in the script?"

"Probably not."

"Well, if we're finished here," said Caffrey, "let's head to the dining room. I'm sure the chef will serve lunch shortly."

I could hear my stomach rumble at the mere thought of food, not to mention the fantastic aroma wafting throughout the lodge. "Mmmm! It smells like onions and garlic."

"I'm so hungry I could eat my left shoe," said Jason.

Jason was an intimidating character, not because he was dressed like a New York City mob boss (although he did manage to pull that off quite nicely). No. He didn't need the pinstriped suit, the white-band fedora, *or* the unlit cigar hanging from his mouth; he had a compelling enough presence without props.

Now, Mrs. Parrish, on the other hand, was anything but a ditsy girlfriend. Annoying? Yes. But Madeline Parrish knew precisely what she was doing, and the fact that she had Jason wrapped around her baby finger proved she was well aware of her persuasive ways.

Jason nearly ripped the seams of his suit jacket, wrapping his muscular arm around Madeline to escort her to the dining room. "C'mon, Mads. Let's go get some food."

THE HEAVENLY AROMA guided us to the dining room, and I could hardly wait to see what the chef had in store for us. But after nearly plowing into Elenor for the second time in one day, I'd have to wait.

"We have to stop meeting like this," said Elenor.

Again, I steadied her from falling. "Sorry, Elenor. What's going on?"

"I'm not sure, dear."

I pushed my way to the front of the line and discovered Caffrey standing at the foot of the stairs. He appeared to be in a trance of some kind. Mesmerized. Like he'd been zapped with a stun gun.

What is he looking at?

And then I realized that the object of his affection was not a what but a who.

The maid. The same maid I had seen having a deep conversation with Caffrey earlier was now gliding down the staircase as though on a hoverboard. I realized what had him so enamored.

She was beautiful.

But in a fresh, earthy way. The kind of beauty that comes from spending countless hours outdoors, hiking, planting gardens, or possibly horseback riding on an acreage in the middle of the prairies.

Her lips were rosy pink, and her cheeks had a healthy glow. Yet, as far as I could tell, she wasn't wearing any makeup. However, the luster in her teal-green eyes spoke volumes when she looked back at Caffrey.

A love affair, perhaps?

"Ah, Miss Hale, perfect timing." Caffrey waved his arm over the tops of our heads. "These are the guests who will be joining us this weekend. And this,"—he redirected his arm as if presenting us with a gift—"is Victoria Hale. Miss Hale is here to help you with anything you need. Isn't that right?"

She tossed him a humorless look. "Well, I wouldn't say *anything*, but if you need fresh towels, I'm happy to help."

"Alright then, we'll leave you to it. I was about to take the guests to the dining room for lunch."

"Oh, you'll enjoy Chef Sébastien's meals. He knows his way around a kitchen, that's for sure. I should know. I've been benefiting from his cuisine for years. Enjoy!"

I noticed a smirk form on Quinn's face after walking past Victoria. She was on to something.

"I'm guessing you're thinking the same thing I am?" I said.

"Well, if you think Caffrey is completely gaga with the maid, then yes."

"Maybe it's a clue."

"What do you mean?"

"I'm sure the staff will be dropping subtle hints throughout the weekend as to the motive of the killer. We have to keep our eyes open."

"This is going to be fun," said Quinn. "I already feel like a detective."

"Good. Now, all we have to do is wait for the murder."

Caffrey had developed a pep in his step after his encounter with Victoria, not to mention the sudden change in mood. The stony disposition that accompanied him for most of the morning had suddenly shifted to a more playful one.

He swung both arms over his head, pointed his fingers like an air traffic controller, and cheerfully sang his orders. "Okay, everyone, this way to the dining room."

That was music to my ears.

14

Pardon my French

I FOLLOWED THE crowd into the dining area—a spacious room with wooden floors, a rustic oak table set for eight, and a breathtaking view of the property.

The smell was intoxicating. Then again, anything emanating from a hot kitchen usually filled my senses with giddy anticipation.

To the left of the table was a large bar, four stools on one side, and a wall of bottles (varying in colors, shapes, and sizes) on the other. Three large windows, surrounded by a feature stone wall, looked out onto a wrap-around veranda with stairs leading down to an enticing tub of steam and bubbles.

"You didn't mention a hot tub," said Gretchen, peering out the window.

Caffrey sighed, his fingers running through his thick, black hair. "You are correct, Ms. Burke," he said. "You were in such a hurry to get back to the lodge I had to cut the tour short."

"So…does this mean we can take a dip after lunch?" Truman said, joining Gretchen at the window.

"Yes, Professor, you can. But I must warn you: the weather is intensifying by the minute. I'm not sure I'd risk the journey for a few moments in the tub if I were you."

"Nah!" Truman said with a wave of his hand. "A little cold weather never hurt anybody. Besides, I could use a little pampering this weekend. I might even walk around the back of the lodge to see what else this place has to offer."

As if on cue, a gust of wind kicked up an enormous mound of ice and snow, thrashing it against the windows. After that intimidating display of nature, there was no way I'd be joining the professor—or anyone else, for that matter—on *that* glacial excursion.

At the back of the room, dressed in a fitted black jacket and matching pants, a woman with long dark hair pulled back in a ponytail stood quietly with a towel folded over her arm. A tendril of hair fell from the black beanie she wore on her head, which she quickly tucked back in place.

"That must be Rebecca," I said to Quinn.

"That would be my guess."

As Caffrey moved in to make the introduction, I didn't miss his subtle touch on the small of her back, causing her mouth to move slightly upward.

"Excuse me," he said. "Before you sit down, let me introduce you to Rebecca, the chef's assistant."

Rebecca nodded and smiled. "I'm sure I'll meet with you all individually. Enjoy your lunch." With that, she disappeared into the kitchen through swinging doors.

The subtle exchange between her and Caffrey was more flirtatious than I expected of co-workers.

But maybe I was reading too much into it.

No sooner had the doors stopped swinging when a man barreled through with as much excitement and charisma as a ringmaster.

"Welcome! *Bienvenue!*"

"And this is Chef Sébastien," said Caffrey.

The chef leaped out from behind the bar with gusto. A very animated man who might have been the life-size replica of the chef figurine sitting on my shelf at home. A large floppy hat rested precariously on his bald head, which glistened nicely under the warm, incandescent glow of the mason jar chandelier hanging above the bar. When he smiled, thin, curly whiskers from an impressive handlebar mustache tickled the tips of his eyelashes, making his eyes flutter constantly.

"It's time to eat," he said, waving a checkered towel back and forth. "Sit down, *s'il vous plaît.*"

"It smells wonderful in here," said Elenor.

"*Merci, m'dame.*" He clasped his fingers together over the long red apron tied above his sugar belly and proudly grinned at his culinary creation.

A piping hot bowl of French onion soup—or, as Chef Sébastien called it, *soupe à l'oignon gratinée*—was placed before us. It looked and smelled amazing. And if this was what I had to look forward to at mealtime, I was sure the trip would be well worth it.

"*Bon appétit!*"

His smile was infectious, and I loved how he observed us enjoying the fruits of his labor.

"You decided to go with the soup, Chef," Caffrey shouted sternly across the room. He rubbed the back of his neck and closed his eyes, and I couldn't tell if he was feeling unwell or just irritated.

Gretchen leaned across the table and spoke softly. "Was that a question or a statement?"

"By the expression on the chef's face, he most likely didn't appreciate the comment either way," I said.

Oddly enough, the aroma of French onion soup wasn't the only thing hovering around the table; the tension was so thick you could have eaten it with a spoon.

Without skipping a beat, the chef placed his hands on his hips, stuck out his chest, and said, "I did! What about it?"

Caffrey stumbled across the floor, his hands folded behind him like he was ready for an interrogation. "I thought we agreed on the sandwiches." He wiped his forehead with the back of his hand as moisture beads began to form.

It wasn't as warm in the dining room as in the den, but Caffrey was sweating profusely. *Could he have been drunk?*

The chef grunted and snapped the towel over his leg. *"Harumph. Je ne veux pas te parler!"* He pivoted with such force he nearly toppled over. But after regaining his footing, he stomped into the kitchen, mumbling angrily in French.

Caffrey stared at the doors as they swung back and forth and noticed the captivation as we looked up from our soup bowls. "Enjoy your lunch," he said. His words were cold and sharp and slightly garbled. Then he tugged at the hem of his butler's jacket and staggered out of the room.

"Okay," said Gretchen. "Wonder what that was all about."

"I don't know," Quinn said. "Why does it matter what the chef serves for lunch?"

"Another clue, perhaps?" I was getting into the whole mystery aspect. Who knew it would be so entertaining?

"He looked a little tipsy to me," said Elenor. "But I only smelled coffee on his breath and maybe a hint of nutmeg. He's been sipping out of that thermos all morning."

"All part of the ruse, my dear," said Sam.

"Well, he sure is convincing."

AFTER A BRIEF lull in the conversation, Gretchen started up again with a few questions for Jason. "You're awfully quiet, Mr. Parrish. What brings you and your..."—she paused— "companion to Mystery Ridge?" She pursed her lips together and raised her brows.

"If ya gotta know, me and Mads are on vacation. I got work in New York, but I'm here to, you know, relax."

"I see," said Gretchen. "And what line of work is that, exactly?"

Madeline rolled her eyes. "He does lots of stuff...mostly for *rich* people."

Jason slipped his arm around Madeline. "It's okay, darlin'. I can talk for myself. Like the lady said, I dabble in lots of stuff. Right now, though, I'm on vacation."

Elenor leaned across the table. "I don't think he answered the question, did he? I wonder what he does."

"Probably on the other side of the law," Sam mumbled.

"What about you, Professor?" Quinn asked. "Are you here on business or pleasure?"

"Oh, I'm here for the pleasure. I've taken a few days off. I had hoped to go skiing this weekend in Lake Louise, but when I heard about the storm, I decided to come here instead."

"Ooh, Lake Louise," said Elenor. "I hear that place is beautiful this time of year. I've never been there myself."

"It's a great place to clear the mind," said Truman, leaning back in his chair.

Elenor nodded. "I'm sure it is."

As we nursed our soup, Rebecca came around to see if anyone wanted seconds—everyone except for Gretchen.

"Well, as fascinating as all your lives are, I think I've had enough conversation for one day."

She stood from the table, tossed her napkin on her plate, and darted out of the room.

"Ain't she a piece of work." Madeline snorted.

"I understand you have business with Ms. Burke," Truman said, directing his statement to me.

"I do, actually. We're meeting in the library at two. I'm purchasing a painting and look forward to seeing it."

"I've heard about Ms. Burke," said Quinn. Her glasses fogged when she sipped her soup.

"What have you heard?" Elenor asked.

"There's been a rumor floating the office; she's not who she says she is."

"Oh? And how do you know this?" asked the professor.

"I'm a reporter. My source told me she was coming to the lodge to handle some business. And not the kind that deals with paintings. So, I booked myself a room at Mystery Ridge Lodge to see if I could find out what she's up to. It's what any good reporter would do."

"So," said Madeline, "who is she?"

"I don't know. That's what I'm going to find out."

15

The game is afoot

MY MIND WANDERED as I slurped the last of my lunch. French onion soup was Dominic's favorite, and I couldn't help but think of what he might be doing. More than likely, he was probably sulking in front of the TV, nursing a can of SpaghettiOs and scarfing down the unopened bag of Oreos I had hidden in the pantry.

"Scarlet!"

Quinn gave a quick jab to my arm, which shook me from my reverie.

"Where did you go? I called your name three times."

"Really?"

"Yes, really. What had you so captivated you felt the need to drift away from *this* place?"

"Just thinking."

"Let me guess. Dominic?"

"How'd you know?"

"I'm sure everything's fine. Maybe the time apart will be good for you two."

"You're right...just wallowing in my guilt, that's all."

"Maybe he tried to reach you. You should see if Harrison will let you check your phone."

"Nah, I'll leave it for now. I'll try again before we turn in for the night. By the way, thanks."

"For what?"

"For not punching me harder."

She laughed. "You're welcome."

IT WAS JUST after one o'clock, and only a few people remained at the table. Quinn had sparked a conversation with Jason, leaving Madeline to sulk alone. I'm sure she was annoyed since Jason wasn't giving her his full attention. She twirled a piece of hair between her fingers, staring into space like the lodge was the last place she wanted to be.

The rest of the guests had already left the dining room, leaving Sébastien and Rebecca in the kitchen to clean up.

Since the game seemed to lull, I figured I could do some writing before meeting Gretchen in the library.

I was about to leave, but not before Rebecca returned to the table, holding a pot of coffee. "Would anyone like a top-up?"

"I'd love some," I said, taking what was left in the pot.

"I can perk some more if anyone else wants a cup."

No one seemed interested in her offer, so she left to continue cleaning the kitchen with Sébastien.

After saying my goodbyes, I left the dining room to retrieve my laptop from the safe. But I needed to find Harrison first.

He had the key.

I didn't have to search very far since I found him in the den, deep in thought with his legs stretched out on the coffee table like his shift had ended hours ago. Who knows what he was daydreaming about, but when he saw me approach, he jumped to his feet with a start.

"Ah! Mrs. Lane!"

"Harrison," I said. "What are you doing in here all by yourself? You missed a wonderful meal."

"I'm sure it was brilliant. But I'm not that hungry, I'm afraid. Perhaps one too many strudels." He gave his stomach a few quick taps. "What can I do for you?"

"Just wanna get my laptop, if that's alright. Thought maybe I could do some writing before meeting Ms. Burke. Do you have the key?"

"Of course. May I ask what you are writing?"

"Oh—I, I'm fiddling around with a story idea. It's something I like to do in my spare time. Nothing, really. It relaxes me, that's all."

"Sounds interesting. Maybe you can write about this place. It would be a great setting for a story."

"Perhaps." I smiled. *If he only knew.*

WHEN I REACHED the library, I planted myself on the sofa closest to the fire, hoping the warm blaze would inspire me. But the cushions I sank into were made from leather, which was soft, luxurious, and dangerously comfortable.

It worried me.

If I proceeded with the usual ritual of letting the soothing strings of the philharmonic float through my headphones and into my subconscious, more than likely, I wouldn't be getting much work done. But I had to try. There was only so much free time, and I had to take advantage of every moment. Chase couldn't stay up on that mountain forever. It was up to me to get him down.

The question was, how was I going to wrap it up?

I only had three—maybe four chapters at the most to bring this series to an end. And having it all tied up with a nice little bow would be a challenge.

Alright, Scarlet, let's do this.

With my laptop in front of me and my headphones firmly around my ears, I drank the rest of my coffee and hit play. Instantly, I was transported to a snow-covered mountain where Chase continued his pursuit.

"Now…where was I?"

ONLY EMBERS REMAINED when I opened my eyes. Obviously, the ambiance was too much for my sleep-weary mind. I didn't even remember dozing off.

I peered down at my laptop only to find the cursor in the same spot it had been for weeks.

Why was it so quiet?

As I tried desperately to pull myself from the sofa's grasp, I noted the time on my laptop. "It's after three?"

Wasn't I supposed to meet Gretchen here at two?

Maybe she was here, saw that I had fallen asleep, and decided to leave. I ran my fingers through the knots in my hair before attempting another launch off the couch. As I reached a standing position, I heard what could only be described as a blood-curdling scream.

"What the—"

Blood instantly rushed to my head, causing me to stumble forward. I braced myself on the arm of the sofa, waiting for the sensation to pass before grabbing my laptop and running out of the library.

The maid was already in the den when I arrived. She was disheveled. Her apron was twisted, and parts of her hair had fallen from her bun. She stared at me (probably thought I looked equally disheveled) but didn't say a word and retreated, allowing me to get a closer look.

Sam and Elenor shuffled into the den with curious apprehension, clutching onto their mugs of hot coffee.

At the same time, Madeline came running down the staircase as best she could despite her most uncomfortable, tight-fitting skirt; Jason, not far behind, was taking two steps at a time.

The urgency was palpable. It was like everyone had forgotten why we were there in the first place. I realized I hadn't seen Quinn since lunch and was about to search for her when the outside door flung open. A strong gust of wind pushed her in like a plastic bag, and she was about to climb the stairs when she noticed the huddle in the den.

"What's going on?" she asked.

"Where'd you go?" I said, ignoring her question.

"I needed a snack." She was munching on a pretzel.

"How long were you out there? Didn't you even hear the scream?"

"Oh, no!" She hurried to the den to see everyone peering down at the floor. "What did I miss?"

"It's Ms. Burke, the art dealer," said Elenor.

"Of course, it would be her," Madeline said. "Just had to be the center of attention."

Quinn chuckled and nudged my arm. "She's one to talk."

"Look at her eyes," said Jason. "They're glossed over like she's…dead."

"Don't be ridiculous," Quinn said, "I'm sure it's all part of the game."

"Don't be so sure," said Sam. He knelt beside the victim. "She doesn't have a pulse."

Quinn nudged my elbow again. "Should keep your mind off your problems for a while, eh?"

I smiled.

Then I had an epiphany: it made sense now why Ms. Burke never made it to the library. She had to make herself into the perfect murder victim. This was her moment, her chance to be the center of attention for the remainder of the weekend—or at least until we solved her murder.

A morbid curiosity washed over the faces around the room as we began our collaboration. I suddenly realized how twisted the game of murder truly was.

First, perfect strangers gather together in a remote paradise, eagerly partaking in a beautifully prepared lunch, laughing and carrying on, knowing all too well that someone at the table will meet their untimely doom. The anticipation is exhilarating and ignites something deep within the soul—a sin so unthinkable that it belongs on the pages of a Stephen King novel. Something once thought utterly abhorrent now provokes a fiendish hunger for murder.

Then, once aroused by a chilling scream—not a signal of distress, but rather a proclamation that the game is afoot. Go time. A race to the scene of the crime. Who is the victim? How were they killed? And more importantly…

Who's the killer?

Why *was* murder so fascinating? A nefarious deed that's been trending since Cain killed Abel. Why stop now?

Of course, there was always justification for murder: jealousy, money, and power. But entertainment? It *was* the crux of every novel I (and every other mystery writer) had ever written. I had reached millions of readers with shady characters and ruthless killers *because* murder was so fascinating.

My gaze fell to Ms. Burke's motionless body. Her eyes reflected an opalescent vacancy, like an ethereal portrait hanging mutely on a wall. Her hair was fanned out like wheat. Wisps of golden strands mingled with a splash of red wine spilling from the crystal goblet that teetered between her long, tapered fingers. I was impressed by how much thought she put into her death scene.

"Has anyone seen the professor?" Jason's question broke through the silence.

"He said he was going to go in the hot tub after lunch," said Elenor. "I hope he's not still in there—he'll freeze! And with that wind, it's gotta be minus forty out there."

"I'll go check," I offered. It would give me some time to think about possible suspects.

16

A door that holds secrets

I RAN TO the dining room and looked out the window first. Since it was plastered with so much snow, it was difficult to see anything outside. I huffed warm air over the glass, melting some of the ice that had built up on the inside, then peeked through the clearing. A ghostly vapor arose from the hot tub, but it didn't appear like anyone was out there.

That's a relief!

He would have frozen to death if he had walked back to the lodge wearing only a bathing suit and a towel.

I turned away from the window and looked at the doors leading to the kitchen. Then, realizing I had been left to my own devices (which usually meant getting into trouble), I decided to investigate. I blamed it on Chase. After all, I had created him to be the tenacious gumshoe who got all his pertinent evidence from snooping.

Well, if he can do it.

It was quiet. And because it was quiet, there was a good chance my investigation would go unnoticed. Slowly, I crept past the bar and pushed through the doors. The kitchen was surprisingly big and flaunted some of the best high-end appliances money could buy.

"Nothing outdated in here," I mumbled.

As I observed the modern exhibit, I thought it was odd, seeing that the rest of the lodge was paraded in more colonial decor. The fact that the stainless steel oven displayed a touchscreen interface seemed like a leap into the future rather than a step back in time.

But on the far side of the kitchen, next to the custom-built wine fridge, there was a door. A door that clearly didn't belong in such a modern kitchen. My curiosity was piqued (no surprise there), so I wandered over to investigate. Naturally, a door that old could hold only the best of secrets.

I slowly pulled on the handle. But, as luck would have it, the room's silence was instantly burdened with a long, slow creak, making the hair on my arm stand at attention. "Shhh," I said, reprimanding myself. A quick check over my shoulder confirmed the shrill hadn't alerted anyone. I looked for a light switch. The room was dark; I couldn't make out anything inside. My hand fumbled up and down the wall, hastily looking for a light, but was unsuccessful. An eerie presence crept behind me as I aimlessly swatted against the darkness, trying to find a string to pull.

"What are you doing in here?"

I yelped like an injured puppy and leaped out from behind the door, slamming it shut with my elbow. "Oh, Chef, it's you! You scared me."

"*Excusez-moi*, Mrs. Lane. But again, what were you doing in there?"

"Well, I was looking out the window in the dining room to see if Professor Gladstone was still in the hot tub."

Sébastien placed his hands on his hips and arched one eyebrow. "*Ah oui, madame.* But this is not the dining room, *non?*"

A nervous laugh was all I could muster. I peered out the kitchen window and noticed the steam wafting upward. And knowing the hot tub was much easier to see from the window in the dining room, I had to think of something quick. "Right...I did look out the window. I didn't see anyone. But as I headed back to the den, I could have sworn I heard a rumbling in the kitchen." I knew my face was reddening from my little white lie. I could feel it.

"And...what did you discover?"

"Um, actually...I found the kitchen to be quite impressive. Who knew so many appliances could fit in one kitchen?" I crossed my arms in front of me and smiled.

Sébastien walked to the door and pulled a key from his pocket. "Did your curiosity yield anything interesting?"

I watched the chef lock the mysterious door, convinced I'd stumbled onto something classified.

"I was trying to locate a light switch when you startled me. What do you keep in there, anyway?"

"Nothing that concerns you. Maybe you should return to the den. You don't want the other guests solving the mystery without you, *non?*"

"Of course." I couldn't be sure if this was part of his facade or if there *was* something in there to hide.

I sheepishly walked past Sébastien, feeling silly for getting caught in the act. Rookie move. I'd have to get it together and improve my investigator skills if I had any chance of solving the murder.

"Madame?"

I stopped and turned. "Yes?"

"The professor is in the den with the others."

"Really?"

"Oui, he entered soon after you left."

Sure enough, Truman was hovering over the body with everyone else.

Quinn grabbed my arm and pulled me away from the huddle. "Everything alright? You look green."

"I'm okay. Well, maybe a little spooked. I'll fill you in later."

"You better. I don't want you keeping all the good clues to yourself."

I smiled. "Not a chance." I glanced at Truman, curious as to where he had gone. "Professor, we were going to send out a search party. I thought you were heading to the hot tub."

"That was my plan," he said. "But I had second thoughts the moment I opened the door. That's no southern breeze out there, and I didn't feel like freezing my face off or any other body parts, for that matter."

"I'm glad you changed your mind," said Elenor.

"Who found the body, anyway?" Truman said, gearing the conversation onto someone else.

"It was the maid." I looked around the room, but she was nowhere to be found. "She was here a few minutes ago."

"Actually," said the professor, "she passed me on the stairs on my way to the den. You don't think she had something to do with this, do you?"

"Well, she was the one who found the body... "

"Who was the last to see Ms. Burke?" asked Sam.

"The last place I saw her was in the dining room," said Quinn.

"That's right," Madeline agreed. "But she was gone before dessert was served."

"But that was hours ago," said Sam. "Anyone could have killed her."

"She was in a hurry to go someplace. I know that much," said Jason.

"Yeah," muttered Madeline, "probably thought she was too good for us."

"Well, let's see," said Quinn, "who had it out for her?"

"That could be just about everyone—"

"*A h h h!*"

"What was that?" said Elenor, jumping away from the noise.

Quinn motioned to the lobby. "I don't know, but I think it came from over there."

Ignoring the body lying before us, we huddled closer together, waiting for the impending plot twist.

The room fell silent. However, in the distance, the sound of a lopsided gait barreled toward us like a three-legged rhino.

A moment later, Harrison came into view. He was running. That in itself was a shock, and he appeared as though he'd seen a ghost.

"What's happened?" Elenor blurted out.

Harrison could barely speak. His cane took the total weight of his body—either for emotional support or to steady him from falling. And while coral streams trickled down his cheeks like paint from his sweat-drenched forehead, the words finally dropped out of his mouth like bricks.

"Come quick! There's been a murder!"

17

There's been a murder...no, really!

HARRISON'S PERSISTENT PANTING made it evident he was unfamiliar with the word cardio. Whatever he was running from had him stumbling across the floor and gasping for air. Not to mention, his usual rosy complexion had deepened into an inflamed shade of red.

"What do you mean there's been a murder?" Jason said. "I thought we already had one here." He pointed to the floor.

Still breathing heavily, Harrison placed his hand over his heart, pulled a handkerchief from his pocket, and dabbed the sweat from his upper lip. "I'm quite hesitant to say," he mumbled, "but this isn't part of the caper. There's been an actual murder! And I'm afraid that—that we are *all* suspects."

"Suspects!" said Gretchen, rising to her feet.

There was a collective gasp at the sight of the dead coming to life.

"Do you know how much time and effort it took to perfect this makeup?" She brushed the invisible wrinkles from her dress. "It's not easy transforming into such a convincing corpse, you know."

She glared at us through hollow grey orbs, which made it difficult to take her rebuke too seriously. However, the lurid contacts she chose still sent a chill up my spine.

Elenor draped her fingers over Gretchen's shoulder. "I'm quite sure this isn't about you, dear."

Gretchen rolled her eyes. "Well, it seems I went through all this trouble for nothing. That's all I'm saying."

Was she that self-absorbed? Did she think her costume took precedence over the death of a human being?

Truman turned his focus to Harrison. "Well? Are you going to tell us who was murdered?"

Harrison flopped down on the arm of the sofa and exhaled air as if he had just completed a marathon. "It's Caffrey, I'm afraid."

"The butler?" I said. "Are you sure?"

"Well, he certainly looks dead," snapped Harrison. "It appears he's been knocked on the head with a pool cue."

[Gasp!]

"Who would want to kill the butler?" said Madeline.

"Isn't it *usually* the butler?" Gretchen quipped. "You know, the butler did it."

"He's not a real butler," said Truman.

She rolled her eyes again. "I know that. But I've grown accustomed to calling him the butler."

"Where is he, Harrison?" I asked. "Where's Caffrey?"

"He—he's in the library."

"The library?" I nearly shocked myself for blurting out the words with such force. How could I have missed him? I was a bit groggy when I woke up from my nap, but missing a dead body?

All eyes were now focused on me as though I had heartily confessed to the crime. "I didn't see anyone in the library. Where is he?" I squeezed Harrison's shoulder to comfort him, not knowing whether or not *he* had just killed Caffrey.

"He—he's by the pool table. You can't miss him."

"Where do you think you're going?" Jason barked.

Gretchen huffed and pushed her way past the group. "I'm going to check it out for myself. For all we know, it's part of this stupid game." She pranced across the floor like she was on a runway. "You can all come with me if you want...or just stand there," she yelled, already in the lobby.

"Wait for me," said Truman. "I'm coming with you."

"Maybe we should all go," I offered. "Like Harrison said, we are *all* suspects."

"You're right, Scarlet," agreed Sam. "We should probably stick together."

THE DOOR WHISTLED and shook, struggling to keep the storm's bluster at bay as a *whoosh* of cold air blew across the floor and up my skirt. I immediately found myself coveting a pair of Quinn's leg warmers. "It's been a while since I've seen the wind this angry," I said.

"It reminds me of that storm we had in Mahogany Falls a few summers back," said Quinn. "Remember?"

"How could I forget? The wind blew so ferociously it took the fascia right off our house, whipping it into Mrs. Huxley's rose bushes. Of course, it had to be *her* rose bushes. The prize-winning peach Mother of Pearl roses, which won her first place in the Mahogany Falls Rose Garden competition every year since it began."

"Has she ever forgiven you for that?"

"Nope, still looks at me sideways every time I see her. I don't know if she'll ever forgive me for decapitating her precious roses."

"Let's hope nothing gets decapitated during this storm."

Gretchen stopped short of the library.

"What is it?" asked Jason.

"It's dark in there. I'm not going in a room with a dead body if I can't see anything."

"Dark?" Harrison pushed his way to the front of the line. "Now, that's peculiar. The lights were on a few moments ago."

"Well, it's dark in there now." She stepped aside and waved Harrison through. "After you."

He reached his hand into the shadows, and a moment later, the room brightened into a soft, warm glow.

I entered the library behind Harrison. "So you didn't turn off the lights when you left the library?"

"Of course not," he replied. "Why would I do that? I had just stumbled upon a body. I was not concerned with any lights."

"Interesting, I said, "That means someone came into the library after you left."

"Unless," said Gretchen, "he's making the whole thing up to add a little more mystery to this whole whodunit thing."

Harrison folded his arms and said nothing.

"Why did you come into the library in the first place?" asked Jason.

"No reason. I guess I was making sure everyone was in the den to participate in discovering the body—I mean, the fictitious dead body."

Before going any further, we hesitated to mull over Harrison's story. And after careful consideration, we silently concluded the story was, at least, plausible. I waited for someone to make the first move; however, since my curiosity got the best of me, I inched toward the body, leaving the rest of the group to follow at a safe distance.

I was acting out a scene from one of my books. The spooky library. The creaking hardwood. The macabre scene coming into view. All that was missing was the passionate narrating.

"What do you see?" Sam whispered from the back of the line.

"Do you think he's dead?" asked Madeline.

Ignoring their absurd questions, I pressed on. My heart was beating so hard I could feel the rhythm in my head. With the already unbearable throbbing from my headache, it was as if someone was performing an African drum solo on the top of my brain.

"Oh my goodness!" Elenor cried. She turned away from the scene and into Sam's arms. "Who would do such a thing?"

There he was, lying on his stomach in the middle of the floor. His eyes and mouth open as if startled by his attacker. And from the side of his head flowed a crimson stream. Everything you'd expect to see at a murder scene—except for one crucial component. "I don't see the pool cue."

"Don't be daft!" Harrison waddled past me until he was standing over the body. "Where—where did it go? I can assure you the stick was there!" He pointed to the floor. "It was there! I'm absolutely positive it was there!"

"Well, it's not there now," said Elenor.

While the rest of the guests kept their distance, Gretchen confidently knelt beside the body. "There's something in his hand."

"What is it?" Truman asked.

"It's a key, I think."

"It looks like a skeleton key," I said. "Like our room keys."

"I'm guessing it belongs to the killer," said Madeline. "What color is it?"

"It's the red key," said Gretchen, gently moving the cuff of Caffrey's coat.

"Don't touch it!" I said. If there was one thing I knew about crime scenes, it was don't mess with the evidence. "This is now a crime scene…we can't touch anything."

"Relax, Nancy Drew, I wasn't going to remove it; I was confirming the color."

"Okay," said Jason, "whose key is it?

"Well, that's Caffrey's room," said Harrison. "It must have fallen out of his pocket during the struggle."

"I think Scarlet's right," said Sam. "This is a crime scene now, and we need to call the police immediately."

"The sooner, the better, too," said Gretchen. "I planned on *being* the corpse, not spending my weekend with one."

"Has anyone ever told you how tactless you are?" When Jason shouted, everyone flinched.

"What do you mean?"

"This man is dead. Show some respect."

Gretchen turned to face Jason, leaving only a few inches between their noses. "I don't consider myself tactless, Mr. Parrish. In my experience, people seem to appreciate a more outspoken, direct approach. I don't sugarcoat anything. If I have something to say, I say it. I'm sorry if it offends you, but life is too short to worry about every little thing I say."

Jason seemed genuinely shocked that she spoke to him with such audacity. "I'm just saying, a little decorum goes a long way."

Harrison wedged between Jason and Gretchen and tilted his head back, looking up to speak. "Alright, before this turns into something we can't crawl back from, how about we regain our composure? Unfortunately, this is not how any of us anticipated the weekend playing out. Let's take a breath and figure out our next move, shall we?"

"That sounds like an excellent plan to me," Elenor said, fanning herself with her boa.

18

We need a plan

DURING MY HIGH SCHOOL years, I dreaded speech day the most. I quaked at the mere thought of having to stand up in front of the class and talk for a solid five minutes, all without saying words like "um" or "ah."

The day before the big speech, I couldn't eat. Or sleep. Or do anything, for that matter, but think of the many ways I could make a fool of myself. I strolled up to the podium, my heart pumping so hard that the thought of it exploding out of my chest seemed plausible. Heat radiated from my cheeks, and the closer I got to the front of the class, the more it felt like I was walking through fire. My memory was all I had since the words I wrote on paper melted into a blur because of my sweaty hands. And when I looked at my audience, my brain turned to mush.

I couldn't breathe. I couldn't speak. And the only thing that comforted me at all was (ironically) my fingernails piercing into the palms of my hands.

Needless to say, I was not one to volunteer speeches of any kind, so when I opened my mouth to suggest an option on what to do next, it surprised me as much as it did Quinn.

"I think the first thing we should do is devise a plan."

Quinn peered at me with a sense of bewilderment and nodded. "I agree."

"What kind of plan?" asked Madeline.

"Well—I mean, the fact remains that one of us is the killer, which means nobody can leave the lodge, right?"

Sam stepped up to the body, shoving both hands into his pockets. "Are you saying you want to lead the investigation?"

"Oh, that's not my intention at all," I said, feeling my cheeks flush. "But I'm willing to help."

Elenor tapped Sam's arm. "Just so you know, Sam is a retired detective, I'm sure—"

"Now, dear, the key word here is retired. I gave up catching bad guys a long time ago."

"But I'm sure we could use your expertise in finding the killer," I said.

"Or maybe I can help *you*?"

Truman waved a finger over his head. "Wait a minute! How do we know that Sam or Scarlet didn't kill Caffrey?"

"We don't," said Harrison. "But might I suggest that we all keep one another accountable for the remainder of the weekend? I will go ring the police and inform them of the murder."

"What should the rest of us do?" said Jason.

"Well, I, for one, would love to get out of this skirt."

"I'm with Madeline," said Elenor. "The sequins on my dress catch on everything."

"Fine," said Harrison. "I wouldn't mind a wardrobe change as well. We'll meet back in the den after everyone has had a chance to freshen up. Maybe we can solve this mystery before the police arrive."

I had to agree; slipping into something more comfortable sounded good. All I wanted to do was wrap myself up in a blanket and work on my book. Of course, that didn't seem very likely at this point. Although now we had a murder to solve—an *actual* murder. Writing about it was one thing, but searching for clues to find a killer here at Mystery Ridge Lodge was serious stuff.

While everyone filed out of the library, Quinn hovered over the body with her arms crossed in front of her. I could only imagine what she was feeling.

"Probably not what you expected when you booked us into a murder mystery weekend, huh?"

"Who could have predicted this? I mean, I've never seen a dead body before."

"I don't think many of us have. You okay?"

"Yeah, I'm fine. I just want to get this guy. It's unsettling to know we're about to spend the weekend with a murderer."

"Agreed," I said. "So, I know I didn't kill Caffrey, and I'm ninety-nine percent sure you didn't kill him."

"Gee, thanks."

"Sorry, a little nervous humor."

"It's okay. I could use some humor right about now. But if I'm not the killer and you're not the killer, that means—"

"That means there are ten other possible suspects, and *one* is the murderer."

"But why would any of them want to kill Caffrey? I mean, I had my suspicions about who the killer was when I thought this was a game. Now I'm not sure what was real or in the script."

"That's what we need to find out. Even though the game is over, there will still be clues; we just have to find them." I walked around the body, quietly observing until something stopped me.

"What is it?"

I bent down and looked underneath the pool table. "That's odd."

"What do you see?" Quinn said, her patience dwindling.

"Can you hand me a tissue from the shelf over there? I probably shouldn't be moving this, but at least my prints won't be on it."

"On what?"

I held up a small bottle, twisted off the cap, and sniffed. "Hmm."

"Perfume?"

"No." I smelled it again. "I think it's…nutmeg." I rolled the empty jar between my fingers. "Yep, it's embossed with the word 'nutmeg' on the front."

"That is odd. Wonder why it's in the library."

"It's definitely out of place in here."

 What should we do with it?"

"We're going to put it back. When the police arrive, I'll tell them where to find it. Hopefully, they'll forgive me for touching it." After returning the bottle, I glanced down at Caffrey. His eyes were open and piercing with conviction. Since I didn't feel like being judged by a corpse, I grabbed a blanket and quickly draped it over the body.

"Your crime-solving juices are flowing, aren't they?"

"How could they not?"

"By the way," said Quinn, "what had you so spooked after coming out of the dining room?"

"Oh, that's right! I've been wanting to tell you. There's a door in the kitchen that Sébastien doesn't want me anywhere near, and I don't think it's the pantry. Initially, I thought it was all part of the game, but now I'm not so sure."

"What do you think it is?"

"I don't know, but I'm game to find out if you are."

"Careful, Scarlet. You're trudging through uncharted waters on this one. It's one thing to write about murders, but to be a part of one? There's a killer here! You need to be careful."

"You mean *we* need to be careful."

"Right! Now, let's get out of these ridiculous costumes and into something comfy so we can solve this murder."

19

Madeline

MADELINE WAS PLEASANTLY surprised Jason had packed her favorite velour sweatpants and matching hoodie. It was a relief to peel out of the tight skirt.

Jason was changing into something more comfortable, too. But something was wrong. It wasn't like him to be so quiet. Sure, seeing a dead body would upset anyone, but he was supposed to be strong enough for the both of them. Tell her everything will be alright. Did he even console her or ask her if *she* was okay? What kind of husband neglects to check on his wife after witnessing such an event? And now it was up to her to make sure *he* was alright?

"Is something wrong?" she said in her sweetest voice.

"Just thinking." He grabbed a navy blue hoodie from the duffle bag, pulled it over his head, and sat on the bed.

Madeline plopped beside him and scratched the nape of his neck with her long, manicured fingernails. She admired the vibrant orange polish Genji had chosen for her at the salon. It was the color that was supposed to coordinate with her newly purchased bathing suits. Now, it just clashed with her current outfit. The irritation began to bubble again at the thought of missing out on precious beach time; however, she needed to find out what was bothering Jason.

"What's wrong, babe? I *know* when something's wrong."

Jason sighed. "I'm not sure I should say anything?"

"Why not?"

"I don't need you complaining about anything else on this trip."

"Well, you can't keep it to yourself. You know how you get when you try to keep secrets from me. Your stomach gets all tied up in knots."

"Fine! It's not like you'll let it go. You'll probably find out sooner or later anyway."

Madeline grinned. *He was still pliable.*

"You know the contract I have with Mr. Whitmore?"

"How could I forget? It's why we're here, isn't it?"

"Well, there are some things I haven't told you."

She removed her hand from his neck, twisting herself to face him. "What do you mean…like what?"

He swallowed. "Well, first off, I haven't actually met Mr. Whitmore."

"What do you mean you haven't met him? I thought you got the contract a few days ago."

He clung to her knee and squeezed as though she might float away. "I know."

"You said he's the one who paid for this trip, and now you're saying you've never met the guy. What's going on, Jason?"

"It's true; he did pay for us to be here this weekend. And it's also true that we've never met face to face. We've only communicated through emails. He said he got my contact from some guy I worked for a few years ago. But he didn't say who."

"I don't understand. Who exactly is this guy? And why is he so mysterious? Is he in prison? Is he connected to the mob in some way?"

Jason got up from the bed and walked over to the window. He paused as the *rat-tat-tat* rattled the branches against the pane.

"Of course not. Mr. Whitmore's eccentric, that's all. That's how he likes to do business. Stays behind the scenes; the less interaction with people, the better. At least, that's what he says. But I *was* supposed to meet him here this weekend."

"Well, who is he? Why be so secretive?"

"He told me he's in fear for his life. That someone's been sending him ominous messages."

Madeline sprang from the bed. "What do you mean, ominous messages?"

"I mean, he's getting threats."

"Threats? Well, we need to tell somebody."

"And what good would that do? We don't even know who he is."

"Maybe we've already met him and don't know it. Do you think he's one of the other guests?"

"Don't know, maybe. And maybe he's not even at the lodge. He could've gotten caught in the storm. Who knows?"

"There could be another explanation. Caffrey could be Mr. Whitmore."

Jason tapped his fingers against his chin. "That was my initial thought, too. But we don't know that for sure."

"Have you tried to reach him?"

"Like I said, my only communication is a couple of emails. I don't even have a phone number for him. I tried sending an email, but I haven't gotten a response yet."

"I can't believe you took on this strange man as a client. Who conducts business this way? What did he say he wanted you to do?"

"He had me look into a few people. Wanted to know everything I'd learned about them before we met. I admit, I found it kinda strange, but he paid me upfront. What was I supposed to do?"

"I still think he's some kind of criminal, maybe a fugitive or something."

"You're getting carried away—"

"No, I'm not. You got us into this mess. If you had stuck with our plan, we'd be in Hawaii right now instead of suspects in a murder."

Bang, bang, bang!

They spun around and glared at the bright blue door as though it had spoken to them.

"Yeah?" Jason yelled.

"You two almost ready?"

Jason grabbed both of Madeline's hands and gave a slight squeeze. "For now," he whispered, "we keep this between us. We don't know who we can trust."

"Fine."

20

Harrison

HARRISON WAS ANXIOUS to unleash himself from the woolen toggery that had held him hostage for the past eight hours. It angered his sensitive skin. He threw his jacket on the bed, opened the closet, and looked for something less abrasive. After settling on a plum, zip-up sweater and a pair of navy blue trousers, he hung up his tweed jacket, then opened the refrigerator for a glass of orange juice.

This was a first for him, an actual murder at Mystery Ridge Lodge. He would now have to be responsible for keeping the guests in line and preventing them from turning on one another. To spend the weekend with an actual murderer was a daunting thought, he realized, but then again, what was he to do? He couldn't leave. Therefore, no one could leave.

He had to take charge and keep everyone calm. They'd be expecting him to contact the police, but of course, he couldn't do that.

He pushed back the curtain with his pinky finger, slowly sipping his orange juice. He could barely see anything out the window. The snow was thick and steady, and the wind blew about like calamitous gossip. It was a stroke of bad luck, he concluded. Now, he was trapped with the others with no means of escape.

Of course, he had no way of knowing the police would be called out to the lodge so soon after the last debacle. He believed there'd be time. One wrong move could be disastrous; the last thing he needed was a kink in his plan.

But, all was not lost. If his approach to the problem went off without a hitch, there would be no reason to focus on him.

He placed his glass in the sink and wiped the orange mustache from his face. To think about failure at this point was not an option. He had to hope the twenty-two years of blood, sweat, and tears he poured into this place would not be in vain—especially over something as ill-timed as murder.

He had to hold it together and assure the others he had everything under control.

But first things first.

He opened a drawer and pulled out a screwdriver.

"We can't have anyone calling the police now, can we?"

21

There's a killer among us

I TRIED TO WRAP my brain around the fact I was now spending the weekend with a cold-blooded killer. Since I had yet to meet a cold-blooded killer, I wondered what one might look like.

While the room began to fill with potential suspects, I took it upon myself to surmise the possible culpability of each person—strictly based on what little knowledge I'd gleaned over the past few hours. And although, on countless occasions, my mother would say to me, "Don't judge a book by its cover," that's exactly what I was about to do.

I first set my gaze on Sam and Elenor, a seemingly adorable couple who sipped coffee religiously from oversized mugs that never seemed to empty. They appeared to be taking the current situation in stride, acting more like sightseers on vacation than suspects in a murder. In my opinion, Elenor was the sweetest person at the lodge, and Sam was like the designated grandpa, telling stories from his past as though they were ripped from the headlines.

It couldn't possibly be either one of them, could it?

Besides, Sam was a retired detective; why would he kill Caffrey?

Then there was Truman. Slumped back in his seat with his arms folded tightly across his chest, he seemed to analyze the room as intently as I was. Somewhat agitated, his eyes darted from one body to the next, unsure who should receive his full attention. Until his gaze met mine. We locked eyes for precisely two seconds before quickly averting his focus to an imaginary piece of lint on his jeans. Was it an abundance of caffeine or a guilty conscience? I couldn't be sure. He had a way of taking the focus off himself and onto someone else. The question was, what was he hiding?

Gretchen, on the other hand, appeared unfazed by our predicament. She was brooding. Probably because her death scene had been thwarted. Her vibe was highly unlikeable. But enough to kill? Of all the people at the lodge, she appeared to be the most cold-blooded of the bunch.

In the middle of my sanctimonious evaluation, I concluded I might very well be suspect number one. After all, I was in the library during the murder, or so it would seem. When I settled in to do some writing, the last thing I expected to see was a dead body. My focus was strictly on my book. But the fact that I fell asleep so quickly was so unlike me.

Almost too unlikely.

Sleep-deprived or not, I don't think I could sleep through a murder. *Could I have been drugged? Was someone setting me up?* Everyone knew I'd be meeting Gretchen in the library at two. It was in the script, for goodness' sake!

I grabbed my water bottle and took a long gulp, knowing I had just worked myself into a frenzy. There was no proof. It was one thing to be at the scene, but with no motive or evidence, what else was there? Nothing, that's what. I didn't even know Caffrey. Who was this guy, anyway? I wondered. And what kind of name was Caffrey?

Victoria entered the den, Sébastien not far behind her. He placed his arm around her shoulders and guided her to the loveseat. She tried to appear as though she hadn't been crying, but her red, puffy eyes had given her away.

Harrison entered a few minutes later, appearing more relaxed than when he came barging in shouting, "Murder!" It might have been because he was now dressed like Mr. Rogers rather than Mr. Bean. It was noteworthy to see him so unperturbed.

"Have you called the police?" Elenor asked.

"I have not," said Harrison. "I figured I'd ask Mr. Parrish to join me."

"You can call me Jason. I think we're done playing games at this point."

"Right, Jason, it is. Let's go ring the police then, shall we?"

"Don't bother," said Truman. "The phones are dead."

"What do you mean the phones are dead?" Madeline cried.

"I tried to make a call when I returned to my room, and there was no dial tone…the phones are dead!"

"Are you telling me we're trapped here with a dead body, and we can't even let the police know? This can't be happening." She placed her hand on her forehead and huffed.

"What about our cell phones? Can't we use those to call the police?" Gretchen asked.

"We can try," said Harrison, "but I'm not convinced it will result in a desired outcome. In the best of times, we can only get reception on our cell phones if we hike up the path away from the lodge. And that's if the weather cooperates. I'm afraid the storm has put a damper on that plan."

"So we're stuck here?" Madeline pushed back the curtains and gazed out the window as if the sun would never return.

"I'm afraid so." Harrison pulled out an old wooden rocking chair from the far corner of the room and dragged it closer to the group. He slowly lowered himself down until he was safely seated. The rickety wood creaked while he leisurely rocked back and forth. "We'll just have to wait out the storm."

"Maybe that's the best thing we can do right now," I said. "The snow is falling pretty heavily, and it's probably not likely the police could even get up the mountain tonight."

"And what about the killer?" said Truman. "Should we ignore that he—or she is sitting in this room?"

"We stick together," said Sam. "Like Scarlet said."

"And who made her boss?" Gretchen hissed.

"She's trying to help," Jason said. "Maybe you should try helping instead of criticizing anyone with a suggestion."

"Alright, alright," Harrison said, again acting as a go-between. "Let's just take a breath and stop acting like immature adolescents. I know tensions are a bit high, and we all want answers. In the meantime, I suggest we sit down and get to know one another."

Gretchen rolled her eyes so dramatically that I was sure they'd get stuck mid-roll. It was a talent she succeeded in.

"What do *you* think we should do, Gretchen?" I asked, hoping she appreciated the gesture of giving her the floor.

"I think we should be discussing what to do with the body in the other room. He can't stay there."

"For now," said Harrison, "that's exactly where he will stay. Until the police arrive, there are not many options, I'm afraid." He gave a slight nod to Sébastien. "Who's up for some coffee?"

"How 'bout something a little stronger?" Jason said.

"*Oui*," said Sébastien, waving his arm. "Anybody else? *Viens avec moi!*"

"Thank you, Chef," said Harrison.

Once everyone had their desired drink, I decided to mingle about the room. Rebecca was lingering at the back and seemed agitated.

"Can I get you anything?" I asked.

"No thanks, don't seem to have much of an appetite."

"It's hard to wrap your head around, isn't it?" I said, trying to get a sense of who she was. Was she a friend or foe? Did she have some deep-seated hatred toward the victim? Or perhaps she was experiencing an unbearable ache over the loss of someone she loved? Or maybe it was somewhere in between.

"Did you know Caffrey well?

She dropped her head and folded her arms in front of her. She wasn't inconsolable or even crying, but she *did* seem upset.

"You could say that."

I waited for her to elaborate, but she was content to leave it at that. I let a few seconds pass before I pushed.

"Did you know him long?"

She sighed. "We've been seeing each other for about six months."

"Oh, I'm so sorry. I wasn't aware that you and Caffrey were in a relationship."

"It's not something we shared with the guests. We wanted to keep our private lives private."

"I can understand that."

"It was mostly because of this stupid game. Caffrey thought it might distract the guests from the plot if they knew we were a couple."

I sipped my coffee while eyeing the chocolate cherry bars Sébastien brought in from the kitchen. I picked one up and sunk my teeth into the decadent chocolate, physically restraining myself from moaning as it melted like butter.

After successfully composing myself, I took another sip of coffee, dabbed my mouth with a napkin, and refocused on Rebecca. "Have you been working here very long?"

She twisted the tissue between her hands like she was wringing out a dishcloth. "I haven't, no. But, Caffrey worked here for years."

"Is this where you two met?"

"You sure ask a lot of questions."

"Sorry about that. I'm not usually this bold when talking with someone I hardly know, but you seem a bit shaken, and I wanted to make sure you were okay."

"It's fine," she said. "And the answer is no. I didn't meet Caffrey here. Six months ago, my sister set me up with him on a blind date, and we hit it off immediately."

"How did you end up here, if you don't mind me asking?"

"Well, at the time, I was looking for work and asked him if he knew of any restaurants that were hiring. He said he would talk to Sébastien about a job at the lodge. I was thrilled when he said he was looking for an assistant. That's how I ended up here."

"That's a lovely—"

"Excuse me," she said. "I need a minute."

That was odd. I thought we were having an enjoyable conversation.

At the same time, Sam strolled to the center of the room. He cleared his throat and said, "To move this investigation along, might I suggest we start by finding out where everyone was at the time of the murder?"

Harrison waved his arm over his head. "I'll start," he said. "Let's see...I do believe I was in the den when lunch was served. Sometimes, when the guests are occupied, I spend a few moments alone. It's relaxing. Besides, I didn't particularly fancy a bowl of soup. I retrieved Mrs. Lane's—uh, Scarlet's laptop from the safe, then made my way up to my room to fix myself a sandwich. I keep a few things in the kitchenette since I often crave a snack during the night. Sometime after, I returned to the lobby, checked my emails, and proceeded down the hall and into the laundry room; I wondered why the dryer was on. I heard Victoria scream a moment or two later, which compelled me to the library."

"Why go there?" Sam asked.

"Like I said before, I wanted to be sure that everyone was in the den for the reveal of the body."

"So, as far as you're concerned," said Sam, "you didn't see anything out of the ordinary?"

"No. Nothing. Except..."

"Except what?" said Jason.

"Well, except for Scarlet running out of the library."

22

I know I didn't kill him

COLD GLARES SHOT through me like ice pellets, and I wasn't sure if I'd be able to convince these strangers I was innocent.

"Yes, I ran out of the library only because I heard Victoria's scream. Isn't that why everyone came running?"

"I think what everyone wants to know," said Gretchen, "is what you were doing in the library? It seems *you* had the best opportunity to kill Caffrey."

The disdain was thick. But she wasn't wrong. The fact that I was in there for nearly two and a half hours placed me at the scene of the crime with no alibi to speak of. Could I expect them to believe I slept through the murder? *I* could barely believe it.

It was curious, however, as to why I had stayed asleep for so long. I had never been a sound sleeper. Dominic says I must sleep with one eye open because no matter what time he gets up to use the bathroom, I'm awake and staring at him with eyes as big as saucers.

"As most of you know, my character was to meet Gretchen in the library at two. But I went there early to do some writing since everyone seemed to be doing their own thing. Apparently, I fell asleep. Must have been the cozy fire and comfortable sofa." I laughed nervously.

"You didn't wake up when Caffrey was fighting for his life?" Rebecca's words stung, and I realized the murder must have been especially hard for her.

"I'm sorry, I—I didn't hear a thing. I opened my eyes just before Victoria screamed. I wish I could help."

Rebecca wiped a tear from her eye and left the den before I could say anything to stop her.

"That's a rather convenient explanation if you ask me."

"Well, no one's asking you, Gretchen," said Jason.

She smirked and said, "How do we even know what time the murder took place?"

"What do you mean?" said Sam, raising an eyebrow.

"I mean, how do we know the exact time Caffrey died? The only person who would know that would be the killer. It's not like there's a coroner around here to tell us the precise time of death. And I'm pretty sure the killer isn't going to offer up any information."

"Perhaps," said Harrison, "a good place to start is to find out where everyone went after lunch." He looked at Sam. "Isn't that right?"

"Thank you, Harrison. Yes, good idea. From what I understand, Caffrey was in the dining room with us just after Sébastien served the soup. Then he left."

Gretchen began rubbing her eyes; they were red and puffy again. She hauled a bottle from her pocket and placed a few drops in each eye.

"You okay, Gretchen?" I asked.

"I'm fine. I'm allergic to wood smoke."

"Really?" said Jason. "Never heard of that one before."

"Well, it's rare," she hissed.

"What about you?" I asked. "You were the first to leave the dining room after lunch. Where did you go?"

Gretchen scoffed. "Of course, you'd point the finger at me." She made a show of dramatically crossing her arms and swinging her leg over her knee, committed to being difficult.

"Answer the question!" Jason shouted.

Jason was no fan of Gretchen.

"Fine!" she snapped. "I was preparing for my death scene." She flipped her hair to the side. "I told you, achieving the look I wanted took time. Once content with my character, I went to the den and took my spot on the floor, where you all found me minutes later."

"That's not true, though, is it?" said Jason. "You came back into the dining room around one-thirty."

"Right, and as you probably saw, I went into the kitchen for a glass of water, then went back upstairs to finish getting ready."

"So you're telling me it took you three hours to put white makeup on your face and place contacts into your eyes?"

"Like I said...everything had to be perfect: my hair, makeup, costume...everything! Do you think that magically happens? It takes work, you know!"

She began to seethe at this point, turning her wrath on Sam. "What about you? I seem to recall you anxious to leave the table as well."

Sam glanced at Elenor and bit the inside of his cheek. "I ahh—I decided to have a nap."

"You don't seem that sure of yourself."

"Well—"

"Lunch didn't agree with Sam," Elenor said, placing her hand on his leg before he could say anything. "He wanted to be close to a bathroom, that's all."

"Thanks, dear."

Elenor smiled back.

"I assume you were in the room together, Elenor?" I asked.

"Yes. I pulled out my knitting while Sam was…"—she paused—"indisposed. After that, I took a nap while Sam went to find Truman. They were going to play pool in the library."

"So, you *were* in the library," I said. "What time was that?"

"Yes, it was around 1:45 or so, but only for a brief moment. I went down to see if Truman was there, but he wasn't. I checked the dining room and peeked out the window, thinking maybe he'd gone out to the hot tub. When I couldn't find him, I joined Elenor for a nap. Figured Truman did the same."

"That's right," said Elenor, giving Sam a nod. "After our naps, I convinced him to go downstairs for another cup of coffee."

"And nothing out of the ordinary?" asked Madeline.

"Uhh—"

"*I* was in the kitchen," Sébastien interrupted. "I was busy creating—*un magnifique dîner.*"

"You were in the kitchen the whole time?" Jason piped in.

"*Mais oui*, apart from my afternoon smoke break…I was in the kitchen the whole time."

"You smoke?" Elenor asked, as though she was surprised that anyone did that anymore.

"I do," he said. "I admit it's an awful habit, but one I am trying to kick. I've managed to get it down to one a day; I save that one for my afternoon break. Twenty minutes, every day at two. I take my coffee and cigarette, and outside I go so no one can see."

"You do this every day at the same time?" Sam asked. "Even when there's a storm blowing outside?" He pointed his finger out the window.

"Without fail. I bundle up nice and warm, leave through the laundry room door, and head to the shed where I'm out of the elements."

I couldn't help but notice the look Sam gave to Elenor and wondered if Quinn picked up on it, too. But as I was about to question him, Rebecca returned to the den.

"What about you, Rebecca?" Sam said without skipping a beat. "I gather you were also in the kitchen?"

"Yes," she said. "After cleaning up lunch, I started chopping vegetables for dinner. Once I finished with those, I began prepping for the chocolate cherry bars, but I had a headache, so when Chef returned from his break, I asked if I could go to my room to lie down. "

"What time would you say that was?" I asked.

"I guess it was around two-thirty? I'm not entirely sure of the time. My focus was getting rid of my headache."

I empathetically rubbed the bump on the side of my head. The headache had subsided but was lingering around like a bad date.

"Victoria," said Sam, "what about you? You were the one to let out the horrifying scream?"

"Yes, that's what I was supposed to do. I had no idea that Gretchen would be playing the role of the victim; none of us did. All I knew was that a body would be in the den at 3:15, and I was to alert everyone with my scream. I've done it hundreds of times."

"Who knew that Gretchen was going to be the victim? Truman asked. "Someone knew."

"Yes," said Victoria, "Harrison usually mails out the character descriptions to the guests. But this weekend, the owner wanted to be in charge. I guess it was so the staff could also play the game."

"Who's the owner?" I asked.

"Mr. Whitmore," she answered.

23

The mysterious Mr. Whitmore

THE MYSTERY WAS getting more riveting by the minute, and the new person of interest was as peculiar as the lodge.

"And does Mr. Whitmore usually take part in these murder mysteries?" I asked.

"Actually," said Harrison, "I've worked at this lodge for twenty-two years and have yet to meet the man."

"That's weird," said Quinn. "What about when he hired you? You must have met him during the interview."

"That's the thing," said Harrison, "I didn't have an interview. The position was just offered to me."

As usual, Quinn scrunched her nose when things didn't add up. "It was just offered to you?"

"Yes. It sounds rather peculiar, doesn't it? But it's true. Twenty-two years ago, I worked as the manager at the Delta Hotel in Calgary. Out of the blue, I received a phone call from someone granting me a delightful position at Mystery Ridge

Lodge. If I agreed to his terms, I could stay in a suite, earn twice the wage of my current salary, and hire my own staff. In addition, I'd acquire a generous expense account to procure the necessary items for each mystery game conducted at the lodge."

"Who was the man on the other end of the phone?" Jason asked.

"Why, it was Mr. Whitmore, of course."

"Who's Mr. Whitmore, and what were his terms?" I asked.

Harrison smiled at me and sighed. It was like he had no idea how to answer the question. "The only thing I know is that Mr. Whitmore is very generous. He only requested two things from me before accepting the job. First, I had to create intriguing murder mysteries for the guests at the lodge, and second, I could only communicate with him by email. If I agreed to the terms, then the job, the expense account, the bump in pay was mine."

"Seems a little far-fetched to me," said Truman. "Some stranger calls you out of nowhere and offers you a job, and you have no idea who he is?"

"Yes. And everything went according to plan until this weekend."

"If you don't mind me asking," said Jason, "why did he choose you? How could he trust you to care for his hotel if you had never met him?"

Harrison gazed out the window, gently rocking to the sway of the pine trees outside. He seemed to bask in his newly acquired celebrity, his audience hanging on to his every word.

"Well, as I've already informed you, I have never met Mr. Whitmore and have only ever spoken to him on the phone once. However, I did ask him that same question. "Why me?" He said he knew exactly who I was and was confident I was the perfect choice for the job. He knew everything about me: where I worked, where I lived, and the fact that my wife was sick. I won't lie, I was rather flabbergasted. But I couldn't think of anything keeping me from taking the job."

"I guess there could be worse places to work," said Jason.

"Not to mention," Harrison continued, "when someone offers you a suite with mountain views in a magnificent lodge, masquerading in costumes in one of the most scenic places in Canada, *and* is willing to pay a handsome wage to boot then he could be the next king of England for all I care."

"So you say," said Sam, "that you only communicate through emails? What if there's an emergency? Like *murder*, for example?"

"Not to worry, Detective. I've sent an email. He's remarkably punctual…answers within minutes."

"Have you told him about Caffrey?"

"No, Detective, I have not had the chance."

"Oh, you can call me Sam. I'm a guest like everyone else here."

Harrison nodded. "Sam."

"I have one more question: Has Mr. Whitmore ever taken over the game in the past? And if not, why do you think he chose this weekend?"

Harrison chuckled. "Over the years, I've learned that Mr. Whitmore expects things to be done a certain way. He also likes to keep a low profile. So if he desires more of a hands-on approach, I oblige without any questions."

"He must trust you," I said.

He paused, and his eyes narrowed as though musing over his incalculable worth. "Yes, quite."

"Enough about Mr. Whitmore already," said Gretchen. "I want to know where the rest of you people were during the murder."

The fact that Gretchen had as much couth as a trucker at an etiquette conference didn't stop me from agreeing with her. For one thing, my curiosity had clung to Truman the minute I noticed him missing from the first crime scene.

He was a puzzle. One minute, he was a frantic hornet. The next, he was quiet and subdued as though pondering his next move in a chess game. I watched as he anxiously chewed his fingernails down to the quick and wondered what had him so concerned.

"You alright, Truman?" I asked. "You seem nervous."

He quickly removed his fingers from his mouth and slid them under his armpit. "Isn't everyone? I don't know about you guys, but this murder has my stomach in knots."

"I agree...it's awful!"

"So," said Gretchen, "where were *you* when the butler was killed?"

Truman swung one leg over the top of his knee, holding his foot with both hands. If it was to prevent his leg from shaking, it wasn't working.

"After lunch, I had planned to sit in the hot tub, relax, and maybe listen to music. But as I was about to change into my swimsuit, I remembered I was supposed to play pool with Sam in the library. When I opened the door, I heard faint voices coming from the other end of the hall. Possibly a woman's voice."

"Voices?" said Elenor. "Who was it?"

"I'm not sure," he said, turning toward Victoria. "Whoever it was, I think the sound was coming from the staff quarters."

Victoria's posture straightened. "Why are you looking at me?"

"What?" said Truman. "I'm not accusing you of anything; I'm just saying I heard a woman's voice. Not to mention, after lunch, when I passed you on the stairs, you looked a little—"

"A little what?"

"Frazzled."

Victoria shrugged her shoulders. "I don't know who or what you heard in your room, but it wasn't me. And as far as how I looked after lunch, I was trying to get into character. I had a role to play; part of that role was looking the part. Finding a dead body in the den can make one appear somewhat…frazzled." She peered around the room. "As you all can imagine, I'm sure."

"Okay, again, not accusing you. It was just an observation."

"What were you doing before you were to sound the alarm, so to speak?" I asked.

"I always go to my room before I set the stage. It gives me a chance to relax before all the excitement begins. I poured myself a glass of wine. It's something I do before the game is about to begin. It loosens me up, you know? However, I accidentally bumped the glass with my elbow, spilling red wine all over my apron and causing an unsightly stain. Hoping I could treat it before it began to set, I quickly rushed down to the laundry room. When I got there, I noticed some sheets still in the dryer, so I began folding while waiting for the stain remover to do its job. After that, I threw my apron and a few towels into the washer. I must have been in there for half an hour or so." She glared at Truman. "So if you heard a woman's voice, I assure you it wasn't mine."

"Did anyone see you in the laundry room?" Sam asked.

"Actually, yes. When I came out with an armload of sheets, Madeline came into the lobby from outside; she even asked me for an extra blanket for her room."

"What were you doing outside?" asked Jason.

Madeline sighed. "What's the big deal? I was curious to see if Harrison would let me have my phone. If you must know, that's where I went. I hoped to get a few bars by going up to the trees like he said when we checked in. But I didn't get very far; it was too cold. So I came back to the lodge."

"I thought we had to give up our cells this weekend," said Truman.

Madeline sheepishly looked at Jason. "When I saw that Harrison gave Scarlet her laptop, I figured he'd let me check my phone. I promised to hand it over as soon as I got back. No big deal."

"And did you?" Sam asked.

"I—um...well... ."

"So, no!" said Jason. "What was so important, anyway, that you just *had* to check your phone only hours after giving it up?"

"You don't understand. I *need* my phone!"

"Why didn't you return it?"

"It's just that...when I returned to the lodge, Harrison wasn't at the desk; I figured he probably forgot. I stuck it in the waistband of my skirt and brought it up to my room."

"You're unbelievable, Mads"

"What? I'm not breaking the law. It's a cell phone, for goodness' sake. It didn't matter anyway; I couldn't get any bars."

"That's not the point."

"And what about you, Jason?" Gretchen said smugly.

She was definitely entertained.

"I was in the dining room talking with Quinn."

"Oh really?" said Madeline.

Quinn jumped into the conversation before Madeline could give Jason the third degree. "We were discussing our shared interest in photography. It's always been a hobby of mine."

"What do you do for work, Jason?" Elenor asked.

"I own a security company for high-end clients."

"Like a bodyguard?"

"Something like that...usually requires confidentiality," he said, attempting to nip the conversation in the bud.

Truman perked up. "So movie stars, politicians, lawyers?"

Jason fiddled with the ring on his finger. "Anyone, really. Whoever feels they need some kind of security measures, I'm the guy. Anyway, after our conversation, I went upstairs to my room to read."

Sam nodded his head toward Quinn. "I guess that leaves you, my dear. Where did you go after lunch?"

"Well, I also wanted to read. I went upstairs to get my book but realized I had left it in my car. I wanted to get it before the snow completely buried it. I noticed the passenger side door was open when I got out there. Figured Scarlet didn't shut it hard enough. I like to keep a few things in there, you know, for emergencies. I didn't notice anything out of the ordinary."

She glanced at me and grinned. Her saying she kept "a few things" was the understatement of the year.

"The wind was cold. I didn't want to spend any more time outside than I needed to. I grabbed my book and beelined for the den, where I spent the next couple of hours reading in front of the fire. After a bit, I wanted a snack and remembered leaving a bag of pretzels in the car. When I returned, I saw everyone gathered around the body—I mean, Gretchen."

At that very moment, a whiff of something heavenly filled the room. The aroma of Chef Sébastien's French cuisine wafted into the den like a comfy blanket. And yes, I *was* undergoing a tinge of guilt for thinking of my stomach amidst a murder investigation; however, I managed to subdue it since I'd been looking forward to dinner since lunch.

"Maybe we should take a break," said Harrison. "I'm sure the chef needs to check on dinner."

"*Ah oui,*" Sébastien said, pushing himself off his chair. "It smells good, *non? Confit de Canard* is on the menu for tonight. And it will be served at six-thirty. Sharp!"

"What do you think?" said Quinn, stretching her arms over her head.

"Not sure what I think," I said. "But I know one thing."

"What's that?

"I have more questions now than I had before we started."

24

Someone's been busy

IT WAS ALREADY half past five, and the body had been lying in the library for the better part of the afternoon. Once the odor started permeating the entire lodge, conditions would turn tense. And if the police couldn't make it up the mountain for a day or two, it would only add to an already stressful situation.

The guests were milling about, waiting for Sébastien to finish preparing dinner, so I thought it would be an ideal time to take another look at the crime scene.

I had to tap Quinn on the leg when I noticed her fighting with her eyelids. "I'm going back to the library to see if we missed anything."

"What? You sure you wanna do that?" she said, attempting to stifle a yawn.

"Yes. It will allow me to examine the scene more closely while everyone's occupied. Cover me, okay?"

"Cover you? Who are you?"

"I need to burn off some nervous energy. I can't sit here and do nothing, knowing the killer might get away with murder."

"Maybe I should come, too."

"The company would be nice, but it might seem suspicious if we both take off. Besides, I already look like the prime suspect. If they catch me snooping around the library, it might look like I'm trying to destroy evidence. That's why you need to cover me."

She sighed and discreetly looked around the room. "Fine. Promise me you'll be careful! And don't get yourself into any trouble. Gretchen's probably monitoring everyone; you know how she sticks her nose where it doesn't belong. I wouldn't be surprised if she's even a bit miffed that you're in charge of the investigation."

"Oh, please! I'm not in charge of anything. I'll leave that to Sam or Harrison. I'm curious, that's all. Not planning to step on any toes."

"Hey," Quinn said in a low whisper, "You make a pretty awesome detective."

I laughed. "I admit, it's been quite exhilarating being thrust into an actual murder investigation. Be back soon."

"Be careful."

"I will."

As I ducked out of the den and into the lobby, I glanced out the window. I had to admire the storm. The sun had clocked out hours ago, yet a white, wintery glow illuminated the sky as though it was mid-morning. Drifts had formed in front of the door and down the stairs like ocean waves, and anything visible beyond that was a pure white blanket of snow.

I snuck a quick peek behind me; the coast was clear, so I hurried down the hall to continue my investigation.

I almost had second thoughts when I entered the library. Approaching a dead body with an enthusiastic entourage was one thing, but scoping out a death scene with nothing but mood lighting and the company of my own shadow was a whole other story. Every time the floor creaked, I was sure I sensed someone behind me. "It's just my mind playing tricks," I said under my breath, convincing myself it was all in my head.

But when I reached the other side of the pool table, I wasn't so sure. Caffrey lay in the same spot as before but with another critical piece of evidence missing.

"The nutmeg!" I whispered. I crouched down, looking for anything else that might be out of place. I was about to remove the blanket from Caffrey's face when my heart nearly jumped out of my chest for the third time that day.

"What are you doing in here?"

I squealed and nearly came into contact with the body. When I turned around, Truman was hovering over me like a cloud. "Truman! What are *you* doing here?"

"I asked you first."

I had to play this smart. Either he was curious (like I was), or Truman was the killer and followed me into the library to keep an eye on me. Or worse, *take care of me* (as they say in the movies.) Either way, I couldn't trust him. "I'm guessing I'm here for the same reason you are."

"Find anything interesting?"

As far as I knew, he had no idea about the bottle I found earlier. I needed to keep it that way. "Looks like he's right where we left him."

Truman took a step back, arms folded in front of him. "You know, discovering someone crouched over the body like that makes them look kinda guilty."

I kept forgetting I was a suspect—and a good one at that, and I figured a few people probably already had me convicted and sentenced to life in prison. It didn't matter what I did; I was going to look suspicious, so the only thing I could do was try to convince Truman I was innocent. For all I knew, he was planning on blabbing to the others that he found me lurking over the body.

"All I can say is I didn't kill Caffrey, and I certainly wasn't in here trying to mess with the crime scene."

Truman's chuckle was a tad sinister for my liking. "That's what a killer might say."

"I can't make you believe me, but I am *not* the killer."

"I guess we'll find out soon enough," he said.

"Now it's your turn...why did *you* come back here?"

"Wouldn't you like to know?"

"Yes, I would."

"I watched as you left the den and figured you were up to something. I decided to follow you to see where you'd end up. Didn't think I'd find you back here, though, looking guilty as sin."

I planted my hands on my hips and threw him a look. "I guess it does look pretty bad," I said. "But that's exactly why I came back here...to find out who killed Caffrey so I can clear my name."

"I don't think you're cut out for this kind of work, Scarlet," he said, leaving the library. "Perhaps you should leave the investigation to the police."

So this is how it was going to be. I was numero uno on the list of suspects. And for some reason, it was easy to believe I could have killed the butler. Me. What did people think when they looked at me? *Now that looks like a killer.* That in itself was enough incentive to test out my investigative skills. If anything, to clear my name.

WHEN I RETURNED to the den, half expecting Sam to put me under citizen's arrest, I was surprised to see everyone still in deep conversation; even Truman had resumed his spot on the sofa as if he'd been there all along.

"Well?" said Quinn, bouncing on the balls of her feet. "What did you discover? Anything new?"

Of course, I didn't hear a word Quinn was saying. Instead, I focused on Truman, wondering what he was discussing with Sam and Elenor. *Was he hanging me out to dry?*

"Scarlet?"

"Sorry—yes."

"Yes, what? You okay?"

"I think so, but I may have made myself an even bigger suspect."

"What do you mean?"

I said it as quietly as I could. "The nutmeg is missing from underneath the pool table."

"What?"

I placed my finger to my lips. "Quinn! Try to keep it to a dull roar."

"Sorry. I wasn't expecting you to say that."

"No, it was a shock for me as well. I'm guessing the killer returned to remove it when we all went upstairs to change out of our costumes."

Quinn folded her arms and grabbed her chin. "So, the killer returned to the crime scene not once, but twice?"

I raised my eyebrows and nodded. "Exactly! They've been busy."

"Why do you think this has made you more of a suspect? I'm the only other person that knows, right?"

"Not exactly." I threw Truman a glance. "Unfortunately, Truman entered the library as I discovered the missing bottle."

"Oops. I thought he was going to the bathroom. Sorry about that."

"Don't worry about it. He followed me to see where I was going. Perhaps he's as curious as we are."

"Or maybe he wanted to see your reaction when you noticed the crime scene had been tampered with."

"Could be. But whoever killed Caffrey is either a very sloppy killer or a killer who plans to frame someone for the murder."

"You could be right." Quinn glared at Truman. "Although it doesn't appear like he's pointing any fingers. Do you think we should tell the others?"

"As far I know, only two of us know about the nutmeg... besides the killer. For now, let's keep that little nugget between us. It might come in handy later."

25

Gossips are the spies of life

ALTHOUGH I HADN'T written one word in over a month, I was sure I could write a book based on current events unfolding over the past twelve hours. I wondered what had given me such confidence to snoop around like that. Maybe I *was* channeling Chase Ridgeway's investigative skills. However, returning from the library only inundated my brain with more questions. For example, the significance of the nutmeg. It stumped me. Why was it in the library in the first place? Who put it there? Was it a calling card of some kind? And if so, why remove it?

The pool cue was another stumper. It wouldn't have been my first choice of weaponry, but it was the killer's. Why? Or was it used out of mere convenience? If so, why would the killer remove it instead of wiping off their prints? It would have been easier to give it a rubdown with the back of their sleeve than risk being seen taking it out of the library. Which brings me to a more puzzling question: How did no one notice the killer moving about the lodge with the murder weapon?

I decided to get up and meander discreetly throughout the crowd; being sedentary was not good for productivity. I grabbed my water bottle, took a few gulps, and proceeded to pace: den, lobby, den, lobby.

Quinn also moved about the room, but she was more of a social butterfly than I was—consistently inserting herself into conversations, whether by invitation or not.

I decided to kick it up a notch, trying to capitalize on an increasing heart rate because, in my experience, it usually served as a favorable catalyst for creative introspection. But as I continued to stride across the hardwood, my curiosity was piqued when I observed Jason and Madeline engaged in what appeared to be a weighty conversation. Whatever had them speaking through clenched teeth and low volumes, I considered it my duty as a co-investigator to monitor the situation.

I deliberately lingered around the painting on the wall, hoping my feigned interest in a moose walking across the highway wouldn't arouse any suspicion.

"Jason, are you listening to me?" Madeline said, shaking his arm.

"What?"

"I said, don't you think it's crazy that Harrison is working for Mr. Whitmore? Do you think he's the same guy you're working for?"

"I don't know, Mads."

"You must have some idea as to who he is, Jason. When was he supposed to meet you here? Today? Tomorrow? You've gotta know *something* about the guy."

"You know as much as I do. I wish I could tell you more, but I—"

As if a spotlight ignited over my head, Jason broke eye contact with Madeline and zeroed in on me.

Not again. I was terrible at this eavesdropping thing; I'd been found out twice in one day. I needed to make my way over to Quinn without bringing any more attention to myself. I peered over my shoulder to see if Jason was following me and was relieved he hadn't moved.

Quinn was either taking a break, or she managed to talk the ear off of everyone in the room. "Learn anything?" I said, taking one last glance behind me.

"I did. Quite an interesting bunch, I'd say."

"What'd you find out?"

"Well, for starters, did you know Elenor is a retired forensic pathology technician?"

"Wow! That's impressive."

"I know. For some reason, I can't picture Elenor performing autopsies in a morgue."

I looked at the elderly couple sipping coffee and holding hands like a couple of lovesick teenagers. They were adorable. And probably two of the most respected guests at the lodge. "Nope," I said, "I can't picture it either."

"And then there's Gretchen."

"Gretchen? How'd you manage to get *her* to open up? She doesn't seem like the get-to-know-you type."

"I overheard her talking with Truman. Apparently, she separated from her husband and decided to come here to deal with the break-up."

"Really? Now I feel bad for her."

"Me too. At least it makes sense, now, why Gretchen is so irritable. I'd be cranky, too, if anything happened with Brian and me."

"Everyone has a story, I guess. Speaking of story, I'm pretty sure I overheard Jason and Madeline saying something I wasn't supposed to hear."

"Ooh! Do tell."

"Well, Jason and Madeline were talking about Mr. Whitmore and—"

Before I could dish out any more gossip, Quinn's eyebrows began to flip out like an imaginary string was pulling them up and down. What was happening? Was it Morse code? Did she lose the ability to speak? I was about to ask her if she was having a stroke when she abruptly stood up and said, "Oh, hey Jason, how's it going?"

Jason had a bone to pick with me; at least, that's what it looked like as I watched him approach. A chastisement was brewing; I could feel it.

"I saw that you left the den."

It was a statement I wasn't quite sure how to respond to. So I didn't.

"Where did you go? The library? Care to share what you found?"

"What makes you think I found anything?"

He grinned. "I watched as you came bouncing into the den. You were anxious to inform Quinn about something, am I right?"

I wondered if he knew about the missing items. Could *he* have taken them?

"I don't feel comfortable telling you anything. You could be the killer."

Jason plunged his hands into his jeans and bent forward as though trying to intimidate me.

"And for all I know, one of you killed him. Perhaps we might be able to help each other. I know something that might prove valuable to the investigation."

"I'm listening," I said, intrigued by the cloak-and-dagger.

He discretely looked in Madeline's direction. "I'd like to keep this between us if you don't mind."

"I assume Madeline is unaware of what you're about to tell me?"

"She knows enough. But not everything."

"What's your secret, Jason," said Quinn.

"Okay, well, today is not the first day hearing about Mr. Whitmore. He hired me a few days ago."

Ah, so that's what they were talking about. "For what?"

"I'm not sure, exactly. Security…maybe."

"What kind of security? Was he being threatened?"

"Yes. And he hired me to find out who. But, like Harrison, I've only been communicating with him through emails. He paid for Madeline and me to attend this murder mystery thing, which I realize sounds ridiculous."

"Why did he do that?"

"He said he wanted to meet face to face and thought this would be a good place to do it. I found that odd."

"Why?"

"Because Mr. Whitmore is someone who likes to keep a low profile. At least that's what he said to me when he hired me. I think he's eccentric or something. I don't know. For being as wealthy as I assume he is, I found it impossible to dig up anything on the guy. He's like a ghost."

"That *is* strange," I said.

"That's not the strangest part."

He sighed. "This is going to sound crazy, but through our email correspondence, he agreed to pay me half up front and the other half when I uncovered who threatened him. I assumed he would send me an email transfer or something. However, I noticed a black limousine pull into our driveway while pouring my morning coffee. An older man with white hair stepped out of the car and approached my front step. I was intrigued. Before he could knock, I opened the door."

"Was it Mr. Whitmore?"

"I thought he was, at first. But after handing me a big yellow envelope, he turned around without saying a word. Before getting into the limo, he placed a black hat on his head. I guessed he was the chauffeur, which led me to believe Mr. Whitmore was in the back seat."

"What was in the envelope?" Quinn asked.

"This is the crazy part. When I opened it, I nearly had a heart attack. There were two stacks of cash adding up to twenty thousand dollars and a note inside that said I'd get the other twenty grand this weekend—assuming I made progress on the case."

Quinn gasped. "Forty thousand dollars to find out who was threatening him? Security pays well."

"Not that well," said Jason. "Our agreement was for a fraction of that...so yeah, you could say I was somewhat stunned."

"Don't you specialize in security?" I asked. "Sounds like you were hired to be more of a private eye."

"That's what I wanted to talk to him about, but when I saw the money, I thought it best to keep my mouth shut and do whatever he wanted me to do."

"Why would he give you so much?" I asked.

"No idea. But I knew I had to meet the man behind the emails. Thought he'd be here by now."

"So I'm guessing Madeline has been left in the dark as far as the amount of money is concerned?"

"Yeah," said Jason, "if you don't mind, I'd like to keep it that way. She's not exactly thrilled about bringing her here this weekend. She kinda had her heart set on Hawaii."

Quinn sucked air in through her teeth. "Ouch! Betcha that cost ya."

"You have no idea. Now, it's your turn; what did you learn from your trip to the library?"

For a moment, I gazed deep into his eyes. Were they the eyes of a killer? At this point, I couldn't be sure of anything. However, I concluded that having someone other than Quinn to feed me information might be in my best interest. I wasn't willing to put all my cards on the table just yet.

"I guess I can tell you," I said. "I beelined it to Quinn because I wanted to tell her that Truman followed me to the library. He found me standing over the body and thought I might be messing with evidence, or so he said. Of course, I was doing no such thing. I wanted to see if we missed anything, that's all."

Jason studied me briefly before saying, "Fine, you don't have to tell me. I'm sure whatever it is, I'll find out one way or another."

Well, that went well.

"Heads up," said Quinn, "we're getting company."

"And what's going on over here?"

"It's none of your business, Gretchen," seethed Jason.

"We're just chatting," I said.

"Yep," chirped Quinn. "Trying to figure out what *confit de canard* is."

"It's duck," said Gretchen matter-of-factly.

"Oh, you speak French," I said.

"Well, I picked up a little in France last year."

"You've been to France?" Quinn said with a surprising squeal. "I've always wanted to go there. I'm trying to get my husband to take me on our anniversary. Did you go on your own?"

"No," she said curtly. "I was there with my…husband. But we're not together anymore."

"Sorry," I said.

And I meant it.

I knew the pain of break-ups. Not my own, of course. Norma (the owner of The Happy Bean) was married to the love of her life for nearly twenty-five years. That is until her loving husband decided to run off to Vancouver with a college graduate a week before their silver anniversary. Let's just say the beans were a little less happy over the next few months.

"Don't be sorry," said Gretchen. "It didn't work—"

"There's someone outside!" Madeline yelled, leaping to her feet.

A sudden swarm ensued around her as everyone tried to get a glimpse out the window.

Jason ran back to the den. "Are you sure it's not the wind? Something could have blown in front of the window."

"Yes, I'm sure. I'm not an idiot," she said emphatically.

I did a mental tally, confirming everyone (except Rebecca and Sébastien) was in the den. They, I assumed, were in the kitchen.

Madeline cupped her hands around her eyes and peered through the glass. "I saw him by the window before he took off around the back of the lodge."

Jason craned his neck over the sea of heads. "He? You sure? It's pretty dark out there."

"He was enormous, so I don't think it was a woman."

"Maybe it was a bear," said Sam. "Caffrey did say there's a lot of animals here."

"Could that have been it, Mads...could it have been a bear?"

"No—I mean...of course it was a man." Madeline moved away from the window. "At least I think it was a man, but—I don't know. I guess it could have been a bear."

Jason darted from the den and headed for the stairs.

"Where are you going?" Madeline yelled.

"To get my coat."

26

In search of a mystery man…or maybe a bear

BAILING ON THE warmth of the den and into a full-blown deep freeze to look for a mysterious intruder had not been high on my to-do list. However, I couldn't let Jason have all the fun, and it wasn't likely that anyone else would jump at the chance to find out who or what was lurking cold.

"I'm coming, too," said Quinn.

"Of course you are. I wouldn't dream of going out there without you."

"Do you think we should bring a weapon?"

"Like what?" I asked. "There are no guns here…well, none that I know of. And it's not like a cast iron frying pan would do us any good if we encounter a bear. If he's a human intruder, I don't even want to think about whether or not he has a weapon."

"Not sure what's worse, confronting a man with a gun or a bear."

"At least Jason will be out there with us. He's kinda like a bear."

Quinn laughed. "He's built like one, that's for sure."

Bundled from head to toe, we were (yet again) about to step into a relentless storm. The wind whistled through the door like a possessed tea kettle while nearby trees clawed at the cedar roof, desperate to tear it apart.

Why was I doing this again?

Jason pushed the door open, pausing before going any further. "We're going to need a shovel."

"Hold on," said Harrison. He wobbled down the hall and returned a few seconds later, holding a bright red shovel. "If you need a bigger one, there's a heavy-duty scoop in the skating shed."

"Thanks," said Jason. "This will do, for now. I just need to find the steps."

I crouched down to re-tie one of my laces. "I think ankle boots might have been a bad idea."

Quinn smirked, flaunting her taupe-colored Sorels, which hugged her calves in waterproof suede. "I warned you to dress for the weather, didn't I?"

"Yes, you did. And shame on me for thinking a nice pair of leather booties would be more than adequate for a weekend *inside.*"

She laughed. "Come on! It's probably best we use Jason as a shield. That wind is brutal."

Everything was white: the trees, the sky, and even the cars in the parking lot had morphed into oddly shaped igloos.

"I can't see anything out here," Quinn shouted.

"Let's go over by the window; there might be tracks." Jason continued to push the shovel, making a narrow path for us to trudge through.

As the feeling in my toes slowly slipped away, I wondered why Madeline wasn't out here with us. It was her sighting, after all. I deduced it was probably another ploy for Jason to jump at her request. From what I gathered, it was pretty indicative of her behavior.

"Look!" Quinn said. "Over there! Does that look like footprints?"

"I'd say so," said Jason. "But the snow has just about covered them up."

As we battled the elements, our focus immediately shifted in the opposite direction when we heard the rev of an engine echoing from the far side of the parking lot.

"Quick! He's getting away!" Jason awkwardly ran back through the path he had just shoveled.

"And what are we supposed to do about it?" Quinn yelled. "Try to keep up? He's gotta a truck!"

We reached the front of the lodge as a faint glint of red vanished into thin air.

"That was a big truck! Look at the size of those...."

"Tires tracks?" said Quinn, finishing my sentence.

"Henry!" We both said in unison.

"What did you say?" Jason yelled. "I can't hear you over this wind. I think we better get back inside before we lose our path. This snow isn't letting up any time soon."

"Good idea!" I bellowed back.

"WELL?" SAID GRETCHEN, bombarding us before we could shed our boots. "Did you see anyone out there?"

Jason pushed his way past Gretchen. "He got away."

"But he left some fresh tire tracks out there...*big* tire tracks." I grabbed a throw off the sofa and sat on the hearth, allowing the fire to warm my bones.

"That doesn't make any sense," said Truman. "Why would someone drive all the way up here just to turn around and leave?"

Quinn sat next to me. "You willing to share your blanket?

"Oh, sure!" I threw half of the blanket over her legs.

"Ahh, the heat feels wonderful," she said. "I'm considering sleeping down here tonight."

"Should we be worried about a stranger roaming the property?" Elenor asked. She linked arms with Sam, who seemed unruffled.

"I think I may know who he was," I said. I hoped Quinn would jump in, but she seemed keen on me taking the lead.

"Who is he?" Madeline asked.

"His name is Henry. On our way up here this morning, we hit a moose and—"

"You hit a moose?" Sam jutted to the edge of his seat. "How are you still alive?"

I was surprised to see Sam so invested. It was the most excitement I'd seen from him all weekend.

"Well, fortunately," I continued, "he leaped over our car without us even knowing. According to Henry, we only clipped one of his legs. He said he'd never seen anything like it in his life. I didn't think moose could even jump that high."

"Oh, yes!" said Sam, standing to his feet. He motioned the approximated height with his hand. "Adult moose would have no problem clearing a four-foot fence. Some even attempt jumps as high as seven or eight feet."

"How do you know so much about moose?" Gretchen asked.

"I spent a week up north a few years back. We were on a hunting trip, and I was determined to catch myself a moose.

My buddy bagged a bull weighing nearly thirteen hundred pounds; unfortunately, I left empty-handed."

"Thirteen hundred pounds?" said Jason. "That's insane!"

"What's insane is that some of them are even bigger than that. I read the record was eighteen hundred pounds up in the Yukon. Anyway,"—he turned his focus back to Quinn and me —"you two are fortunate you weren't killed."

"Agreed," I said. "So, back to Henry, the man who helped pull us out of the ditch. He drove a *huge* truck with the same type of tires that left those tracks out there."

"Who do you think he is?" Truman asked.

"I don't know," I said. "But if the storm continues, I'm guessing he'll be back."

Before I could get the chill out of my bones, Sébastien strolled into the den as animated as ever, waving his arm over his head. *"C'est l'heure de manger!* Time to eat."

I slid off the hearth and peacefully filed in line with the others. The need to fuel my hunger was as strong as the need to find the killer, but I wouldn't be doing much crime-solving until I dealt with my growling stomach.

Harrison was in the lobby, steering everyone to the dining room. He was calm and authoritative, and the color in his cheeks had returned to his usual rosy glow. The story he told about Mr. Whitmore was puzzling, and the fact that both he and Jason only communicated through emails was even more bizarre. I needed to find out more. "Harrison, can I talk to you for a minute?"

"How may I help you, Mrs. Lane?"

"Please, call me Scarlet."

"Alright. How can I help you, Scarlet?"

"I must say, I find your history quite fascinating. I don't think I've ever heard a story as interesting as yours. I still can't believe you've never met Mr. Whitmore."

He slipped both hands into his trousers, teetering on the heels of his feet. "As bizarre as it is, my tale is very true."

"How long were you married?"

The question seemed to startle him. "Why do you ask?"

"You said earlier that Mr. Whitmore knew that your wife was sick. I assumed—"

"My wife passed away soon after I accepted the job at the lodge. Cancer, I'm afraid."

"I'm so sorry, Harrison."

"You don't need to be sorry, Scarlet. Cancer is a formidable beast, gnawing at you from the inside out. I was relieved when I no longer had to watch my wife suffer."

"I'm sure you miss her every day."

"Indeed I do."

"Did she ever spend time with you here at the lodge?"

"Unfortunately, she was too sick to travel for any length of time. She would have loved it here, though."

"I'm sure she would have." I gently placed my hand on his shoulder.

"It would be nice if she were here to celebrate with me."

"Celebrate?"

He lowered his voice. "Keep this under your hat, will you?"

"What is it?" I was beginning to feel like the secret keeper.

"If my hunch is right, I'll be taking over this place in the next few days."

"Taking over? Are you purchasing the lodge?"

"On the contrary, Scarlet. Mr. Whitmore has decided to *give* me the lodge, no strings attached."

"How so?"

"He wrote me an email a week ago. He praised me for doing such a marvelous job over the past twenty-two years that he wanted to discuss passing the lodge down to someone he cared deeply for. I was flattered and frankly dumbfounded that he thought of me. But after the shock had worn off, I realized I *had* been a real asset to Mr. Whitmore."

"I see," I said, trying not to sound too skeptical. "And what makes you think this will happen in the next few days?"

"Well, it just so happens that he plans on coming out here this weekend. I assume it's to make the big announcement. However, the storm may have prevented that, I'm afraid. I expect an email soon letting me know of his intentions."

"What about the rest of the staff? Do they know you're about to be the new owner?"

"Well, I didn't broadcast it if that's what you mean. But I may have let it slip once or twice that things were about to change; they could be sure of that. Now, if you don't mind, Scarlet, I have things to attend to."

"Just one more question, Harrison," I said, reaching for his arm. "Were you aware of the relationship between Caffrey and Rebecca?"

"Relationship? As far as I could tell, they hardly spoke."

27

The Great Pretender

QUINN LINGERED BY the stairs, waiting for me to catch up

"So?" she said, linking arms with me.

"So, what?"

"I'm guessing you have news, so spill. I can tell you have something to say. You look like you're ready to burst."

"I've got news, alright! I'll get to Harrison in a minute, but I haven't had a chance to tell you what I learned from Rebecca."

"Okay," she said, firmly squeezing my arm, "go on."

"According to Rebecca, she and Caffrey had a thing."

"What kind of thing?"

"Well, *she* says they'd been dating for the past six months. But according to Harrison, they hardly spoke to each other."

"Strange. Wonder why they were trying to keep their relationship a secret?"

"Rebecca said they liked to keep things private, but mostly, Caffrey didn't want their relationship to interfere with the game. Although, I'm not sure what one has to do with the other."

"Odd."

"Which brings me to Harrison."

"Oh, I'm sure he's got a good story."

"He thinks Mr. Whitmore is coming to the lodge this weekend to make a big announcement. Take a guess what that announcement might be."

"One lucky guest is about to win an all-expense-paid trip to Mexico?"

"No," I said, trying to hide my amusement. "Harrison thinks that Mr. Whitmore is giving him the lodge."

"What do you mean…like selling it to him?"

"No, like giving it to him as in, here ya go, enjoy your new hotel."

"Can he even do that? Why would he give it to Harrison?"

"No idea."

"So who is this, Mr. Whitmore, anyway? And where is he?"

"Like Jason, Harrison figures he got caught in the storm but still expects an email from him. So we'll see where that goes."

Quinn did a quick peek over her shoulder to see if anyone was nearby. "So, who's on the top of your suspect list?"

"I'm not sure. Finding someone with the means, motive, *and* opportunity is a challenge. But now that I know Caffrey and Rebecca were a couple, that does open up the possibility of a love triangle."

"You mean Victoria?"

"You saw how he looked at her. I'm sure he pictured her floating down those stairs in slow motion. Maybe he was having an affair with Victoria, and Rebecca found out."

"Ahh, one of the oldest motives in the book. Rebecca's a good choice."

"Sure, however, my mind keeps turning to Truman. Something about that guy intrigues me, and I don't know why. He has a secret, and he's attempting to keep it from everyone here. What do you think about him?"

"Not my type."

"Ha!" I said, rolling my eyes. I mean, do you think he's hiding something? He's jittery and constantly moves the focus off himself and onto somebody else."

"Maybe he's shy."

"Shy?" I said sarcastically.

"Well, he's kinda nerdy. The only thing missing is a piece of tape between those absurd, hipster glasses of his. He's gotta be an accountant or something. But I see what you mean; he's a bit tight-lipped."

"Right…and who says nerds can't be secretive?"

"Or even killers."

I shrugged and nodded. "Curious, though, isn't it, that he decided to come to a murder mystery weekend alone? Not something a typical guy would do."

"Gretchen is here by herself," said Quinn. "But then again, she did just break up with her husband."

"Perhaps Truman is recuperating from a failed relationship as well. I did see him schmoozing with Gretchen at the meet and greet earlier. Maybe they were comparing notes."

Quinn scoffed. "Oh, Scarlet, she *schmoozed* with all the men."

"Probably part of her persona," I said.

"Right, but the last time I checked, the need for pretending came to a crashing halt when we found a dead body in the library."

"Ah, but that's where you're mistaken, my friend," I said, stepping into the dining room. "Someone is *still* pretending."

28

Roasted duck and conspiracy theories

AFTER PULLING OUT the solid oak, high-back chair (exquisitely upholstered in coffee-brown leather), I settled in next to Quinn. Beholding the entrée sitting before me, I inhaled deeply. The steam carried a melange of savory herbs and spices that made my mouth water, and it immediately took me back to the little French restaurant we visited on our first anniversary.

I closed my eyes, and for a brief moment, time stood still. There was no denying it; I loved food: French, Italian, Chinese. It didn't matter where it came from; food was my love language.

The feeling soon passed, however, when I opened my eyes and found myself back at the table with an array of nonchalant murder suspects.

What a strange day, I thought. A day in which I *knew* there'd be a murder. Strangely enough, I even prepared myself to solve said murder and was looking forward to it. And now, here I was, eating a delightful meal, hobnobbing with a charming circle of strangers who seemed to ignore that the butler lay dead in the library.

Quinn rested her elbows in front of her and began observing Rebecca, who had been staring longingly at her ice water as if debating whether or not to take a sip.

A quick bump to Quinn's shoulder startled her. "You're staring. She's going to think we suspect her."

"Well,…don't we?"

"Yes, but we can't let *her* know that. Plus, we don't have any proof. It's a hunch at this point. We can't even be sure Caffrey was having an affair."

Quinn cut through the perfectly crisp, golden brown duck and stabbed it with a fork. "Think about it," she said. "Truman insisted he heard a woman's voice when heading to the library to meet Sam. Maybe she confronted Victoria. It seems obvious to me, at least, that Caffrey and Victoria had *something* going on, whether we can confirm it or not. It's possible that after speaking with Victoria, she squared off with Caffrey and, in the heat of the moment, picked up the pool cue and hit him over the head."

"But if Rebecca were angry enough to accuse Victoria of an affair, Truman would have heard more than just voices. There would have been shouting for sure."

"Good point. Maybe it was Victoria. She probably didn't know they were a couple since they'd kept it hush-hush. She couldn't face the fact that Caffrey dismissed her. Feeling embarrassed and utterly rejected, she flew into a rage, found Caffrey in the library, and killed him."

"But Victoria stated she was in the laundry room at the time of the murder. If it *were* a crime of passion, don't you think she would have killed Caffrey first, then put in a load of whites?"

Quinn placed her chin in her hand while twirling her fork with the other. "Of course, but she could have lied about how long she was in the laundry room."

I scooped a spoonful of mashed potatoes into my mouth, closing my eyes to relish their savory goodness. Then, after gracefully dabbing the sides of my mouth with the red linen napkin I'd yanked from my lap, I turned to Quinn and said, "True, but Madeline saw her coming out of the laundry room with an armload of sheets. At *some* point, she was in the laundry room."

"She could have an accomplice," said Quinn, soaking up the juices on her plate with some brioche bread. "What if she *and* Rebecca were in on it together?" She turned to face me. "I still can't believe you didn't hear anything. There would have been a struggle for sure."

"I've been thinking about that. What if he wasn't killed in the library? What if the crime scene was somewhere else, and the killer or killers moved the body to the library."

"But why do that?"

"I don't know…to throw us off somehow?"

"Do you think Rebecca *or* Victoria would even be strong enough to move a hundred and seventy pounds of dead weight to another location?"

We eyed Victoria at the other end of the table, who pensively pushed potatoes with the tines of her fork as if it were a zen garden.

"It's unlikely," I said.

"This is like solving the murder in one of your books."

"Although Chase is usually at the helm solving the cases."

"You realize, don't you, that you're at the helm? You're giving all the credit to him: a fictitious character. Who you yourself pioneered into the crime-busting, murder-solving hunk of a man he is. You forget that you *are* Chase Ridgeway."

I am?

I never thought of it that way. Sure, I forged Chase out of my imagination, giving him savvy investigative skills and a composed, laid-back, cool-as-a-cucumber outlook on life. But he was nothing like me.

Or was he?

I put a pin in my self-doubt, turning my attention to an ornate vintage goblet. It had been enticing me from the moment I sat down. Unable to ignore it any longer, I picked up the glass, swirled the crimson liquid, and gave it a spirited sniff. A wine connoisseur I was not. *But it's what they do on TV, right?*

"Exquisite, isn't it?" Elenor raised her goblet and sipped.

"Oh, it sure is." I mimicked her technique. "Do I detect a slight hint of cherry?" I was only guessing at this point.

"Of course," she said as if I should have known better. "I'm also picking up on a sensual undertone of rich chocolate, layered with notes of clove and vanilla."

"Wow! You know your wine."

"Sam and I have traveled quite extensively over the last few years. Since then, I've learned to appreciate a good glass of wine."

I put down my glass and twisted in my chair to face her. "May I ask you a question?"

"Ask away, my dear."

"I noticed you gave Sam an awkward glance when the chef said he was in the kitchen during the murder. Is there something you're not saying?"

"Oh, I don't want to get anyone in trouble." She nervously looked around the room.

"I'm sure you have nothing to worry about, Elenor. Was he in the kitchen the whole time?"

She sighed and set her goblet on the table. "Alright, my dear. I'll tell you. I must say, holding on to something like this tends to eat at you. It will be good to get it off my chest."

I placed both elbows on the table, gearing up to hear a story that could catapult this investigation in a whole other direction. And from how Elenor was acting, it would probably be a good one.

"After Sam started to feel better, I convinced him to go to the dining room for another cup of coffee. We are quite the coffee drinkers, you know. Some days, it's close to six or seven cups. We know we should probably cut it back to two or three cups a day. Like the doctor says, *That much caffeine at your age isn't good.* You'd think it would keep us up at night, but ironically, we sleep like—"

"Elenor!"

"Sorry, dear. Anyway, we reached the dining room and found it empty. We thought that maybe the chef was in the kitchen preparing food, so we helped ourselves to the coffee carafe sitting on the table. Truth be told," she said with her hand up to her mouth, "we wanted another one of those strudels. We peeked inside the kitchen to see if Rebecca had moved them in there." She took a sip of wine. A long sip.

"And?"

"Well, he wasn't in there. We were surprised to see that big, beautiful kitchen empty. Have you been inside there, dear? I can only imagine the treats I could bake."

"So you're saying he lied about being in the kitchen?"

"Well, not exactly. We decided to leave after checking out all those appliances and sneaking a few extra strudels for later."

"I'm confused. You left the kitchen without seeing the chef?"

"No, I said we *decided* to leave. But before we could, Chef Sébastien barreled through the door."

"You mean the swinging doors?"

"No, dear, the other one."

I knew the exact door. "On the other side of the kitchen? By the wine cooler?"

"Yes, that door."

I leaned in even further. "Did you ask him where that door led?"

"Yes! Sam asked him that very question. I told him not to be so nosy. I'm sure the staff want to be left alone sometimes. You know how it is, dear: you deal with people all day. The last thing you want is to have a conversation when you're all peopled out."

"And?" I was trying very hard to be patient. "Where did he say the door led to?"

"Oh, let me tell you, he was perturbed that we were in his kitchen. He probably thinks of it as his office. You know men, dear, so possessive."

"Right."

"Anyway, we found it quite peculiar."

"Peculiar?"

"Yes. Before crashing through the door, it sounded like he was running up some stairs. It was quite a racket, I tell you."

"Interesting," I said.

"And that's not the most interesting part." Elenor moved in so close I could detect the hint of chocolate on her breath. "He was hiding something under his apron."

"What was it?"

"Well, dear, if I knew that, I would tell you. But I haven't the foggiest. Now, please excuse me. I must find the little girl's room. Wine tends to run right through me."

As exhausting as her story was, I was intrigued. I leaned back in my chair and folded my arms across my chest, considering the facts I'd attained.

"What was that all about?" Quinn asked.

I filled Quinn in.

"So we have another possible suspect?"

"Perhaps," I said, "but something's off with the timeline."

"How do ya figure?"

"We were all in the den when Harrison ran in to alert us of the murder, right?"

"Right."

"And Elenor and Sam saw Sébastien before Victoria screamed."

"Okay."

"So that would mean if Sébastien were the killer, he would have had to leave the kitchen, run to the library, kill Caffrey, and escape before Harrison caught him red-handed. That doesn't leave him much time. Not to mention, someone would have seen him running from the library."

"Hmm," Quinn also leaned back and folded her arms.

"Unless..." I said, pointing my finger straight in the air. "Harrison and Sébastien are the killers."

"You think Sébastien could have killed Caffrey?"

"Well, we did witness some tension between the two of them at lunch…maybe there was something more to it than acting out a part in a mystery game?"

"Why mention the pool cue at all? If they were in on it together, why remove it from the library and tell us about it?"

"I don't know. Possibly to take suspicion off Sébastien?"

"So, you think what Elenor saw behind his apron was the pool cue?"

"I can't be sure. But it's enough to put Chef Sébastien at the top of the suspect list."

29

He's on to me

DESSERT WAS AS heavenly as the main course—*mousse au chocolat*. It was a far cry from the chocolate mousse I had stored in my refrigerator back home. Somehow, chocolate (anything) in a plastic container with a tinfoil lid did not scream decadence. But this creation was sheer perfection.

It briefly gave me pause. How could I possibly believe Sébastien—talented, creative, and unbelievably gifted with food—could be involved with something so nefarious as murder? Could he even survive in prison? To be ripped away from his kitchen—his sanctuary, where mere ingredients are transformed from ordinary to positively awe-inspiring. It would be as bad as stripping an artist from his canvas, a musician from his instrument, or an author from her laptop.

I gave my head a shake, realizing I was getting carried away.

Get a grip, Scarlet!

Before condemning the guy to a life sentence, I needed to at least talk to him first.

Meanwhile, the chef had popped out of the kitchen, confident he had perfected another mouthwatering meal. He certainly didn't appear as though he'd just committed murder. But then again, no one did. And that was the problem.

"I'm going to talk to the chef," I said.

"You're not going to ask him if he's the killer, are you?"

"Of course not. I'm going to ask about that door again. Maybe he'll be more forthcoming now that the game is over. It will give me an idea if he's hiding something."

"You want some backup?"

"I'm good. He might feel ganged up on if we both go." I got up from the table. "Eat your dessert…it's fabulous," I said, breathing so deep that I hoped it would impede my jitters.

I walked across the dining room with confidence (well, as much as I could muster). When I arrived at the bar, I cleared my throat and said, "Excuse me, Chef?"

He turned around. *"Oui?"*

"I've gotta say…that was one of the best meals I've had in a long time."

"Merci, Madame." He pushed back his shoulders like a proud man would.

"If you don't mind, I'd like to ask you some questions."

"But of course."

"First of all, you said that during the time of the murder, you never left the kitchen; you were busy preparing dinner?"

"Oui. Except for my break, of course."

"Well,….." I swallowed hard enough for the chef to hear me gulp. "Elenor mentioned that while she and Sam were helping themselves to some pastries, they saw you coming in from that door. You know, the door you didn't want me opening." I discretely inched past the bar, hoping he'd offer a tour. But instead, he blocked my path like a bouncer on a power trip. "What's behind that door, Chef?"

"I've already told you, Scarlet, that door is none of your concern. It's for staff only. No guests allowed!"

Aha! He *did* have something to hide. But what could they possibly be hiding? Gold bars? Expensive wine? More dead bodies?

"May I get you something else to eat, *Madame?*"

Interesting. He was trying to get rid of me; I must have hit a nerve. Which meant I needed to get inside that room.

"No thanks," I said. "I couldn't possibly eat another bite. However, I'm looking forward to the breakfast menu."

"You will not be disappointed," he said, disappearing into the kitchen.

I plodded back to my seat, sniffing the aromatic flavors of roasted almonds and maple syrup. The guests seemed to have forgotten the gruesome scene in the other room, devouring their chocolate desserts and sipping specialty coffees as though indulging at a five-star resort. But who was I to judge?

For me, coffee and chocolate had always proven to be a fitting antidote to ease my frazzled nerves; it was one of the reasons why I had chosen to work in a coffee shop in the first place. With decadent syrups and robust bouquets of espresso beans, I could relate to why it brought faithful patrons into The Happy Bean every day. Like zombies, they patiently wait. Tired. Grumpy. Irritable. Until that glorious moment when they wrap their hands around a daily fix that happily escorts them through the day—one sip at a time.

"Well? What'd you find out? Quinn clung to her coffee mug with both hands.

I reached for the carafe and poured myself a cup. "Not as much as I was hoping for. It seems the staff are being quite tight-lipped about that door."

"He wouldn't let you in, eh?"

"Nope. And the fact that he caught me in there earlier, I'm sure I won't find it unlocked again. They're on to me."

"What do you think is in there?"

"No clue. I have some interesting guesses, but that's all they are."

"On another matter, do you think we should start a discussion with everybody about moving the body out of the library? It's hot in there. Hate to think what it might smell like after a few days."

"Harrison wants to leave him where he is, but maybe it would be better if we put him outside...even though he'll probably freeze."

"It's better than the alternative," said Quinn.

I observed Harrison at the end of the table; he appeared to be enjoying a second dessert. "I think I'll go see if he has any suggestions."

"Careful, I'm not positive we should trust him."

"I don't trust anyone."

When I got up from my chair, a sudden thunderous bang startled everyone at the table.

"Is someone at the door?" asked Madeline.

I sat back down, waiting to see if someone more gallant would address the scene unfolding in the lobby. Whoever was frantically banging on the door was adamant about getting inside.

"I'll go check it out," said Jason.

I was thankful we had the brute force of Jason's muscular physique.

"I have an idea who that might be," said Quinn.

Really? I couldn't imagine anyone dumb enough to be out in that weather.

Then it dawned on me when I heard him shout, "Let me in; it's cold out here!"

"Of course," I said. "Who else would be galavanting around in this storm?"

30

Oh, Henry!

ONE PEEK OVER Jason's shoulder confirmed that it was Henry. He pounded on the door like a wild man. Jason turned the deadbolt and pushed it open, allowing Henry to plow through him like a freight train.

"Sorry to be so pushy," said Henry, "but that wind is enough to slice right through ya. Why was the door locked? Aren't you guys open for business?"

It was hard to believe he had pulled us out of the ditch only twelve hours earlier. And he seemed way more menacing than I remembered. Maybe it was his wardrobe. With the green parka, matching trapper hat, and a black mask covering his mouth and nose, no wonder he looked sinister. His eyes, which looked like shiny brown marbles, were the only visible features I could see.

"Henry?" I said. "Is that you?"

He stepped out of his boots and peeled off his snow-soaked garb one piece at a time, dropping it in a pile on the floor. "The one and only. How's the head?"

I reached for the lump, realizing the dull ache had never disappeared. "I'm still having headaches. They come and go, but I can manage as long as I keep on top of the pain with meds. The question is, what are you doing here?"

"Well, I was doing my rounds and wanted to see if everyone was alright. Looking at the parking lot, it doesn't appear that anyone's tried to leave."

"Well, no," said Jason. "Where would we go? It's at least a forty-minute drive to the nearest gas station or more in this weather."

"What do you mean, doing your rounds?" I asked.

"Oh, it's nothing. Figured there's always someone up on this mountain that needs assistance." He raised his eyebrows and nodded. "You can attest to that, I'm sure."

"I guess I can."

"I have the benefit of a big truck. Can usually get through almost anything. That's why I came out tonight...to see if anyone needed my help."

"Were you here earlier?" Jason asked.

"I was. Hope I didn't spook anyone. I was surveying the property when my phone rang."

I thought that was curious, considering *we* couldn't use our phones.

"Your cell phone?" I said. "There isn't much service out here in the mountains."

"Agreed. Only one ring managed to get through, so I hopped into my truck and got back on the road. Thought maybe the wife was trying to get ahold of me. She tends to get nervous when I'm out in these storms. You know how it is," he said, nodding to Jason.

"And was it?" Jason asked.

"Was what?"

"Was it your wife on the phone?"

"As a matter of fact, she wasn't. Don't know *who* it was."

"What about earlier in the afternoon?" said Gretchen. "Say between one-thirty and three?"

"Nope. Once I helped these gals out of the ditch this mornin', I headed home to rest up. Figured that with the storm being as ferocious as it is, I'd be out here for most of the night; I don't think I'm making it down the mountain any time soon. The snow drifts are even too much for my truck. I was hoping I could bunker down here until the storm settles."

"That won't be a problem," said a shaky voice behind me. Harrison came into view and seemed curious about who this Henry guy was.

"I believe I still have one room available.

Henry's gaze seemed to linger. "That's mighty generous of you," he said. "What do I owe ya?"

"Nonsense," said Harrison. He plodded his way behind the desk and began opening random drawers. "Now let me see… where did that key get to? Ah, here it is."

There was visible apprehension among the group, allowing Henry to stay at the lodge. Still, it wasn't like he was any more dangerous than the people we were currently bunking with. What's one more? We didn't have much of a choice, anyway.

"It's alright," I said, "I…well, Quinn and I know this man. This is Henry. He helped get Quinn's car out of the ditch this morning."

"So, *you* were the guy snooping around outside?" Madeline asked.

He raised his arm high in the air. "Guilty. I apologize, again, if I scared anyone."

Quinn moved to the center of the lobby and followed my lead. "It's alright, everyone. We'd still be out there if Henry hadn't come along when he did. I think we can trust him."

"You know," said Madeline, "you could have come into the lodge instead of skulking out there like a homicidal maniac."

Henry chuckled. "Oh, I can assure you, I'm no killer. Just making sure everyone was staying safe."

"Well, it's still creepy."

Harrison held out his hand. "Here's your key. You can stay in the orange room. It's upstairs and to the left. But right now, how about we get you something hearty to eat? I'm sure you could use a good meal."

"I could eat," said Henry. "Smells fantastic! What's on the menu?"

"Duck," said Gretchen.

"Then duck I shall have."

Sébastien led the way, and the rest of us followed out of mere curiosity. "It won't be as good as if fresh, but if you wait a moment, I'll heat it up."

"Oh, I'm sure it'll be just fine."

Rebecca cleared a place for him at the table and put out fresh cutlery and a clean goblet. "You can sit here," she said, pouring wine into his glass.

"Thank you, ma'am."

"It's Rebecca."

"Okay,...thank you, Rebecca."

She forced a smile and headed for the kitchen, probably wasn't in the mood for his country bumpkin idioms. Why was she even serving dinner, I wondered. I wouldn't be able to function if Dominic was lying dead in the library. Yet, Rebecca seemed to be business as usual.

Sébastien bulldozed through the door. He held a plate high above his head, which boasted duck and fixings and a sprig of rosemary for garnish. *"Bon appétit!"* he said, positioning it just so in front of Henry.

"Thanks, Chef, sure beats the can of chicken noodle soup I'd planned for supper. The wife doesn't cook much these days. She's going through a phase of letting me starve, I'm afraid." He chuckled as he lowered his head to the plate and took a big whiff. "Mmm."

"Merci! Eat! This should warm you up from the cold, *non*?"

"Oh, my," said Elenor. "You must be hungry!"

Henry filled his fork with meat and swiped it through the mound of mashed potatoes before shoving it into his mouth. He chewed a couple of times before answering. "Um…yes. Thought I'd be able to make it back down the mountain before it got too bad; guess I was wrong about that."

"Eat as much as you like," said Sébastien. "After you finish your meal, I'll have Rebecca bring you some dessert."

"Much obliged."

Henry continued shoveling food into his mouth, nearly finishing his whole plate before Rebecca could ask him if he needed butter for his bread.

While Rebecca lingered by the window, waiting to clear the rest of the plates, I wanted to check in to make sure she was okay.

"I'm sorry, Rebecca. I can't imagine what you're going through."

"Thank you," she said. "I don't know what I should be doing. All I want to do is curl up into a ball and forget this day even happened."

"Why don't you? The rest of us can help Sébastien if he needs it."

She wiped the condensation from the window with the towel she was firmly clenching. "And then what? Stay in my room for who knows how long? I want to keep my mind off what's waiting for me when I get home. I can't think of funerals and autopsies and murder right now. I need to work. Excuse me." She pushed past me and ran back into the kitchen.

I took my chair and dragged it next to Harrison. I couldn't believe he was on dessert number three.

"Scarlet, how was your dinner?" He scooped the last bit of mousse from his bowl and gobbled it up as if it were his first.

"It was excellent," I said. "One of the tastiest meals I've eaten."

"Good to hear."

I waited until he made eye contact with me; he was in no hurry. When he was finally ready to face me, he put down his spoon. "I assume there's a reason for your proximity?"

I smiled. "I just have one question, if you don't mind."

He took a sip of wine. "Proceed."

"Quinn and I have been talking, and we think it might be a good idea to find a better place to put Caffrey."

"Is that so?"

"It is. I'm sure you've thought a lot about the ambiance of this place and how wonderful that ambiance is. But have you envisioned what it would be like if we kept the body in the library for the next few days, where the fire has been crackling non-stop?"

He paused and scrunched up his nose, visualizing the nightmare. "I haven't given it much thought. I assumed we had no choice in the matter. It is a crime scene, after all. What does Sam say we should do?"

"I don't think he's interested in leading any investigation. He emphasized that he's retired but said he'd be willing to help."

The chair creaked when he leaned back, his arms folded behind his head, content. "I see."

"Besides," I said, "it could be three, maybe four days before anyone can get to us. You heard Henry. He doesn't think his truck will make it down the mountain, let alone a police car climbing it."

Harrison glanced at Henry. The telltale sign of sweat trickled down his sideburns, which led me to believe he was worried about something.

"What do you suggest?"

"At first, we were thinking of outside, although it's quite likely he'd freeze. Unless..." I studied his reaction before I continued.

"Unless what?"

"Unless there's a cold room somewhere in this place?"

"I—I'm not aware of any cold room or—"

"A basement? I'm sure there's gotta be one of those." He was stalling; I didn't know why.

"Well," he said hesitantly. "There is a basement but—"

"Great!"

I pushed myself away from the table before he could object. If he was hiding something, it was only a matter of time before I figured out what it was.

31

Did you say... m u r d e r?

AFTER DINNER, we filed back into the den feeling full and satisfied. Each prod of Harrison's poker sparked a familiar crackle as he tended to the fire, and thanks to his tireless devotion, the room remained nice and toasty.

Henry strolled in from the dining room like he'd succumbed to a hotdog eating contest. His face was red and dewy, and an audible moan escaped through his whiskers as he plummeted to the sofa.

I knew someone had to fill him in on the day's events, and by the looks of all the reluctant eyeballs staring back at me, I was as good as any to deliver the news. I knew how unsettling it would be if he stumbled over the body while taking a tour of the lodge.

"How was dinner?" I asked.

He looked peaked.

"Oh, it was good!" he said, loosening one or two notches of his belt. "Probably overdone it on the dessert, though, but I'm a sucker for holiday spices. Haven't eaten like that in a long time."

"I know what you mean. We sure lucked out having a chef like Sébastien; his meals are fabulous."

I noticed the chatter slowly dissipated into an awkward silence. You know the kind? When everyone else in the room knows the secret except for that one person. It was uncomfortable. But seeing that I'd been deemed the unofficial spokesperson, I had to conjure up the nerve to speak in front of a gawking crowd. Why had everyone clammed up? Because one of them was the killer, that's why. Guilty and sitting brazenly among the innocent, like they'd just gotten away with murder.

Well, not if I can help it.

I cleared my throat. "I'm afraid there's been an incident at the lodge."

"Really? What kind of incident?"

"Well,...there's—there's been a—"

"There's been a murder," Harrison bellowed.

There was something about the way the English said murder.

M - u - u - d - e - r.

As though it signaled a cliffhanger at the end of Act II. I half expected a cacophony of stringed instruments to bellow out overhead. *Dun-dun-dun!*

"A murder? Who was murdered?" Henry looked frantically about the room as if trying to unearth the killer.

"The butler," said Madeline.

"The butler?"

"Actually," said Harrison, "he portrayed the role of butler in the game of murder we play here at the lodge." He paused, frowning as though reliving the scene over in his mind. "I must say, it was quite unfortunate that *I* was the one to discover the body."

"That's terrible. How did he...."

"Someone hit him over the head with a pool cue," said Gretchen.

"And since nobody has had the chance to leave," said Sam, "the murderer is still here."

Henry was stunned into silence. But it was more than that. *Concern perhaps?*

He looked down at the floor and drifted away for several seconds before responding. "Have you called the police?"

"No," said Truman. The phones are dead, and—"

"And we're trapped!" shouted Madeline. "Trapped in this remote ice shack with a corpse just mere feet away from us— with no way of reaching the outside world. I feel like a prisoner."

Jason let out a sigh. "Settle down, Mads. No need to be so dramatic."

"Settle down? Unbelievable."

"You make it sound like we'll never get out of here. There's a storm, so what? We've been in storms before. I think the real reason why you're so upset is because the phones are dead, and there's no cell service. Isn't that right? Deal with it, Mads, like the rest of us are doing."

"Fine! I'm going to my room if it's alright with you. And don't worry; I'll try not to escape from the upstairs window."

Jason shook his head and turned to Henry. "Sorry for that." The color on his face changed slightly. "Did you say you used your cell phone out there?"

"Like I said, it was off and on. But if you like, I can go out there and try again."

"I'll go with you," said Jason, already standing to his feet.

"It'll be nice knowing the police are aware of what's going on up here," said Elenor.

"We'll sure do our best." Henry grabbed his coat off the floor and slid into his boots.

"Hold on a minute!" Harrison hurried to the safe, pulled out the cell phones, and placed them on the desk. "You'll need one of these."

"Oh, right," Jason said. He combed through the mountain of smartphones—most protected in designer cases—until he found his phone. "Okay, be back soon."

Harrison lined up the remainder of the phones on the desk. "I guess there's no real point in keeping these here any longer. Feel free to come and collect your phones."

FORTY MINUTES LATER, Jason and Henry returned from their quest, looking like a couple of abominable snowmen. Small, round, ice balls clung to the cuffs of their sleeves and jeans like a dog's underbelly after frolicking in the snow.

"What happened out there? Sam said. "I thought you took the truck. What did you do, roll around on the ground?"

Henry chuckled. "We weren't out making snowmen if that's what you mean. But we managed to get stuck and had to dig ourselves out." He finished peeling off his coat and boots before heading to the den.

"Did you get through to the police?" Gretchen asked.

"Yes," Henry said. He shook his shaggy head back and forth, flinging ice and snow into the air. "They said they'll do their best to get someone up here. But until the roads clear, nobody's attempting the trek up here. We're looking at two—maybe three days, at best."

Hearing that made my stomach sink. I wished I could reach Dominic and tell him I was okay. He knew I didn't like driving in bad weather. And not being able to talk to him made the situation much more stressful.

"How far up the mountain did you go to get reception?" I seriously contemplated taking the trip myself.

"Not too far," said Henry. "The problem wasn't getting someone on the line; it was keeping them there. The reception was bad. It took four tries to report what had happened."

"Not to mention how easy it is to get stuck," said Jason. "A mountain of snow has already fallen, and it's still snowing."

Quinn grabbed a blanket off the loveseat and handed it to Jason. "Here ya go. Why don't you sit here by the fire? You look cold."

"Thanks." Jason took the blanket and offered Henry an awkward glance. "We're not supposed to share this, are we?"

"Ha, ha. I'm good. It's all yours."

"I can get another blanket," offered Quinn. "But I'd have to get it from the library."

"That's not necessary," insisted Henry. "Besides, isn't that where—um…?"

"Yes," said Harrison. "The body is in the library."

Gretchen adjusted her position on the sofa. "But it sure would be nice if he weren't. If we must hang out together all weekend, I'd rather be in the library than here."

Sam held up his hand. "It might be a good idea to move him outside."

"Actually," said Henry, "I wouldn't mind checking out the crime scene for myself. Maybe I can even help move the body to a better spot."

"I guess that couldn't hurt," said Sam. "I'll come with you."

When I got up to follow the men to the library, I couldn't help but notice the stink eye I was getting from Gretchen.

"If Scarlet's going, I'm coming too."

"Well, I don't want to miss any excitement," said Elenor. Wait for me."

And yet again, a familiar entourage followed Henry back to the library to investigate the scene.

32

Do you have something to hide?

"AND YOU SAY *you* found the body?" Henry said after several minutes of woeful reflection.

"I did," said Harrison.

"And he's always been right here...next to the pool table?"

"Yes, except for the missing pool cue, the scene is as we left it."

Elenor searched around the pool table like the stick had somehow leaped to another part of the room. "I still don't understand why the killer would take it. Why would he do that?"

"I'm guessing he didn't want the evidence to trace back to him," said Gretchen.

Truman jumped in. "So, a sloppy killer."

"Unless..." I considered the scene again as though seeing it for the first time. Although I knew Quinn and I had already discussed it.

"Yes?" urged Truman.

"Unless it was a crime of passion. If it were a premeditated murder, the killer would have worn gloves or, at the very least, wiped off their prints. But maybe it happened so fast that they had to leave all the evidence behind. Perhaps they heard Harrison coming down the hall and panicked."

"But certainly, I would have seen them coming out of the library," said Harrison.

"That's true," said Sam. "But didn't you say the lights were on in the library? If the room was dark, they might have been able to keep themselves hidden, but since the lights were on, I doubt there was a decent place to hide."

"You were in the library too, Scarlet," said Truman. "Were the lights on or off when you heard Victoria scream?"

"They were on."

"So, from when you left the library to when Harrison came in, there wasn't much time."

"That's correct."

"I have a thought." Gretchen slithered beside me, her black leather pants swishing with every stride. "What if the murder happened before Harrison entered the library? Say, sometime between one-fifteen and a little after three."

"What are you trying to say, Gretchen?" Quinn was petite, but she rarely shied away from a good spat

"I'm stating facts, that's all. The fact is, Scarlet was in the library for a couple of hours, 'sleeping.' That doesn't sound like much of an alibi to me. For all we know, she could have killed Caffrey, came out here with the rest of us, and played dumb when Harrison came running into the room."

Quinn stepped closer to Gretchen, but not before Sam could get between them. "Okay," he said, directing Gretchen to the other side of the room.

"Thanks, Quinn," I said through gritted teeth, "but I think I can handle myself." I planted myself in the middle of the group, hoping I could talk some sense into them. "Look, I realize this looks bad. Some of you think I may have killed Caffrey, but I assure you I didn't. I *did* fall asleep, and honestly, I didn't hear anything."

"Quite convenient if you ask me." Gretchen wandered to the seating circle and slumped into one of the cozy sofas.

Chase Ridgeway, I was not; however, if I wanted to get anywhere with this investigation, I'd have to get out of my way and show some bold initiative.

I looked around the room and knew I was quickly losing the battle to convince them of my innocence. But as I basked in the tension of their cynical looks, an idea formed inside my newly acquired detective brain. It was risky, and there was a chance I'd throw all credibility out the window, but it was the only thing I could think of that might turn up some evidence. "Might I suggest that we search everyone's room? Perhaps we might get lucky and find the murder weapon?"

No one said anything—at least not right away. At first, I thought I had spoken too softly. But as I was about to repeat myself, Harrison turned to me and said, "Isn't that a bit presumptuous, Scarlet?"

"Well, it has to be somewhere," I said. "I'm saying that I think we need to cover all our bases, that's all."

Gretchen huffed. "And what do you mean, cover all *our* bases? Are you aligned with some covert police investigation we're not aware of?"

"Of course not, I—"

"I agree with Scarlet," said Sam. "I may be retired, but I still have detective's blood running through my veins."

"Fine," said Gretchen, "I would love to check Scarlet's room." She rewarded me with her evil eye. "You never know; we might find something in there that contradicts the goody-two-shoes persona she's been promoting since she got here.

I smiled. I was all too familiar with the 'Gretchens' of the world. My whole life, I struggled to find the courage to stand up to people who believed they were better than me. Stronger. Savvier. Sexier. It was easier to let them win than to convince myself I was a worthy opponent, which usually ended in embarrassment. I marveled at her icy stare and smug grin as if she had already declared victory.

Not today, Gretchen, not today.

"Listen, Gretchen. I don't know you, and you don't know me, but I can assure you that what you see is what you get. We got off on the wrong foot for some reason, and I'm not sure why. I have no problem letting you into my room to peek into my life. And I'm quite confident you won't find any evidence of a secret life *or* a murder weapon."

At this point, I paused and looked to Quinn for some moral support. And she didn't disappoint. The look on her face was that of a proud mother on graduation day. That alone spurred my confidence.

"By all means, have a look. But let's get one thing straight, Gretchen: if we check *my* room, we check yours."

As I stopped to mentally congratulate myself for putting Gretchen in her place, I realized the irony of the whole situation. Was I hiding a secret life? Of course, I was. But I was an author, for heaven's sake, not a killer.

Gretchen's smirk plunged into a frown, which boosted my sense of accomplishment. I could finally say I stood up to a bully and survived.

"Of course," Gretchen said, her voice patronizing and drawn out. She sighed heavily and folded her arms as though fraternizing with us common folk was beneath her.

"Alright," Henry said, "since I'm a little late to the party, I assume I'm missing something."

Sam mumbled under his breath. "A whole lot of drama."

"Maybe Scarlet is right," said Jason. "We *should* search everyone's room. With any luck, the murder weapon will turn up, and we can be one step closer to the killer."

"I've changed my mind," said Gretchen. "No one is going in my room."

"Do you have something to hide?" Quinn asked.

"Not at all. I just don't want you yahoos looking through my things. I think I'll leave that up to the police."

"Forget it," shouted Jason. "We're checking your room. If you have nothing to hide, it shouldn't be a problem.

"I have nothing to hide," said Truman.

"I'm with Gretchen," said Madeline. "I'd like to wait for the police, too."

"You don't have a choice," said Jason.

As predicted, Madeline huffed and planted herself against the pool table.

"Right, I guess we're doing this," said Harrison. "You all go on ahead. I'll go get Sébastien and Rebecca from the kitchen."

Sam cleared his throat. "If you don't mind, Scarlet...we'll start with your room."

Gretchen pushed herself off the sofa. "Great idea!"

33

Sure, I'd love another cup of coffee

THE STAIRS CREAKED and moaned like they were sick and tired of being stepped on. And by their look and sound, I ventured a guess that they were next on the list of renovations.

An uneasy feeling swept over me, knowing everyone was about to snoop in my things. I had nothing to hide (except a whole other life), but still, nothing to do with the murder.

We ascended the stairs, huddling together like cattle heading for the slaughter, when a thought dawned on me. I allowed Elenor and Sam to pass so I could run a theory by Quinn.

"Is there even a point to this little charade?" I asked as she came up beside me.

"What do you mean?"

"Who would be dumb enough to leave the murder weapon out in plain sight?"

"No one said criminals were smart, Scarlet. You, of all people, should know that."

"Maybe the killer already planted the evidence in someone else's room."

"But how would they even—"

Before Quinn could finish her thought, the lights flickered on and off before going out altogether, marooning us all on the stairs in complete darkness. But it was only pitch black for a moment or two because, within seconds, half a dozen iPhones lit up the staircase with enough lumens to light up the Calgary Tower.

It reminded me of my childhood, living on the South Shore of Nova Scotia. Every year, a power outage was inevitable; it was only a matter. I could almost hear the sounds of the ocean gearing up for a big storm. Angry, restless, like my mother scurrying around the house to find matchbooks and candlesticks. There were no such things as smartphones, so knowing which drawer had what in it ahead of time was a must, especially in the wake of hurricane season.

I pointed my phone in front of me, happy for the technology, and carefully dallied down the stairs and into the den with everyone else.

"Of course, the lights would go out," groaned Madeline. "Just one more thing to add to the murder mystery experience."

"What are we supposed to do now?" said Gretchen.

I noted Harrison entering the den. He appeared winded. It hadn't occurred until now that he wasn't on the stairs when the lights went out. "No need to be alarmed, everyone. We have a generator—although it's a small one—but a generator nonetheless. The only problem is someone will have to go turn it on."

"If you tell me where it is, Harrison, I'll go out and get 'er working." Henry's offer made it sound like he knew his way around machinery.

Harrison let out a sigh of relief. "That would be wonderful. It's behind the lodge, about twenty feet away from the hot tub. If you go down the hallway to the library, you'll see a door leading to the laundry room. From there, you'll find another door leading outside. You'll notice a large red tarp; that's where the generator is. You can't miss it. Although"—he walked to the lobby to get the shovel—"I'm sure the snow will be somewhat troublesome for you as you try to locate it."

"Don't worry, I'll find it." Henry took the shovel from Harrison and headed down the hall.

"Looks like you got lucky, Scarlet." Gretchen rocked back and forth in the chair with her arms crossed.

"As soon as the lights are back on," said Quinn, "we can head back up there. We have nothing to hide."

"I'm sure you don't, but I'll wait for the official tour. I don't want it to be your word against mine. When it comes to the likability factor, you have more votes than I do."

A few minutes later, the lights popped on, putting everyone at ease.

"Wonderful," said Elenor.

"I'm not sure how long we have with this generator," said Harrison. "It's a portable one, good for about twenty hours. The shed has another gasoline container, so we should be good for a few days."

Victoria tapped Harrison on the shoulder. "I don't think so, Harrison. I checked it last week, and it was empty."

"Oh, drat! I was supposed to get that filled, wasn't I? I completely forgot."

"I guess you better make sure we have a good fire burning in both fireplaces, Harrison," said Sam.

"You don't have to worry about that. I have a knack for maintaining a good fire going."

"So," said Sam, "we have about twenty hours, give or take. Might I suggest we make a plan to use the generator only when necessary?"

"We need to have enough power to cook our meals for tomorrow," Rebecca said.

"But we don't need power while we sleep," said Jason. "We can turn off the generator after we head upstairs for the night and not have to turn it on again until morning."

"Good," said Harrison, "that will save some energy."

"Can I get anyone anything?" asked Rebecca. "I'm sure there won't be much sleeping tonight. I can make some coffee."

"I could use a cup," said Elenor.

She wasn't kidding about being a coffee drinker. How many cups was that, I wondered.

"I will fetch the snack," said Sébastien.

I had already polished off enough sugar to fill my left boot; it was only day one. If I continued on this path, I'd be up ten pounds before the end of the weekend. But, to the best of my knowledge, I couldn't recall the last time I refused a fresh mug of coffee accompanied by an irresistible sweet.

REBECCA PLACED A tray of mugs on the table before retreating to the kitchen to fetch the coffee. Sébastien entered with an assortment of fancy cookies and put them next to the mugs. He fanned out some napkins along with spoons to stir the coffee.

"What if our phones die...then what?" Madeline was somewhat hysterical.

"If we need to charge our phones," said Jason, "we could always go out to our vehicles and charge them. We should probably go start our cars up anyway."

Quinn placed her cookie on the table beside her and headed for the lobby. "You know, that sounds like a great idea. I'm going to go see if my baby will start."

"We just have to wait until Henry returns with the shovel," said Jason. He went to the window to look outside. "Still coming down. I'll try to make a path to the parking lot. Didn't you say there was a big scoop in the shed, Harrison?"

"Yes. It should be inside the door. Hopefully, you'll be able to get out there."

Henry strolled around the corner, leaving icy, wet puddles in his wake. "Sorry about the mess. Glad to see the lights are on, though."

"Any trouble finding it?" Harrison asked.

Henry took off his boots and carried them to the lobby entrance. "It took me a minute, but once I got it working, I cleared as much snow around it as possible. Figured I'd make it easy for anyone who has to find their way back there. Where y'all headed?"

"If you're up for it," said Jason, "you could come and help me shovel out the front steps. Thought we'd start our vehicles and charge up our cell phones before we turn in for the night."

Henry stepped back into his boots and zipped up his coat. "Sounds like a plan. Lead the way."

"You can have the first shift with the scoop; I'll take the shovel."

34

The game is afoot…again.

THE TEMPERATURE HAD fallen to a grueling depth, and my face felt like it had been injected with a syringe full of ice-cold Novocaine.

Once I finished my turn with the shovel, I was eager to thaw in Quinn's heated car. "Brrr," I said, rubbing my cheeks with my mittens. "There's so much snow out there; not sure we've made much of a dent."

Quinn leaned over the steering wheel to look at the sky. "Looks like it might be letting up, though."

"Now, if only that wind would stop blowing."

She picked up her phone and checked how much more it needed to charge. She gazed out into the parking lot. "So? Are we any closer to figuring out who the murderer is?"

"No, and we still need answers to some questions."

"I agree," said Quinn. "Like, was Victoria having an affair with Caffrey? Why did Henry decide to come to the lodge?

And who the heck is Mr. Whitmore? I believe this place has secrets, and what's with that door?"

"Yes!" I probably shouted that a little too loudly for the inside of a small car. "That door…what is with that door? I need to find out what they're hiding in there." I glanced at the time on the dashboard. "Once I know everyone is asleep tonight, I might go to the kitchen and see if I can get inside."

"Are you crazy? The power will be off, and who knows what might lurk in the shadows."

"Don't worry, I'll have my phone for light, and you could come with me to be my lookout."

"Who are you, and what have you done with my best friend?"

"What do you mean?"

"First of all, standing up to Gretchen like you did earlier? That was amazing! I don't think I've ever heard you say that many assertive words to another person. You were fierce!"

"It did feel kinda good."

"Yeah, it did," Quinn said in her most "you-go-girl" voice. She wiped the condensation off the windshield with her fist. "And secondly, you are basically taking the lead in a murder investigation…and people are listening to you. You are coming out of your shell with tenacity, girlfriend! Tenacity!" She held up her hand, coaxing me into a high-five.

I laughed and indulged her with a silent thwack against her mitten. I loved her energy and goofiness, not to mention her relentless cheerleading. What would I do without her? I imagined it would be rather dull.

"So, is that a yes? Will you come with me to do some snooping?"

"Of course!" She picked up her phone and disconnected the charger. "After all, it *was* my idea for a murder mystery weekend, and if we have to look for clues to find out who the killer is, count me in."

AFTER SHOVELING A path to everyone's car, it was nearly midnight. The snow had finally tapered off, giving way to a celestial parade of shining stars that twinkled against a carbon sky. It was still freezing, but at least the wind had died down.

As Harrison stood at the door, ushering people into the warmth, I couldn't help but chuckle at the icicles that had formed on the ends of his eyelashes. "That's the last of us, Harrison. Do you have someone who usually clears the parking lot?"

"I do, but it's not likely we'll see him for a few days. Our hope lies with the snowplows. Now, let's get inside so we can defrost our faces, shall we?"

"You don't have to ask me twice; I'm right behind you."

Once inside, Harrison gathered us into the den like sheep. He pulled out his pocket watch and closed his eyes like he was doing a mental calculation. "Okay, people, settle down. As discussed earlier, we must be smart about how much time we use the generator. For all we know, we could be stranded here for a couple more days, and we want to be able to cook our meals. Having said that,"—he turned and focused on Henry—"could you give the guests fifteen minutes to settle into their rooms before turning off the generator? I'll wait downstairs until you return."

"I can do that." Henry grabbed his gloves and slipped them over his large, callused hands.

"I'll come with you," said Jason.

"Can always use an extra pair of hands."

"Great," said Harrison. "And remember, it's going to get extremely chilly tonight. There should be extra blankets in the closet if you need them." Before heading to the staircase, he checked the fire one last time. "If there's nothing else, let's try and get some sleep. I'll be up early tomorrow and turn on the generator in time for Sébastien to make us a wonderful breakfast."

"I will be up by five o'clock," said Sébastien. "If that's too early for you, Harrison, I will turn on the generator."

Harrison raised his eyebrows. "That might be a bit early for me, so yes, if you wouldn't mind."

"Pas de problème."

"Right, we have a plan," said Harrison, waving the guests toward the staircase. "Rest well, everyone. We shall see you all at breakfast."

35

Sleuthing by moonlight

I GRABBED MY phone from the nightstand and turned the alarm off. Quinn (already dressed and standing with her ear pressed against the door) was ready for the mission. It was eerily quiet and dark as tar.

"Did you sleep?" I asked.

"Couldn't. Too excited."

"Hear anything?"

"Sounds pretty quiet…I think we're a go."

I rolled out of bed and threw on a pair of jeans and a sweatshirt. I grabbed my hair and twisted it into a bun, leaving a few unruly strands to do whatever they pleased. After splashing my face with cold water, I slid into my slippers and headed for the door. "Okay, ready when you are."

Quinn opened the door and peeked outside. "Coast is clear."

We crept across the old hardwood to the top of the stairs, instigating only a few minor groans.

"Sit on your bottom," I whispered. "Maybe the stairs won't creak as much.

The lobby was quiet. The door no longer rattled since the wind had calmed, enhancing the chilling hush.

Tiptoeing into the dining room, we pushed through the swinging doors that led to the kitchen. Metal bowls and whisks lined the countertops, along with breadboards, measuring cups, and an assortment of knives. Whatever the chef had in store for breakfast, his tools were ready.

I shone the light over the marble slab, marveling again at the impressive kitchen. It seemed like yesterday that I was drooling over the very same oven while perusing kitchen renovations on some obscure website.

My eyes bounced from one shiny thing to the next but stopped when I came to the spice rack. "Hey," I said softly, "notice anything familiar about these bottles?"

Quinn moved in for a closer look. She took out one bottle and brought it to her face. "Yeah, it's like the one we found in the library."

"Interesting. Is there any nutmeg there?"

She ran her finger up and down the bottles. "Hmm," she said, pulling a vial from the rack and shaking it. "I'm not sure, but this one is empty." She brought it up to the light to examine it a little closer. "It's not engraved."

I held out my hand. "Let me see that for a second." I popped off the cork and sniffed. "There's no trace of nutmeg in this one."

"Interesting," said Quinn. "And all the rest of these bottles have names of spices engraved on them…all but that one."

I returned the vial to its rack. "Hmm…a conundrum."

"It is a mystery," said Quinn.

I aimed the light at the door—the whole reason for our mission—and imagined what could be on the other side. "So, you think you can unlock it?"

Quinn scoffed. "Do you need to ask?"

I rolled my eyes. "Tell me again how you got so good at this."

"All thanks to my big brother. It's the one thing he taught me that has come in handy."

"How is he, anyway? Have you been up to see him?"

"Nope. Been wanting to, but I hate seeing him like that."

"I'm sorry."

"Don't be…you're not the one who got caught trying to break into his ex-boss's house. He should have known there would be a high-tech security system in a house like that. It was careless. Enough about my brother; let's see if we can find out where this door leads."

She pulled a black leather case from her back pocket and laid it on the floor. It opened to a cornucopia of stainless steel picks. It seemed to energize her. She thoughtfully ran her index finger over the tools, settling on one suitable for the job. It was fascinating watching her work. Such focus. I almost didn't recognize her. Was she my best friend or a seasoned thief?

I realized that her upbringing was a far cry from mine, but it still astounded me whenever she did certain things. Like whipping out a set of lock picks from her back pocket, as though it was common practice for women in their forties. "Who brings lock picks with them on a girl's weekend?"

With one pick between her lips and another at the ready, she carefully examined the lock before proceeding with her extraordinary skills of breaking and entering. She removed the pick from her mouth and grinned. "I always carry them with me…you never know when you might need them."

"How often do you need to break into places?"

She laughed. "Just shine the light on the lock."

As soon as Quinn unlocked the door, we heard a noise.

"What was that?" My legs had turned to noodles at the thump echoing from somewhere in the lodge; I thought I might drop where I stood.

"I don't know," Quinn whispered, frantically placing her tools back in the case. "But it sounded like it came from the lobby."

"What should we do?"

"We should go check it out; that's what we should do."

"That's not a good idea…what if we get caught?"

"The way I see it," said Quinn, "someone else is skulking around here, too. Maybe it's the killer."

"Well, that doesn't make me feel any better."

She grabbed my arm and pulled me toward the dining room. "Come on, let's go catch' em!"

"You don't happen to have any weapons in your back pocket, do ya?"

"Very funny."

"I thought so."

Quinn led the way, which didn't make me feel safe at all. It wasn't like anyone would feel threatened by a petite-sized woman wielding an iPhone and a set of lock picks; however, she did possess enough backbone for the both of us, so I guess, at this point, I was content with forging ahead.

According to the time on my phone, it was almost two in the morning, and I wondered if someone else had the same idea to snoop around while everyone slept. And if so, what were they doing on the opposite end of the lodge?

"Shhh!" Quinn stopped and held her hand up.

"What is it?"

"I think the noise is coming from the library."

"Maybe someone's in there looking for a good book to read."

"Or maybe someone has gone to see the body again."

As we passed by the lobby door, I glanced out to see a very bright, very full moon. It was breathtaking. A pure white snow shimmered under a golden globe; it was like peeking into a Thomas Kinkade painting. Now that ambient light poured in through the windows, it was much easier to prowl around the lodge without bumping into anything.

And it was quiet. Very quiet.

As we entered the library, I realized we had infringed on something we weren't supposed to see.

A door.

It was a secret door hidden behind one of the bookshelves.

"Did you see that?" I rushed past Quinn, pointing my phone toward the pool table. I shivered at the sight of Caffrey still lying on the floor. Was someone in here messing with the crime scene again? I wondered. And if so, where did they go?

"I think someone went through that wall," Quinn said. "But...that's impossible."

"Well, not exactly," I said. "I think there's a door here, but that would mean it should lead into the hall, and I'm pretty sure I didn't see a door out there."

"A secret passageway?"

"That's my guess." I inched closer. "The door is well-hidden. I would have never seen it."

"What are you waiting for? Open it!"

I placed my hand on the shelf, looking for a latch. When I didn't find one, I pressed against the wood until it popped open. "Bingo!"

"This is exciting!" Quinn whispered. "It keeps getting better."

"I know, it feels like we're in a movie. I hope someone doesn't jump out of the shadows, which would seem to be the next logical scene."

"That's why I'm letting you go first," she said.

"Gee, thanks."

"Not a problem."

I pulled the door, opening it with my fingertips. It was dark, and there was no ambient light coming from anywhere. I aimed the phone into the blackness and discovered a staircase. "Interesting."

"Be careful."

"I will," I said. "Stay close."

The steps were more precarious than the staircase in the lobby and clearly not recommended for paying guests. I held the railing as if my life depended on it. "I wonder if Caffrey knew this place existed."

"Well, if he did, I can see why he left it off the tour."

A chill ran up my spine when we reached the bottom. It was cold and desolate and looked like something out of an old Alfred Hitchcock movie. Nothing was welcoming about it. In fact, it was the total opposite: cement floors and cracked walls. That was it. Mysterious portals loomed on either side of the stairs, and neither option looked all that enticing. What could be on the other side of them? I wondered.

"This reminds me of when we went through that haunted house, remember?" Quinn was still holding onto the hem of my sweatshirt.

"You mean the spooky house at the end of Cherry Drive? Oh, I remember. I still can't pass a mirror without turning the lights on first."

"That was almost fifteen years ago. Can you believe it? I wonder what happened to the people that lived there?"

I brought the light up to my face and lowered my voice. "Maybe they're here right now. *Wah-ah-ah!*"

"Not funny," said Quinn, pushing the phone away.

I laughed and pointed the light to the right and the left. "Okay, which way should we go?"

"I'm gonna let you choose."

I could hear muffled voices coming from the right. "I say we go this way."

"If we walk through a spider web," said Quinn, "I will lose my mind…just saying."

"Don't think you have anything to worry about since I'm in front of you. You make sure nothing creeps up behind us."

"Oh, great! Now I have to worry about that, too."

The voices were getting louder, and we could see a faint light coming from somewhere. We slowly crept down the hall, stalling at each ominous portal.

"Whoever is down here," I said, "they stopped talking."

"Maybe they heard us coming."

There was no longer a faint light when we reached the end. I peeked my head around the corner.

"What do you see?" she whispered.

"I don't see anything."

We slowly entered, not knowing what we'd find. "Where did they go? I know I heard voices."

"I did, too."

"What's that over there?" I edged along the wall until I came to another staircase. "Well, this is interesting. How many secret staircases are in this place?"

"I bet you anything; this leads to the door to the kitchen."

"You're probably right, so where do these other hallways lead?

"Here, shine the light this way. I'll go up and see if we're right."

Quinn began climbing up the stairs before I could stop her. Whoever *was* here might not be gone for long, and I wanted to check out the rest of the place before they decided to come back.

"Quinn, let's go!" I said, trying to hurry her along.

A long creak echoed down the stairs as she slowly opened the door. Whipping her head around the corner, she whispered back to me. "I was right; this is the mystery door to the kitchen."

"Okay, great! Now, get back down here."

But before she could descend the stairs, a shadowy figure emerged from the other side of the hallway, holding a bright light straight into my eyes that blinded me temporarily. The intruder took off, running in the opposite direction.

"Quick!" I shouted. "They're getting away!"

"How many twists and turns are down here?"

"Keep going. I think I see the light up ahead."

"He went into that room," said Quinn. "We've got 'em; there's nowhere to go!"

We turned the corner, expecting to see our suspect up against the wall, but no one was there. There was nothing there at all. No person. No staircase. No door.

Nothing.

36

Insomnia and chamomile tea

IT WAS MIND-BOGGLING. How could someone disappear into thin air? Of course, they couldn't, so there had to be a reasonable explanation.

Someone was in the basement, meaning they knew all about the secret passageways. But did they know about them this whole time? Or did they stumble onto them haphazardly like we did? The only logical explanation was it had to be one of the staff.

But where did they go?

I rubbed my hands up and down the concrete walls, hoping to find another secret door. "It's got to be around here somewhere. You check on that wall."

"Got it," said Quinn.

With only a tiny circle of light, it was hard to locate anything in the dark, gloomy room, and I couldn't be sure we were even alone. Who knows how many different rodents and creepy crawlers were along for the adventure?

"What do ya think Dominic is up to?" I said, trying to ease some nervous tension.

"My guess? He's sound asleep."

"You don't think he's up pacing the floors because he can't get ahold of me?"

"Nah…he knows you can take care of yourself. You left him a message earlier. So, he's aware that you made it to the lodge safe and sound. I'm sure he's sleeping like a baby."

"You're right," I strained my eyes, hoping to see something curious. "How is it that men can sleep through anything? It doesn't matter what the crisis is; Dominic can fall asleep at the drop of a hat. On the other hand, I struggle to sleep because I'm trying to solve all the world's problems."

"You find anything?"

"Nothing…you?"

"No. But I'm not giving up. There gotta be—"

Crash

"Now what?" I swung myself around in perfect sync with the beam of light.

"It came from the kitchen."

We rushed out of the room, taking the stairs two at a time. When we pushed the door open, the last person we expected to see was standing in the middle of the kitchen, looking like they had seen a ghost.

"Oh my goodness!" said Elenor.

She had a head full of foam curlers and a face slathered in moss-green night cream. "Elenor!" I said. "What are you doing here?"

Elenor's eyes glazed over as though she hadn't heard a word. She was standing over a shattered mug, holding the empty vial of...nutmeg?

Now that's curious.

Finally, she snapped out of it. "Well, I couldn't sleep... thought I'd see if I could find anything to settle my nerves. I may have overdone it on the coffee. You know, dear, I love my coffee, but I think it's time to switch over to herbal tea. Although it doesn't have the same kind of oomph as coffee, that's for sure. I love that full-body roast but decided to go for the tea instead. I was looking for a little nutmeg but was unable to find any. I realize it's a bit unconventional. I got a whiff from Caffrey's coffee when we were on our tour and thought, hmm, I wonder if that would go nice in some tea—"

"Elenor," I said, "can I help you with that?" I helped her safely over the glass, plucked another mug off the rack, and placed a chamomile tea bag inside. I noted the time on the wall clock above her. It was already two-thirty, and I wasn't the least bit tired. How could I be? I was too revved up to even think about sleep.

"Oh, thank you, dear. You two couldn't sleep either?"

"You could say that," said Quinn.

"Well," she said, gingerly sipping her tea, "Sam's sleeping like a baby. He tends to snore rather loudly; he can't help it. Sam has sleep apnea, you know. But, as usual, he forgot his CPAP mask at home again. I keep telling him he needs two, one for home and one for when we go gallivanting across the country. He's forgotten that thing on more than one occasion, and when he does, *I* don't sleep."

As Elenor rambled on, I stared out the window at the steam coming from the hot tub. It looked peaceful. For a moment, I imagined if a quick dunk would help me relax enough to sleep. But something off in the distance caught my eye. I held up my hand to stop Elenor from talking. "How long have you been up for, Elenor?"

"I don't think I had a chance to close my eyes, dear. After completing my nighttime ritual, Sam was already fast asleep. I lay in bed and listened to that dreadful sound until I couldn't take it any longer. I'd say it was about a quarter to one when I decided to take my pillow and blanket and come down to the den to try and fall asleep."

Quinn shot me a look. "You mean you've been in the den since 12:45?"

"I do believe so. Why?"

"And did you fall asleep?"

"I may have dozed off, but something woke me up. I thought I heard voices."

"Do you know what time that was?" I asked.

"Well, it was before I came in here to fix myself some tea."

I looked out the window again. "Where were the voices coming from?"

Elenor casually slurped her hot beverage like she was shooting the breeze with a couple of girlfriends. "I was sure they were coming from outside, but who in their right mind would be out there in this freezing weather?"

"That's what we'd like to know." I grabbed the broom, leaning against the wall, and swept up the shards of glass. "Maybe it would be best if you tried to get some sleep. I'm sure it's nothing; maybe it's animals running around making noise. We'll go take a look before we head back upstairs."

"Are you sure, dear? I could wake up Sam to go out there with you."

I gently guided Elenor toward the door. "Oh, that won't be necessary, Elenor. You have a good night, and we'll see you in the morning."

"Well, okay, dear…if you're sure," she said, yawning into her hand. "Oh my! I do believe this tea is working; I'm already feeling a bit drowsy. Have a good sleep. See you in the morning."

After Elenor headed back upstairs, I took Quinn by the arm and dragged her to the window. "Do you see that?"

"No, what am I looking at?"

It wasn't bright, but it did seem to be moving. *A flashlight, maybe?* "That light over there…isn't that the skating shed?"

She pressed her cheek against the glass, trying to get a better view. "It sure is, and I think someone's in there."

"It's probably the same person we heard downstairs. But how did he get over there so quickly?"

"I know what you're thinking, Scarlet, and I don't think we should be going out there alone. We should probably wait until morning."

"You're right. It's not like they can get away. We'll go out to the shed first thing in the morning; then, we need to have a little chat with Harrison."

37

THE SUNLIGHT POURED in like marmalade. But the beacon of color saturating our room was deceiving; it was freezing. Still, seeing the sunshine beam in after a night of chasing boogymen through the secret tunnels of Mystery Ridge Lodge was comforting.

I lay in bed, agonizing over the thought of placing my feet on the cold hardwood. The idea alone made me shiver. Since the power was out, keeping the entire lodge comfortable with only two fires burning was impossible. I hoped that at least the main floor was warmer than the second. By now, the fire would be roaring, and Sébastien would be cooking up a storm in the kitchen. That thought alone was enough to stick one foot out of the covers. "Nope!" I said, pulling my foot back to safety.

Quinn was still sound asleep and hadn't moved much throughout the night. She was lying on her back with the blankets pulled up to her chin as if she were tucked in tight and told not to move a muscle.

Finally, I willed myself out of bed and into the shower without a stir from Quinn. But when I emerged from the bathroom, she was awake and eagerly rummaging through her suitcase. "Good morning!" I said.

"Oh, hey."

"Lose something?"

"I thought I packed my purple Angora sweater. I can't find it anywhere."

I whipped the wet towel from my head and sifted through my clothes. I settled on high-rise yoga pants and my favorite fleece hoodie. There was no need to impress anyone at this point, so comfort it was. "Maybe it's in the car. I thought I saw a bunch of sweaters in there."

"Maybe, but I swear I put it in my suitcase."

I plugged in my blow dryer, preparing to wage war with my hairbrush. "How about we look for it after breakfast? We can search for it in your car on our way to the shed."

"Yeah, okay," she said, dragging her feet to the bathroom. "If you finish drying your hair before I'm out, go down without me."

IT HAD TO BE one of the most satisfying smells in the world. It brought me back to my childhood and the anticipation of Christmas morning: the tree, the lights, the presents. But the enticing aroma of cinnamon waffles, maple bacon, and perked coffee filling the air with sweet bliss is what fueled my love for food—especially sugary food.

"Good morning, Scarlet," Truman said, scooping scrambled eggs into his mouth like he hadn't eaten in a week.

"Morning." I pulled out a chair next to him.

"Where's your partner in crime?"

"You mean Quinn? She'll be down in a minute." I couldn't help but notice the stares from across the table. *Do I have something on my face?* I did a quick swipe but didn't think that was the issue. "How did everyone sleep?"

"I think the question is, how did *you* sleep?" Gretchen asked.

Hmmm. She's alluding to something.

Gretchen had a way of making you feel guilty, even if you had done nothing wrong. "I slept well, thank you?"

She twirled a strawberry between her fingers and stabbed another with her fork. "As I hear it, you were quite the busy beaver last night."

"Me? Where did you hear that?"

"I'm sorry, dear," Elenor said. "I was telling everyone about our encounter last night. I didn't mean to imply that you and Quinn were up to no good."

"That's okay, Elenor." I helped myself to some waffles, drowning them in a generous amount of maple syrup. "Could you pass the bacon, please, Madeline?" I didn't feel the need to elaborate, at least not until my sidekick could back me up.

"Well? Are you going to tell us what you two were up to last night?" Gretchen asked.

"Mmm…smells wonderful in here!"

Perfect timing!

"Oh, Quinn. You can sit here." I tapped the empty seat next to me.

"Nice of you to join us." Gretchen was extra surly this morning. Complete with a smile dripping in sarcasm.

Quinn turned to me, puzzled. "What'd I miss?"

"I believe," said Truman, "Scarlet was about to fill us all in on your shenanigans."

"Shenanigans?"

I held up my hand. "Okay, okay. If you must know, we were curious about the mystery door in the kitchen. There seems to be a lot of secrecy surrounding it, and we wanted to check it out, that's all."

"What mystery door?" Gretchen said, looking toward the kitchen.

"I noticed it yesterday."

Jason downed his glass of orange juice in one gulp. "What were you doing in the kitchen?"

"I went in there yesterday when I was looking for Truman. The plan was to sneak a peek, but instead, I was pulled in by my incessant curiosity."

"Uh-huh," said Gretchen. "So your curiosity brought you to a closed door?"

I could feel my cheeks flush; I despised the spotlight. "You caught me." I held up my hands, trying to make light of the situation. "But in my defense, the door was unlocked. I was curious what was inside."

"Don't keep us in suspense," said Madeline. "What'd you find?"

"Nothing. I mean…before I could find the light switch, Sébastien entered the kitchen, nearly scaring me half to death. When I asked him what was in there, he said it was for staff only and locked the door. So, being that I have a very inquisitive mind, I had to find out what he was hiding."

"And…" said Gretchen, crossing her arms. "…instead of filling the rest of us in on your plans to investigate, you and your little co-conspirator over there decided to go it alone?"

When she put it that way, it sounded way more devious than it was. What was I supposed to do? Should I have posted an announcement that I was executing a covert mission?

"Actually, yes," I said. "We still don't know who to trust, and in case you've all forgotten, there's a killer among us."

Truman reached for another slice of bacon, escorting it through the trace of maple syrup on his plate. From the lack of love handles above his waistline, I'm sure he didn't indulge in such elaborate breakfasts very often. "Out with it," he said, licking the sweetness off his fingers. "Don't keep us in suspense...what did you find out? What's behind the door?"

The only thing we had going for us at that point was that none of the staff were in the dining room.

Where were they anyway?

They might have been on to us, especially now that everyone knew what we'd been up to. I had to be careful, but I also needed answers. "It's true," I said, glancing at Quinn, who stuffed a considerable forkful of waffles into her mouth. She wouldn't be jumping in anytime soon. She looked like a chipmunk.

I continued. "While everyone was sound asleep, we decided to investigate, but we heard a noise when we got to the kitchen. It sounded like it was coming from the library."

"Was someone messing with the crime scene again?" Jason asked.

"No," said Quinn. "But we *did* find something very intriguing." She nodded for me to continue and slapped another waffle onto her plate.

"There's a door in the library...a secret door," I said.

Elenor reached her arm across the table, grabbing the tips of my fingers. "You mean like in the movies?"

"Kinda, yeah. It took a while to figure out how to open it, but we found a very spooky staircase leading to the basement once we did. We used our phones to light the way and headed down, not knowing who or what we'd find. Once we reached the bottom, we heard voices and chased someone to a room where they disappeared into thin air."

"What do you mean, disappeared?" Truman asked.

"When we got to the room," said Quinn, "nobody was there. Nada. Zilch. Zip."

"Now, that's curious," said Sam.

"Before we could investigate more," I said, "we heard Elenor dropping her mug on the floor."

Jason stood, pushing his chair away from the table with his calves. "I don't know about you guys, but I'd like to check out this secret, underground, who-knows-what-it-is basement."

A chorus of "Me too" resonated across the table as the guests stood from their seats, determined to conduct their own investigation.

It's not like we could stop them. They had every right to know what was going on as much as we did, and maybe if they were all busy exploring, we could check out the shed.

"I'd be happy to show you where the hidden door is in the library," I said.

"But that means we gotta see the body again, right?"

"No point in whining about it, Mads," said Jason. "There's nothing anyone can do about it."

"I know," she griped. "All I'm saying is that I wish Caffery were someplace else…someplace where we didn't have to see him just…just lying there."

Elenor wrapped her arm around Madeline's shoulder. They were nearly the same height. "Come on, dear. It'll be alright."

38

It was the manager in the shed with the shovel

WHILE THE OTHERS roamed the basement to uncover more secrets, Quinn and I set forth into the cold to search for clues.

We started at the back of the lodge, where the steam continued to billow high into the cloudless sky.

"Okay," I said. "Let's check the car for your sweater before heading to the shed. You ready?"

"As ready as I'll ever be. You think someone's in there now?"

"I don't know," I said, pulling my scarf over my nose. "We need to be prepared, just in case."

"What'd you suggest? An arsenal of snowballs ready to use at the first sign of trouble?"

"That's not a terrible idea."

We searched the car for Quinn's sweater and came up empty. It had to be somewhere and would probably show up sooner or later. In the meantime, we set out on the daunting trek to the shed. As we struggled to move through the snow, I began to relive Caffrey's story and how he didn't want anyone hiking up to the rock. But nothing prevented us from taking a look now. "Let's go up there," I said, pointing to the memorial.

"Why?" said Quinn. "Do you see something?"

"No. Just curious, aren't you?"

"Of course I am. Do you even have to ask?"

We made it up the hill and immediately noticed an inscription written on a plaque:

"To walk in nature is to witness a thousand miracles" — Mary Davis

"Interesting," said Quinn, "I wonder if someone *did* die out here?"

"Maybe, but I still think it was just a moodsetter."

"Either way, this place is starting to give me the creeps."

"Me too. Let's go."

Eventually, we found ourselves peering through a small, circular window. The door to the shed was weathered, a few rusted nails protruding from the wooden slats. I twisted the knob, relieved to find it unlocked, and pushed my way through. It was warmer than outside, but only by mere degrees. I could still see my breath escaping from the fibers in my alpaca scarf.

"Looks cozy," said Quinn.

My first observation was a long L-shaped bench adorned with red and black plaid cushions, which (not surprisingly) evoked memories of Henry pulling us out of a ditch. After a quick introspection, I spotted a cast iron stove in the corner of the room, plausibly uprooted from the 1920s. I was tempted to grab a few pieces of wood from the antique milk jug and start a fire. But it was only a matter of time before someone decided to come looking for us.

Behind one of the shelves at the back of the shed, there was a door, and not surprisingly, locked.

"How much you wanna bet that whatever they were up to last night has something to do with what's behind here?"

Quinn slipped a hand into her coat pocket, pulling out a familiar aid. "Luckily, there's a pick for that."

"You really do take that thing everywhere, don't you?"

"Never leave home without it."

Quinn masterfully picked the lock, then immediately tucked the case back in her pocket. Slowly, we emerged into a small room with floor-to-ceiling shelves housing cardboard boxes, plastic crates, and (from the look of a few ornaments and stringed lights attempting an escape from a few Rubbermaid containers) Christmas decorations.

"So this is where they keep all the good stuff," said Quinn.

I selected a box from one of the shelves and opened it with all the excitement of Christmas morning. Using two fingers, I plucked out a long red and white scarf. "Harrison's, maybe?"

"Or not. What do you make of this?" She held up a purple sweater.

"That's a sweater," I said, stating the obvious.

"Yes, a sweater that looks a lot like *my* sweater."

"Sure, but yours isn't the only purple sweater. Maybe some of the staff keep extra clothes out here. They do live here."

"Would you store your clothes outside in minus forty weather?"

I wouldn't, actually. If clothes hung in my closet for six months without so much a glance, I promptly brought them to the donation bin outside Louise La Bella's hair salon.

"Do you think it's yours?"

She shook it out a few times and held it up to her body. "Well, for starters, it's an Angora sweater." She proceeded to inspect the sweater, turning it this way and that. "Ah, ha! I know it's mine, and I can prove it." She turned it inside out and pointed to the stitching along one of the cuffs. "See? Do you see this stitching? Dark purple. But the stitching of this sleeve is light purple. It was a manufacturing error, but because it was on the inside of the cuff, it didn't matter."

"Okay," I said slowly. "I guess my question would be, what is your sweater doing in these boxes, and who put it there?"

I opened another box and began searching the contents, wondering if I would spot any of my clothes. Not only were there articles of clothing—from beautiful sweaters to baseball hats—but a whole bunch of other stuff that didn't belong in the back of a shed.

"I don't know about you," said Quinn, "but somehow, I don't think these belong in the Christmas decorations." She pulled out a pair of bright orange pants and held them to her waist.

"No, I should say not," I said, trying to appreciate what went into the thought process of even buying a pair of tangerine pants.

"And what about these?" she said, placing a pair of Ray-Ban sunglasses on her face. "I don't see these sitting on a tree either."

I had to admit, rummaging through all those boxes gave me a slight thrill. I took another one off the shelf, eager to see what was inside. But before I could take inventory of the box, a voice blared out behind me, scaring me yet again.

"What are you doing in here?"

I jumped and dropped the box, spilling the suspicious plunder everywhere. Harrison stood in the doorway, holding a shovel over his head like a maniac. I'm sure his intent was to be threatening; however, I almost laughed out loud. Somehow, he had managed to squeeze his pudgy body into an ill-fitting, bright red parka while the teeth of the zipper held on for dear life. His white, fluffy mittens (probably made out of rabbit fur) reminded me of the ones I had sewn in home economics class in junior high. The ensemble was peculiar (but then again, so was Harrison) and anything but intimidating.

"I'll ask again. What are you two ladies doing in here? If I recall, that door was locked, was it not?"

I picked up the purple sweater and held it up to his face. "I think we have a few questions of our own, Harrison."

"What are you talking about?"

"We're talking about how my sweater managed to get from my suitcase to this box here. And don't tell me you don't know what we're talking about. We know you were in here last night doing something. We saw a light on in the shed."

"I'm afraid you are mistaken. If you don't mind, please come out of there."

"No," said Quinn. "We will not come out of here until we get some answers. In fact, I'm sure we need to see what's in the rest of these boxes, don't you, Scarlet?"

"I'd have to agree with my friend, Mr. Hightower. You and your staff have been secretive from the moment we arrived. I first chalked it up to being part of the whole mystery weekend thing. But, no! You have a secret, and we're here to find out what that secret is. So, unless you want to stand there and watch us empty out the contents of every box here, you'll tell us what we want to know."

Whoa! What's gotten into me?

Since arriving at the lodge, I acquired a boldness I'd never had before. Would I have ever talked to anyone like that back home? Heavens, no. But for some reason, a sudden outbreak of unexplainable courage allowed me to do it here. *Who was I becoming?*

Harrison rested the shovel against the wall and collapsed on the wooden bench. "It was only a matter of time before anyone found out."

I sat down next to him. "Found out about what, exactly?"

"I'm afraid it's not my secret to tell."

"Oh?" Quinn said. "And whose secret is it?"

"It's Victoria's."

"What does she have to do with this?"

"If you don't mind, I would rather keep this between us. I don't think the rest of the guests need to know."

"Well, that depends," I said. "Are we going to find anything in those boxes that belong to them?"

Harrison lowered his head. "I can't be sure you won't," he said.

I placed my hand on his furry mitten. "How about we start from the beginning."

The secret he'd been holding on to must have been a doozy; why else would he go through so much trouble to hide all those boxes? But for the life of me I couldn't understand why.

Harrison was jittery. His feet bounced up and down while he pulled his bunny hand from under mine and placed it under his armpits. Although it felt like we were sitting in an icebox, a familiar dew had presented on his forehead.

"You okay, Harrison?" I was concerned he might pass out.

"Oh, yes," he said, "but maybe we should go inside and fetch Victoria. Like I said, it's not my secret to tell."

Quinn opened the door. "I'm with you, Harrison. I would love nothing more than to sit and chat while my toes thaw by the fire."

39

Has anyone seen Henry?

WHEN WE RETURNED from the shed, I sensed a swell of restlessness bubbling through the lodge; something significant had happened. I could hardly hear myself think over the clamor of voices arising from the den.

"Settle down!" Harrison yelled, trying to compete with the pandemonium. "What's going on in here?"

"I think you have some explaining to do, Harrison," said Elenor.

"I'm sure I don't know what you're talking about?"

"Really?" said Madeline, placing her hands firmly on her hips. "Why haven't you told us about those secret doors?"

"Well, frankly," Harrison said, "there was no reason to tell you about them, and I'm appalled that you all felt the need to go snooping around when it's none of your business."

"Actually," said Jason, "it became our business once we found the butler in the library. Dead."

"The door in the library leads to the basement," said Sam. "Which suggests someone could have killed Caffrey, headed down to the basement, and proceeded through another door, making it look like they were never in the library in the first place."

"And the fact that you kept that from us," said Madeline, "means that one of four people killed the butler: you, Victoria, Rebecca, or Sébastien."

"Now, you wait a minute. I have been at this lodge for twenty-two years, and no one has *ever* accused me of such a horrible crime. And I can assure you our staff at Mystery Ridge Lodge could never and *would* never commit a murder." Harrison wiped the steady trickle from his brow.

"Harrison," I said, "I think now would be a good time to get the rest of the staff and meet back in the den."

"Fine," he said with a huff.

I reached out for Harrison's arm and squeezed it before he could run off. "And don't think we've forgotten about the shed. We still need to talk to you and Victoria about those crates."

"Of course...I'll go get her right away."

AS WE SAT quietly for the staff to join us in the den, I felt like I was attending a town hall meeting in Mahogany Falls; the demand for answers was intensifying. Who could blame them? I needed answers, too.

Anticipating what rousing tale Harrison and his staff would conjure up, I immediately realized someone was missing. "Where's Henry?"

We searched the room as if he could be hiding among the furniture.

"Come to think of it," said Sam, "I don't think I've seen him since last night."

"Did *anyone* see Henry this morning?" I asked.

As I listened to the guests plead ignorance of Henry's whereabouts, the staff paraded through the den as though being escorted to the defense table in a courtroom.

"Before we start this little…inquiry, has anyone seen Henry this morning?"

"He was not a breakfast?" asked Sébastien.

"As far as we can tell," said Jason, "no one has seen him since last night."

Truman cocked his head and stared intently at Jason. "And if I'm not mistaken, you were the last to see him."

"Me?"

"Well, you went out with Henry to turn off the generator, did you not?"

"Yes, but—"

"Then you were the last to see him," insisted Truman.

"What are you getting at?" Madeline sprang up and loomed over Truman.

"Sit down, Mads," said Jason. "You're not as intimidating as you think you are. Besides, I wasn't the last person to see Henry last night. Harrison was."

"I don't appreciate your tone, Mr. Parrish. And Henry was alive and well the last time I saw him."

"Says you!" Gretchen snipped.

"Before we start pointing fingers again, how about we check his room? For all we know, he decided to sleep in." Of course, I didn't believe that for one minute, but someone had to be the voice of reason.

Harrison stood to his feet. "Victoria, you come with me. We'll check his room. Scarlet, why don't you and Quinn check the library? Truman and Gretchen can check the dining room and kitchen." He pointed a finger at Jason. "If you don't mind, you and Sebastien can search outside beside the generator. The rest of you stay here in case he decides to show up. He couldn't have toddled off very far."

40

This looks familiar

I KNEW HENRY wouldn't be in the library. But we still did a good sweep of the room just the same. "He's not here." I walked to the hidden door and popped it open. "But he could be down there."

"Seriously, Scarlet? Why would you want to go back down to that creepy basement? If he was down there, I'm sure someone would have said something when they were searching the basement earlier. Henry's hard to miss."

"But now we can do a more thorough investigation, don't you think? We were interrupted last night and still don't know how Harrison, or whoever it was, vanished into thin air. At least now, we can turn on a light. What'd ya say?"

"You're making my head spin. You know that, right?" Quinn pushed me forward. "Okay, I'll go. But you're going first."

Scanning every square inch along the way, we cautiously approached the room. Even though there was enough light to see where we were going, it was still pretty gloomy. And there was still the fear of someone lurking behind a corner, ready to pounce.

I stood at the entrance of the room, hesitant, until my eyes settled on something dark. "Over here!"

Quinn swung around. "What is it?"

One of the concrete blocks, darker than the others, stood out like a sore thumb. I squatted down, moved my hand over the rough surface, and pushed. Like the door in the library, a hidden exit appeared. "Help me pull it open," I said, placing my fingers inside the crack.

We grunted and pulled, finally opening the door to a long, dark tunnel. "Well, this looks ominous."

"Wonder where it leads?"

"Only one way to find out." I steadied my nerves and aimed the flashlight into the abyss. We crept through the darkness until we came upon another door.

"Why'd you stop?"

"Because I'm not exactly sure I want to find out what's behind here."

"But we've come so far," Quinn said blithely.

I turned the knob and pushed the heavy, steel door. As we paused and gazed at our surroundings, it seemed oddly familiar. "Isn't this—"

"The shed?"

"At least we know how they got here so fast."

"An underground tunnel? Didn't see that coming."

The door was conveniently camouflaged behind a stack of crates. That's why we hadn't noticed it when searching the boxes earlier. "So, a door in the kitchen that's off limits, a secret door in the library, and an underground tunnel that leads to the shed. I can understand why this place is called Mystery Ridge Lodge."

"So what? Did the staff use the tunnel to move these boxes into the shed without the guest's knowledge? Why? As far as I can tell, these have nothing to do with the murder."

"It would appear that way," I said. "But things don't make much sense here."

"One being...where's Henry?"

"Right! Henry! We better get back to the lodge."

EVERYONE EXCEPT FOR Harrison and Victoria had returned to the den.

"Nothing?"

"*We* had no luck," said Madeline.

"Where's Harrison?" asked Quinn.

"They're still upstairs," said Jason.

I began heading for the stairs. "I'll go check."

"I'll come with you," Quinn said, running alongside me.

We noticed Harrison standing outside Henry's room when we reached the top of the stairs. Something was wrong.

"Harrison! What's happened?"

There was a look in Harrison's eyes. A combination of confusion and dread. He took a few steps back, pointing in front of him. "See for yourselves."

Victoria had her back against the wall, her face as white as a ghost. Henry was kneeling at the side of the bed, grasping his neck, while the other hand rested on the side table like he'd been reaching for something.

"Is this how you found him?" I asked.

Harrison strolled into the room next to Victoria. "Yes. And we didn't touch anything." He held onto Victoria's hand.

"No," Victoria agreed, "we didn't touch anything."

Quinn moved closer. "Odd that he's still wearing his coat and boots."

"That's what I thought," said Harrison.

"You were the last person to see him last night, right?"

"Well, yes. I watched him go down the hall to his room before I headed to mine."

"And nothing seemed out of the ordinary?" asked Quinn.

"Nothing."

A quick scan of the body hadn't revealed any visible wounds, but that didn't mean there were none.

"What are you looking for?"

"I'm not entirely sure," I said.

"It could be a heart attack," said Victoria. "He was a fairly large man, after all."

"That could be the reason," I said, "but I don't think Henry died of natural causes."

"What makes you say that?" Harrison queried.

I took one step closer to the body and leaned in. "Because I do believe he's been poisoned."

41

Poison anyone?

SINCE MY VOCATION granted me a unique insight into murder (strictly from prolonged research), I entertained a few educated guesses. And my conclusion was that Henry was most *definitely* poisoned.

Now, we had two bodies in need of a medical examiner: a handsome butler bludgeoned to death in the library and a shaggy stranger who succumbed to a mysterious poison in the bedroom. But what did one have to do with the other? I was stumped.

"How could you possibly know he was murdered?" said Harrison. "And at the hand of poison, nonetheless?"

I pointed to Henry's hand. "Notice his fingernails?"

Victoria took a timid step forward. "They're blue."

"And so are his lips," I said, moving my finger to his face. "From what I *do* know about poison, it's possible that some sort of toxin caused it. Something he ate or drank, perhaps?"

"This wasn't an accident?" Victoria shuddered.

I shook my head. "No. I believe he was murdered."

"We should tell the others," said Quinn. "I'm sure they're curious as to what's happened."

"I agree," said Harrison. "We need to get to the bottom of these bloody murders." He made a point of kicking the bed before dramatically storming out of the room.

Victoria ran after him. "I'll go see if he's alright."

"I'm not surprised Harrison is so upset," I said. "Finding not one, but two bodies over the last couple of days, I can't imagine what he's going through."

"Anyone would be," said Quinn. "But it could all be an act."

Before I pulled the blanket over Henry, I noted the almost peaceful look on his face. Unlike Caffrey's troubling posture (which implied a state of shock), Henry appeared to be too tired to remove his clothes and collapsed before he could get into bed.

"Harrison *did* have time to perfect his performance," I said, continuing our conversation.

"Twenty-two years, to be exact," said Quinn. "That's a lot of time pretending to be someone you're not."

"But why Caffrey? As far as we know, they got along."

"Right, as far as we know. And what about Henry? Before yesterday, nobody even knew who he was—as far as we know."

"It's quite the puzzle," I said, reaching for the phone on the nightstand.

"Anything?"

"Nothing." I hung up the phone and noticed the contents on the bedside table: a cell phone, a mug, his room key tied with an orange ribbon, and another set of keys, most likely for his home and truck. "He had enough time to empty his pockets before the poison took effect." I picked up the mug and sniffed. "Hmm."

"What is it?"

"Smells like nutmeg."

"Really? What's with everyone putting nutmeg in their beverages? Do you think that's what killed him?"

"It's possible," I said, examining the residue around the lip of the mug. "But you would need a considerable dose to kill a man Henry's size. And I'm pretty sure nutmeg wouldn't make your lips turn blue."

"What could have killed him?"

"I don't know, but let's keep the nutmeg to ourselves."

WE RETURNED TO the den before Harrison could deliver the bad news. More than likely, he was stalling.

"What's going on?" asked Gretchen. "Harrison won't tell us anything."

The den had become the meeting place for revealing unsettling news. Everyone slumped in their seats, eagerly waiting for details on Henry.

Meanwhile, Harrison vented his frustration by throwing logs on the fire. I noticed there were only two logs left in the box. At some point, someone would have to replenish the wood from an additional stockpile somewhere. *Right?* Dealing with urgent matters without the welcoming warmth of a fire would be more unpleasant than usual.

Harrison kept his back to the group. "We found him," he said without elaborating.

"What Harrison means to say is...is...I mean—I'm afraid he's dead."

"What?" Madeline shouted. "Dead? Where did you find him?"

"He was in his bedroom," said Quinn.

Rebecca was standing at the back of the room with her arms crossed, her demeanor as consistent as when she learned of Caffery's death. She quietly spoke. "Was it some sort of heart attack or something?"

"It wasn't," I said, shaking my head. "In fact, there's strong evidence to suggest he, too, was murdered."

"Murdered!" Elenor said with her hands over her cheeks. "But how do you know?"

I considered that sharing suspicions of poison might not be the way to go, but I wondered if it would help prompt a reaction from the killer. I decided to go with my gut.

"He was poisoned," I said matter-of-factly. I waited for the guilt-ridden to give themselves away. Swiftly, I scanned the eyes of everyone in the room, thinking that the killer would reveal themselves at any moment. However, the outcome was not at all what I expected.

"Not surprising," said Sébastien.

"I agree," said Truman. "It would be easy to slip something into a drink unnoticed."

"Yes," said Sam. "There's enough coffee drinkers here."

"I would be drawn to poison," said Elenor. "But only if I was planning on murdering someone."

"There's a lot of ways to do it," said Gretchen.

"I read that the Canadian Toad is quite toxic if ingested," said Elenor. "Although, who would want to eat such a thing."

"Ah oui, les cuisses de grenouille sont délicieuses."

Gretchen translated. "He said, "Frog legs are delicious.""

"But probably not Canadian Toads, though."

"No, dear, probably not," said Sam.

"There are poinsettias all around here," said Madeline. "What if someone put some leaves in his food...and that's what killed him."

Harrison shook his head. "No. Poinsettias can't kill you. You can get sick if you overeat anything, I suppose, but they can't kill you."

"I know Oleander plants are quite poisonous," said Elenor.

"Yes," said Harrison. "Quite."

What was happening? All of a sudden, I was in a room full of toxicologists.

"Have you people lost your mind?" shouted Rebecca. "We've just found out there's been another murder, and all you can do is sit there, playing name that poison?" She buried her head in her hands and began to cry. Her outburst was unexpected and immediately stunned the crowd into an awkward silence.

Harrison gently tapped his hand on her shoulder. "It's going to be alright, my dear."

"How do you know Henry was poisoned, Scarlet?" asked Jason.

"Well...I'm no expert, by any means, but I have researched the subject for a—a short story." *Now was not the time to divulge the secrets of my alter ego.*

"At first," I said, "I too thought he may have suffered a heart attack; however, I noticed a slight blue tinge to his lips, which could be a sign he was poisoned."

"Does that tell you the kind of poison they used?" Jason asked.

"No, it doesn't." I turned to Elenor, hoping she could validate my theory. "Elenor might be able to shed some light."

She giggled. "Oh, heavens! It's been years since I've been in a lab. And even then, I've only assisted with autopsies. But considering his lips *and* fingernails are blue, I guess poison is possible."

"Maybe the two murders aren't even related," Quinn said.

"Perhaps," I said. "But what if we missed something when we inspected Caffrey's body? Maybe we were distracted by the missing pool cue."

"We should go take another look," said Quinn.

Gretchen scoffed. "How many times do you have to *check the body?*" She held up her fingers in air quotes. "So much for steering clear of the crime scene; it's like a regular tourist attraction."

"Gretchen's right," said Truman. "Maybe we should wait until the police get here. More than likely, we've already contaminated the scene."

I nodded my head in agreement. "I know it's the last thing we should be doing, but we have no idea when the police will arrive. And I don't know about you, but I'm curious to see if Caffrey was also poisoned. If you'd like to join me, I'm going to see what I can find out."

AGAIN, I LEAD the procession to the library. It didn't matter how often we approached the body; it never got any easier. But at least now he was covered up. I was thankful for that. A tingling ran down my neck at the thought of removing the blanket. We had no idea what the body would look like after a day of lying by a fire, but I knew it wouldn't be pleasant.

I held my breath and slowly removed the blanket from Caffrey's face while the others hovered nearby, and just as I thought, my suspicions were...*wrong?*

If his facial features had any color remaining, it wasn't blue.

Sébastien took a step back after the unveiling of the body. "Was he poisoned?"

"I can't say for sure," I said, distancing myself from the deceased. "There may not have been the same amount of poison in Caffrey's system as there was with Henry's."

"And that's why the killer had to resort to hitting him with the pool cue?" Truman asked. "Because the poison was taking too long?"

"That's a great theory," said Sam. "But why not wait for the poison to work? Why risk it by introducing a murder weapon?"

"Maybe," said Madeline, "he had to hit him with the pool cue because Caffrey caught him with the poison."

"What makes you think it was a he?" asked Truman. "It could have easily been a woman."

"I don't know," she said, glancing at Harrison.

"You don't think *I* had anything to do with Caffrey's murder, do you, Madeline?" Harrison dramatically placed his fingertips over his heart.

"I didn't say I did."

"You implied it with your look."

"Did I? Well, I do find it curious that you discovered both bodies."

Harrison huffed. "A mere coincidence, Madeline. That doesn't mean I killed them. It would have taken some time for the poison to work. I didn't hand him a cup of tea and say, 'drink.'"

"Well, someone did," said Elenor.

"The only time I saw him eat anything was at dinner," said Rebecca.

Instinctively, all eyes darted toward Sébastien. *"Moi?"* He shook his head vigorously. "It was not me! I would never poison my food; that would be a travesty!"

"Anyone could have doused his food with some sort of poison," said Jason.

"Yes, but why?" I placed my hands on my hips and paced around the body. I needed to think. "Why would someone kill a man they had only just met? Unless..." Now, the wheels were turning.

Quinn finished the thought. "Unless he wasn't a stranger to everyone."

"Exactly," said Gretchen. "But that still doesn't give a motive. Just because you recognize someone doesn't mean you're going to kill them."

"No, but maybe he was a witness to something," I said. "Something he shouldn't have witnessed. In the wrong place at the wrong time, perhaps?"

"But why kill him here?" Truman asked. "Why not get rid of him before coming to the lodge?"

"This doesn't make any sense," said Elenor. "If I knew someone had done something wrong, I would have gone to the police."

Gretchen yelled from across the room. "Maybe he did." She plopped on the sofa, stretching her feet across the coffee table. "How would we even know? It's not like the man told us his life's story before he croaked."

"This is all a bunch of guesswork," said Jason, rolling his eyes. "Maybe the killer had it out for Henry. Fine. But that doesn't explain why Caffrey was killed."

"That's what we need to find out," I said. "I believe these two murders are connected. And sooner or later, we'll know what and *who* that connection is."

42

It was the maid in the bedroom with the sweater

EVERY YEAR ON my birthday, Dominic would convince himself that he had devised the perfect surprise. And every year, he would fail.

His plans were not faulty; on the contrary, some of them were downright brilliant. But no matter how much effort he put into his schemes, he couldn't catch me off guard. It wasn't *his* fault my senses were on high alert a month before my birthday. Every question was curious. Every phone call reeked of conspiracy. For the whole month of November, I'd envision myself as a savvy secret agent, lurking in the shadows of my own house, collecting valuable information until I uncovered what futile plan my husband concocted.

Since Dominic put so much hard work into these surprises, I had to at least pretend to be amazed. I didn't have the heart to tell him I'd known what he'd been planning the whole time. What fun would that be? And as it turns out, searching for clues and getting him to slip up one way or another made my birthday fun.

It was like these murders; there were clues everywhere.

I just had to find them.

I picked up the linen napkin from my lap and dabbed the corners of my mouth. It was another satisfying meal. *I could get used to this*, I thought, placing the napkin on top of my plate. *Croque Monsieur:* a toasted ham and cheese sandwich imbued with a milky béchamel sauce—or so said Sébastien.

As I downed the last of my water, the chef popped out of the kitchen with his usual flare. "All finished in here, Harrison. You can turn off the generator now. We won't need it on again until three-thirty."

"Thank you, Chef. I'll go turn it off right away."

"Need any help?" Jason offered.

"Thank you, but I can manage." Harrison smiled and left the dining room to carry out his task.

A few moments later, the room dimmed to a more natural glow, leaving the low winter sun the only light for the next few hours.

"I think I'll start my car again," said Gretchen. "The minute those roads get cleared, I'm outta here."

"None of us can leave Gretchen," I said. "I'm sure you haven't forgotten you're a suspect in a murder investigation?"

"I didn't forget." She mumbled while strutting out of the room.

Victoria sat at the other end of the table, trying not to make eye contact with me. It was evident Harrison filled her in on what we discovered in the shed, so I figured now would be an excellent time to question her about the crates.

I nudged Quinn and nodded toward Victoria. "Shall we have a chat with Miss Hale?"

"Let's do this," she said, pounding her fist into her hand like a gangster ready to break some kneecaps. "I'm anxious to hear her explain how my sweater got in the shed."

"Settle down, Capone."

Victoria's eyes bounced from the table to the chandelier above the bar. An invasion was imminent, and she was probably looking for a quick escape.

"Mind if we sit?" Quinn said, trying out her most intimidating voice.

"Sure," said Victoria.

We cozied up on either side of her, preventing her from a quick getaway. I sensed she was intimidated when her voice began to crack. "I know what you're going to ask," she said.

"And what is that, exactly?" asked Quinn.

"You want to know where all that stuff came from."

"More importantly, how did my sweater go from being folded neatly in my suitcase to being stuffed in a plastic crate in the freezing cold shed?"

"Maybe we should take this conversation someplace a little more private." Harrison and Sébastien crept up behind us like a couple of bodyguards.

"After you," I said, following them into the den.

FOR NOW, THE DEN was empty and, again, the muster station for another crisis. While Harrison, Sébastien, and Victoria settled in, I wondered why Rebecca wasn't invited to this little powwow. Had she been kept in the dark about Victoria?

"Go ahead," said Sébastien. He reassured Victoria with a nod and a smile and hovered over her like an umbrella.

"I'm sorry for taking your sweater. I—I didn't mean to..." Her jaw clenched, and she squeezed her hands together so hard they began to turn white.

"What do you mean, you didn't mean to?" I asked.

Harrison jumped in. "She means she couldn't help it." He turned to Victoria and smiled. "She's been diagnosed with kleptomania."

I rested my chin on my fist, realizing my mouth had fallen open. I wasn't expecting a confession like that. "So, all that stuff in the shed...."

Victoria nodded. "Yes, I took it."

"There must be years worth of stuff in there," said Quinn. "Has no one ever wondered where their missing belongings ended up? I'm sure someone had to complain."

"There have been many complaints," said Harrison. "But, we try to convince them they must not have packed the item."

"Seriously...they actually fall for that? I'm sorry," said Quinn, "but if I'm missing a pair of tangerine pants, there's no way you can convince me that I didn't pack them."

Harrison pushed himself off the sofa and ambled across the room. He grabbed the poker from its cast iron stand and raked through the embers, causing them to glow. "Usually, they give up trying to convince us they brought the item. However, we did have one complaint concerning a cashmere scarf. It was a designer scarf worth more than four thousand dollars."

"Four thousand dollars! What happened?" I couldn't possibly imagine spending that much money on a scarf. I didn't even pay that much for my Italian leather sofa.

"They filed a claim but couldn't prove the maid stole the items while cleaning their room. In fact," said Harrison, "if I understand correctly, they discovered their missing item after they had left the lodge, so they could never accuse the maid of stealing."

"So they just left it at that?" I asked.

"What else could they do? At check-in, I ask each guest if they would like to keep any valuables in the safe—"

Quinn scoffed. "You mean the one behind the check-in desk?"

"Yes! And since almost everyone declines, saying they have nothing valuable, they can't say we didn't provide sufficient security. And because there's no proof the items were ever here, they have no choice but to leave." Harrison sat down on the hearth and stretched out his legs. The longer he sat by the fire, the redder his face became.

"Just so you know," said Victoria, her hands firmly clasped in her lap, "I don't take these things because I want them. It's an unbearable itch to soothe until I take something."

"Are you aware of what you're doing?" I asked.

"Most of the time, yes. Once in a while, I take something without realizing it until I empty my pockets at the end of the day. Even then, I have no idea where it came from."

"Did Caffrey and Rebecca know about your certain... proclivities?"

I had never met a kleptomaniac before and knew nothing about the disorder. Did they feel guilty? Did they steal something every day? It probably wasn't a good idea to ask personal questions at this point—just the pertinent ones.

"I assume so," said Victoria, glancing at Sébastien. "I'm sure they've seen us going down to the basement. I figured Sébastien had filled them in."

"You didn't confide in Rebecca?"

"No. With the guilt I feel from the disorder, the fewer people who know, the better. Besides, Rebecca and I never clicked. It's not that I have anything against her. It's just...she keeps to herself."

"Did she and Caffrey know about the secret doors?"

"Yes," said Harrison.

"So, only the four of you knew about the tunnel?" Quinn asked.

Guilt splayed across Victoria's face like she was about to drop another bombshell. "Well, there *was* someone...."

"Who?" Harrison seemed shocked that someone else had uncovered their secret.

"Truman saw me. I don't know for sure, but the way he looked at me, I think he caught me closing the door in the library."

"When did this happen?" I asked.

"Yesterday, before strudel and coffee."

"Why was he in the library?"

"I don't know. But he left right after he spotted me. And oddly enough, he never confronted me either."

"Hmm," said Quinn. "Why *didn't* he call you out after we discovered the body?"

"Maybe Truman was scoping out the library for the perfect place to attack Caffrey." *Again, with my educated guess.*

"Might be why he's been acting so weird, too," said Quinn.

"I know what you mean," said Sébastien. "He asked me a strange question."

"Is that so?"

"*Oui.* When everybody went upstairs, he pulled me aside."

"What did he want?"

"He asked if I got along with Caffrey and if I would mind him being in charge."

"Weird question. What did you say?" asked Quinn.

"I had no clue what to say. The fact is, I *didn't* like Caffrey. He was rude and obnoxious, obsessed with everything I did. On more than one occasion, he insisted on lecturing me about my food. No one tells me how to prepare my food!"

"Well," I said, shocked at his impetuous reply, "I could see how that would upset you. Have you always felt that way about Caffrey?"

"*Non*. Only the last few months. Something was different about him."

"Did you notice a change in Caffrey, Harrison?"

"Not really. He seemed fine to me."

"Strange," said Quinn. "I wonder what his beef was with Sébastien?"

"Also," I said, "why would Truman ask you about Caffrey being in charge?"

"I don't know," said Sébastien

"That *is* peculiar," said Harrison, uttering a subtle grunt when he stood. He clasped his hands behind his back and casually changed the subject. "Can I trust you two to keep this little indiscretion quiet? I don't think informing the other guests is necessary, do you?"

"I don't know, Harrison. I feel uncomfortable keeping the others in the dark regarding Victoria's secrets."

Quinn chuckled. "Good one, Scarlet."

I smiled at my unintended pun.

"Keeping the others in the dark about what?"

At that moment, Gretchen appeared in the den, oozing cold-blooded curiosity.

43

Confession is good for the soul

GRETCHEN YANKED THE white slouchy beanie from her head, allowing a few wayward strands to linger like feathers from a Silkie chicken. After several unsuccessful attempts to tame the persistent static, she draped her coat over the side of the sofa. With one hip emphatically dipped to the side like a bendy straw and her eyebrows pitched as far as they would go, she folded her arms across her chest and said, "Well?"

Gretchen was the last person on earth to whom I wanted to divulge any secrets. Our most recent encounters uncovered a less-than-harmonious rapport, and now I was faced with a question I couldn't possibly answer. Hoping for an empathy rescue, I turned to Harrison, who was already shaking his head and mouthing the word 'no.'

A lot of help he was.

"It's a private matter," I said with conviction.

She scoffed. "Oh? A private matter among the five of you?"

"Yes," said Victoria.

"You look upset, Victoria. Is everything alright?"

"It doesn't concern you, Gretchen," said Harrison.

"Fine!" She abruptly snatched up her things, her fingernails scraping the leather like a cat's claws. "Well, a girl knows when she's not wanted. I'm sure whatever you're hiding will come to light soon enough." She flung her hair off her neck and turned on her heels.

Gretchen sailed out of the den while Victoria scowled, squinting and puckering her lips. "An interesting woman, that one."

"What do you mean by interesting?" asked Quinn. She's not easy to like, but it's probably because of the breakup."

"Right," said Harrison. "I heard something about that. If I'm not mistaken, she separated from her husband."

"Maybe she needed some time to herself," I suggested.

"How much time does she need?" said Victoria.

"What do you mean?"

"Well, for starters, she packed quite an extensive wardrobe. Creams, lotions, perfume, there's enough in there to anoint a boatload of supermodels."

"She comes across as a little high maintenance," said Quinn. "Changing outfits two or three times a day *is* a bit much."

"I noticed that, too," Victoria said. "And the way she makes an entrance when she strolls in for dinner."

"So," said Quinn, "you rummaged through Gretchen's room, and we *know* you were in our room. What about the other guests? Did you "check" their rooms as well?"

"Uh—yes, sort of—but just to be sure everything was in order. Gretchen's room was the last, but when I heard someone running up the stairs, I thought I was toast. I didn't know what to do. Luckily, no one came in, and I hurried out of there as fast as I could." Victoria stood to her feet, inching her way out of the den, indicating she was done answering our questions. "I've told you what I know."

"Wait!" said Quinn. "We should probably have a look inside your room."

"What for?"

"To make sure you didn't take anything from the other guests. Like the murder weapon, perhaps?"

"Seriously? I'm pretty sure the sweater is the only thing."

"Pretty sure?"

"Do you think that's necessary?" asked Harrison. By this point, his arm was firmly around Victoria's shoulders.

"Well, we *could* fill everyone in on our conversation," I said. "But somehow, I don't think that's what you want right now."

Victoria stopped and appeared to conduct the scenario in her head. What would an already tense crowd do if they found out she'd searched their rooms without their knowledge. It wouldn't be a far leap to accuse her of murder.

"I'm not saying I won't keep your secret. I will. For now. But you realize, at some point, you'll have to come clean, right?"

"I know," she said, head bowed.

"Look at it this way," said Harrison. "We were going to search everyone's room at some point anyway; you can be the first."

I wondered what her silence implied. Was she guilty of taking other items? Or was she worked up over something far more sinister?

"When you put it that way…what choice do I have?"

WHEN THE WHITE DOOR opened, I expected to see a modest, nondescript dwelling with subtle hints of Victoria's pure, understated life; however, it was anything but understated. I was amazed by the blatant, saturated spectacle that could have easily been ripped from the pages of a modern design magazine. Everywhere you looked, there was color. Lime green and bright orange throw cushions. A yellow wingback chair as bright as the sun. Vibrant oil paintings on every wall.

I stumbled into a type of clandestine paradox. Multi-colored studio meets monochromatic maid.

"Looks like you put a lot of effort into this space," I said, pondering one of the paintings.

"I love a good color pallet," said Victoria, disappearing into her bedroom. "For my wardrobe, on the other hand, I tend to stick to more neutral tones."

I followed her into the bedroom, observing much of the same: color, color, and more color. I guess you never know what goes on behind closed doors.

"I'm not sure what you expect to find," said Victoria. "If I *did* manage to take something from the other rooms, it's probably in the shed. And it's not like I would put any of it on display."

"But there is still the matter of the missing pool cue," I said.

"You don't think I'd be stupid enough to keep that in my room, do you? I got rid of the stolen goods, so what makes you think I'd stash the murder weapon here?"

"So what you're saying," said Quinn, "is that we need to do a better sweep of the shed."

"That's not what I'm saying." Victoria left the bedroom to perch herself on one of the red leather stools adjacent to the countertop. "Do what you need to do; there's no murder weapon here."

I briefly scanned the bedroom for anything resembling a pool cue. But after a quick rummage through the closet, I was satisfied that Victoria was telling the truth. Though there probably wasn't a thief alive that would proudly display their stolen swag in plain view, there was still a chance she stashed the murder weapon somewhere in the lodge no one would think to look. No one was in the clear.

I followed Harrison out of the bedroom and wondered how well he knew Victoria. "When did you know that Victoria had...?"

"Kleptomania?"

"Right. Kleptomania."

"We only just learned about it a couple of winters ago."

"We?" Quinn queried.

"Yes," said Harrison, "me and Sébastien." He smiled at the chef, and since all the stools at the bar had been taken, he propped himself against the wall. "I guess you could say Victoria had become quite the collector."

"What Harrison means to say is, yes, I took many things that didn't belong to me, and because of that, I kept my disorder to myself. But when these guys"—she tapped Sébastien on the arm—"found out, I thought for sure I'd be kicked out of here. I didn't want anyone else to find out; it would have made them uncomfortable. And since I already intruded on their privacy, I couldn't bear the thought of having them feel sorry for me, too."

Sébastien took her hand and kissed it. "I think everyone would have understood, Victoria."

"Not everyone is as understanding as you guys." She smiled.

"How *did* you guys find out?" I asked.

"One weekend," said Victoria, "I had come down with one of the worst chest colds ever. I spent three long days in my room. I couldn't even get out of bed. Sébastien brought meals to my room because taking the stairs to the kitchen was daunting. And that's when—"

"That's when I noticed the crates in her closet," Sebastien interrupted. "I was not snooping. *Non*! There were big containers on the floor. One of the covers had come loose. I was curious and looked inside."

The chef gave me a crooked smile. Most likely to remind me of the earlier incident concerning the secret door.

"He found a pair of purple mittens that he noticed one of the guests wearing when they arrived." Victoria smiled as if remembering the encounter. "He immediately woke me from a deep sleep to confront me."

"I was shocked," said Sébastien. "I found so many things."

"He convinced me to tell Harrison, which I did. They never judge me. Ever. But they were concerned that someone else might if they found out."

"That's when we decided to move the crates to the basement," continued Harrison. "We figured no one would ever go down there, and as far as the door in the kitchen, nobody ever questioned it." Again, he glared at me. "Until you, Scarlet."

I let out a tentative chuckle. "Sorry about that."

"I'm sure you were relieved they were so understanding," said Quinn, "but don't you think you should have tried to get help? I mean, technically, it *is* stealing."

"I *have* been seeing someone," Victoria said. "Actually, I've been doing quite well. I haven't taken anything in over two months."

"Until this weekend," I said.

"Yes, I admit I slipped. It's just that when I went into one of the rooms, which I assumed was Gretchen's, I had this overwhelming compulsion to take something. Especially after noticing that bright pink suitcase. As you can see," she said with her arm out to the side, "I have a weakness for colorful things."

"That you do," I said, glancing one more time around the room.

But did that weakness lead her to murder?

44

Why is the killer still here?

QUINN AND I ducked into our room to digest the latest revelation. I wouldn't necessarily consider myself a gossip, but Quinn had always been my go-to person when soliciting dependable feedback. It was time to bounce a few ideas off her to see where her head was at.

"Well, I wasn't expecting that," she said, falling backward onto her bed.

"I know! I'm as surprised as you. Kleptomania? Nope. Never saw that coming."

Quinn pulled herself off the bed and ran to the closet, pushing hangers across the bar, like she was rummaging a sales rack. "Maybe you should check your stuff, too. She could have taken something without you knowing it. I like Victoria. I do. But I wouldn't trust her as far as I could throw her."

After blithely combing through my luggage, I did a more comprehensive search of the bathroom, hoping nothing of importance (like my frizz-taming conditioner) had gone missing. "Everything seems to be where I left it," I yelled from the shower. "Is the sweater the only thing you're missing?"

"As far as I can tell."

I exited the bathroom and immediately zoomed in on the plumped-up pillows stacked halfway up the headboard. They were like luxurious clouds coercing me into a much-needed nap. I kicked off my shoes and climbed under the covers. Whether a nap was in my near future or not, it was nice to lie down. The bump on my head was still throbbing, and I was beginning to think Quinn was right.

Did I have a concussion?

As I welcomed the heaviness in my eyes, I drifted into a dream-like state, wondering if Dominic was thinking about me too. I hated the fact I couldn't reach him.

But instead of falling asleep, I had a thought that catapulted me out of bed like an army cadet at roll call. I felt guilty for scaring the living daylights out of Quinn, considering the book she was reading flew clear across the room.

"What?" she shouted.

"I have an idea."

"Can you warn me you're about to have a eureka moment before jumping out of bed like a maniac? I thought maybe a mouse scurried across your face."

"Sorry, didn't mean to startle you."

Pulling the elastic from my head and letting the curls spring freely from their prison, I quickly corralled it back with my fingers before placing it back in restraints. I'd often do this ritual when I had problems to sort out.

"We should go and get the keys to Henry's truck."

"You wanna do what now?"

"I need to call Dominic to let him know we're okay. I can't stop thinking about him. Maybe I can get the truck far enough up the mountain to get a signal on my phone."

Quinn strolled across the room to retrieve her book, staring at me like I had two heads. "There are two things wrong with that plan, Scarlet. First of all, have you ever driven a truck that big in your life? You wouldn't have a clue how to maneuver it over those snowy roads."

"That's insulting."

"You know it's true."

I begrudgingly conceded. "It's a little true." She had a way of getting straight to the point.

She smirked and raised her eyebrows. "And secondly, I'm pretty sure we're not allowed to leave the lodge. If spotted, it might look like we're trying to escape, and I'm sure the killer will follow suit if they think there's a chance to make a run for it."

"Usually, it's me that provides the voice of reason, isn't it?"

"Like I said, this new you? It's gonna take me a minute. Watching you run around here with so much spunk? Let's just say it's an adjustment."

"That's a nice way of putting it."

"I'm excited to see where this new attitude takes you when we get back to Mahogany Falls."

"We need to make it through the weekend first."

"True."

"It's strange, though, don't you think?"

"What?"

"Why *hasn't* the killer tried to leave?"

"I'm guessing it's because of the weather?"

"Right," I said, pacing the room. "But if poison was the weapon of choice, it was most likely premeditated. Don't you think the storm would have played into the preliminary outline of the crime? Why was there no get-away plan?"

"This is Alberta...no one is sure of the weather. Maybe when the killer concocted his plan, he envisioned clear skies."

"Maybe." I looked out into the parking lot through the frosted window. It was pretty. "But if *I* had killed someone, I'd either be looking for the first opportunity to escape, or I would be so guilt-ridden you'd be able to read it all over my face."

Quinn laughed. "That's only because you have a tell."

I rolled my eyes. "I know, my face gives me away, but whoever killed Caffrey and Henry knew exactly what they were doing. And they have no intentions of leaving. Just yet."

"That's a little unnerving."

"I agree. The killer feels confident. They think they're going to get away with it. And that's mistake number two."

"What was mistake number one?"

"Removing the murder weapon from the crime scene. We find that; we find the killer."

45

It'll be like moving a bookcase

I FOUND MYSELF gazing out the window again, trying to determine how a killer could mingle about so nonchalantly. Like they were schmoozing with fellow parishioners at a church picnic or something. At this point in my investigation, it could have been anyone. But who?

As I fantasized about bringing the evildoer to justice for several uninterrupted minutes, my quiet time came to a thunderous halt when Harrison barged through the front doors, his cane in one hand and an armload of firewood in the other. He shuffled into the den, dropping the wood into a rustic wrought iron rack.

Jason had just turned on the generator, and we were again basking in the glow of artificial light. From what I had calculated, we still had about twelve hours, give or take.

"It's too bad you have to keep the fire going in the library," said Truman, "I'm starting to get whiffs of something not so pleasant."

"We don't have much choice," said Harrison. "If we don't keep on top of it before you know, there'll be icicles forming on the tips of our noses. We only get so much heat from the generator, so keeping the fires going is necessary if we don't want to freeze to death."

"Which makes all the more reason to get Caffrey out of the library and to a colder climate," said Gretchen.

"Do *you* want to be the one to touch him after he's been in there for over a day?" Jason asked.

"Heavens, no!" she said, wrinkling her nose. "But someone should."

"At this point," I said, "it might be worse leaving him in the heat than dragging him into the cold."

"We should take a vote," Madeline said, raising her hand. "All in favor of moving Caffrey outside?"

Naturally, it was unanimous. It was amazing what one would do with a foul odor as an incentive. A flash-back of marinating in pickle juice came to mind.

"Well," said Quinn, "now that that's settled, who's going to do the deed?"

"It's going to take at least four people to get him outside," said Jason.

"I say we put names in a hat," offered Gretchen.

"Agreed. Yours included."

"I thought maybe the men would be the better option, seeing as they are much stronger than us."

"Nice try," said Truman. "You ladies can do anything us men can do…right?"

"Fine!" Gretchen snarled. "Let's get this over with."

We each reached into the chef's hat to determine our fate. Whoever retrieved a sad face had the unfortunate task of carrying the body out of the lodge. A happy face meant you could breathe easily.

I was the second last to reach in. Truman, Sam, and Victoria had already sealed their fate by retrieving a sad face from the hat, which meant one spot left. It was me or Jason.

I shoved my hand into the hat, praying the folded piece of paper I yanked out would exonerate me from participating in the abysmal task. Would I be spared?

No.

I unfolded the paper and saw a deformed circle with the unmistakable arch of a sad face Quinn had so expertly sketched with her ballpoint pen. I sighed.

"I can take your spot," said Jason.

"That's not necessary," I said. "Fair is fair."

THE FOUR OF us gazed down at the body with as much anticipation as jumping into a swamp full of crocodiles.

The smell was beyond revolting.

I would have gladly sat in pickle juice for an entire week rather than do what I was about to do. It wasn't quite the dramatic activity I expected when I started on this adventure; however, rolling with the punches was something I prided myself on, so the quicker we got it done, the better. "Ready?"

Truman removed his sweater and rolled up his sleeves. "Might I make a suggestion? Pulling him across the floor might be easier if we roll him up in one of those larger blankets. Especially if he's fully covered."

"Sounds like a good plan to me," said Sam.

Victoria took the fanciest blanket from the sofa. "Here, we can use this one. I think it's big enough."

I took one end and helped Victoria fan it onto the floor. Sam and Truman stuffed their hands in their sleeves before rolling the body to the center of the blanket. We gathered up both ends—Victoria and I took one side, Truman and Sam taking the other.

We paused.

"Well, here goes nothing," said Truman.

They pulled. We pushed.

The first few steps led me to believe this would be a walk in the park. However, once we reached the hallway, we shared that unsettling feeling that turning a body (in full rigor mortis) would be challenging.

"There's not much give to him, is there?" said Sam.

Ignoring Sam's comment, I estimated the hallway to be five feet long and the library's opening no more than three feet. Caffrey was six-foot-four, give or take an inch.

The rest of the bystanders stood outside the library as though watching a makeover show on HGTV, anticipating how we'd make him fit.

"I don't think you're going to get him through the door," said Elenor.

"Sure we can," said Sam. "All we need to do is lift him to change the angle. A piece of cake, like moving a bookcase."

Really? A bookcase?

"Truman and I will lift him from the arms. Scarlet and Victoria can guide his feet."

I was sure I had a nightmare like this once; it didn't end well. Something was bound to go wrong. It was only a matter of time.

My head was light, my stomach churned, and the noxious vapors repulsed me dearly. And I probably wasn't thinking straight.

I grabbed his thighs, believing that would help alleviate some of the weight, while Victoria hugged his feet. The men, still avoiding the necessary contact with the corpse's skin, secured their grasp around his arms—or so they thought.

I had a sinking feeling as I raked my fingers through the velvety faux mink blanket (with red satin underbelly). Was this particular blanket the best choice for moving a body?

I doubt it.

With great effort, we changed the angle from a hundred and eighty degrees to an impressive forty-five degrees. We were thrown off guard when the body unexpectedly transitioned from a bookcase to a six-foot-four salamander, slipping from our grasp and sliding through the blanket onto the hardwood floor. The sound he made when hitting the floor is what you might imagine.

Thud!

However, the *tink, tink, tink* that followed was a bit of a mystery.

As I looked down to see from what direction the sound was coming, I noticed something familiar rolling across the floor.

"Oh, my!" Elenor gasped.

By this point, everyone had made their way back into the library. And although our mission failed miserably, there was no doubt it was entertaining.

"What is it?" asked Jason.

"It's a spice bottle," I said as we watched it roll past us, stopping in front of the pool table. "Nutmeg, to be exact."

"Where did it come from?" Madeline said, still holding her nose.

"I think it fell out of his pocket," said Truman.

"Why would he have a bottle of nutmeg in his pocket? Gretchen asked.

Of course, I immediately knew someone planted the bottle in Caffrey's pocket, considering it had gone missing from underneath the pool table. But what was with the dramatic reappearance? It was time to shake things up a little.

"Because someone put it there," I said, hoping for a guilt-ridden reaction. However, the only thing that cracked was the sparks from the fire behind me. Not even a flinch.

Nothing.

Well, so *much for luring out a murderer.*

"How do you even know that?" said Truman.

"Because after you all left to change out of your costumes, Quinn and I noticed the vial underneath the pool table. It must have gotten left here during the struggle. We decided to leave it where it was until the police arrived. But when I returned to the library a few hours later, I noticed it had gone missing."

"Interesting," said Gretchen, "that you decided to return to the library alone. How do we know *you* didn't put the vial into Caffrey's pocket?"

"I guess you don't."

"So he *was* doused with nutmeg," said Elenor, bypassing the blatant accusation. "That must mean Henry was, too."

"So it would seem."

"I didn't think it was strange at the time," said Jason, "but I remember hearing Henry say he liked holiday spices. I don't recall any holiday spices at dinner."

"There wasn't any," said Gretchen. "Either the chef sprinkled cinnamon and cloves on his potatoes or—"

"They were *both* poisoned with nutmeg!"

"I'm not so sure about that, Madeline," I said.

"Why's that?" asked Sam.

I walked across the room, picked up the vial with a tissue, and placed it on the pool table. "Because I think the killer put the vial in Caffrey's pocket to make us believe he was poisoned with nutmeg."

Truman had separated from the rest of us, holding his sweater like a security blanket. "You don't think that's what killed him?"

"No. You would need a lot of nutmeg to kill someone Henry's size. And I don't think it would turn your lips and fingernails blue. Someone at the lodge is still playing the game of murder."

But they haven't won yet.

46

Sleep! Oh, how I've missed you!

WE STILL HAD a problem.

The body.

We had enough muscle to move him out of the library and into the cold. We just had to make it work. I decided to kick my female pride to the curb and let the big, strong men take over. Considering it would be a waste of resources not to take advantage of Jason's muscles, what else could I do? "We could probably use your help, Jason. That's if you don't mind."

"Thought you'd never ask," he said, rolling his sleeves.

"Wait!" I shouted. "Perhaps we should try a better gripping blanket or one that's not so slippery."

I considered my options and settled on a wool, two-toned plaid throw. It was a shame we had to use another beautiful blanket to wrap up a dead body, but at least this one promised more resistance.

Again, we unrolled the body from the old blanket and into the new, tightly securing him to the best of our abilities. Jason and Sam took the top half while Sébastien and Truman guided his lower half.

Without incident, they picked him up and efficiently guided him down the hall, into the laundry room, and out the door, where freedom awaited them.

As I watched them gently lay Caffrey's body on the cold, hard ground, I had a troubling thought.

Henry.

I could only imagine how much of a struggle it would be to try and maneuver *his* body down the stairs and out the door. I envisioned broken toes and a surrendered staircase.

Enough imagery for now, Scarlet.

I was determined to piece together the vial's significance. But to do that, I needed a top-up on pain meds.

"SCARLET!"

I rolled over and wiped the drool from my chin. Quinn was standing over me, boasting a delightful grin. In the wake of my groggy disposition, it was evident I had fallen asleep. I gazed at the wry smirk before me, my eyes striving to focus, and pulled myself off the pillow.

"You slept," she said.

"What time is it?"

"It's your favorite time of day." She opened her suitcase and passed me a mirror. "Dinner time! But first, maybe splash a little water on your face. Try and wake yourself up."

I cringed at my reflection; it seemed to be upset with me. Thanks to the wrinkles in my sheets, my face looked like a road map, creases going this way and that. My hair—which usually didn't contend well during nap time—appeared to have given up altogether. And the crust that formed in the corner of my eyes prevented them from opening to their full, almond-shaped glory. I was a mess.

"You're right. I probably should clean myself up before presenting myself to the public. I didn't plan to fall asleep. But my head was pounding so hard I thought if I just closed my eyes until the meds kicked in, I'd be as good as new. Guess I was more tired than I thought."

"Not surprised. You've been fighting sleep for a while now, but at least you gotta nap in. It might help you focus more on the case instead of how sleep-deprived you are."

"About that," I said, corralling my hair into a messy bun. "What are your thoughts on the nutmeg?"

"I was going to ask you the same question. The killer returns to the library and places the bottle in Caffrey's pocket to be discovered? Why do that? If the nutmeg is evidence, why not just remove it altogether?"

"I don't know. But whatever the reasoning, I don't think the nutmeg is the clue. I think it's the vial itself."

"But both Henry and Caffrey drank coffee containing the nutmeg."

"True, but my suspicion is the killer wanted us to think it was the nutmeg that killed them—or, in Caffrey's case, almost killed him. That way, anyone could have taken the vial from the kitchen and doused both coffees with a large amount."

"So if we've established the nutmeg wasn't the poison, what was it?"

"I don't know," I said, climbing out of bed. "We need to revisit the kitchen."

47

Perfecting the skills of espionage

I WASN'T SURE Sébastien would let me in his kitchen while he was creating. Still, I needed to get a read on the staff while stealing another glance at the empty bottle in the spice rack. I was confident that it didn't belong with the other spices; the question was, where did it come from?

I left Quinn in the den with the others while I scoped out the kitchen. I knew she'd pick up on anything suspicious without being detected; she had a way of blending in.

After inhaling so many delectable aromas, I felt compelled to plan a trip to Paris and dine on French cuisine. If I made it out alive, I'd have to plant that bug in Dominic's ear.

I wedged enough of my face through the crack in the door to see Sébastien merrily going about his business. He was a jolly chef; I'll give him that. Rebecca was at the other end of the island slicing a baguette, which I assumed had just been pulled from the oven. It smelled heavenly, like a bakery. I waited patiently for my moment, but before I could will the rest of my body through the door, Sébastien's whistling abruptly stopped.

"Ah, Scarlet. *Entrez!*"

With some apprehension, I pushed my way into the kitchen. I suspected the heat creeping from my neck to my cheeks had created a glorious shade of rouge. "I don't mean to bother you guys. I'm sure you're both very busy. But if you don't mind, I would like to look at your spice rack."

Rebecca finished slicing the bread and placed her knife on the counter. "Why?"

"I noticed something when I was here earlier and wanted another look."

"Be my guest," said Sébastien, waving his arm toward the spices.

I stepped up to the rack, took out the empty vial, and held it up for them to see. Evidence of moisture remained inside like it had been washed clean. "Any idea why this bottle is in here?"

Rebecca took the vial from my hand and looked at it intently. "Oh, this must have been the bottle I saw yesterday. It was on the counter when I came into the kitchen to start on lunch."

"Did it have anything in it?"

"Not that I remember. I was going to ask Sébastien what we needed to fill it with, but I got busy. I probably shoved it in the rack without thinking."

"You didn't need any nutmeg for breakfast this morning, Chef?"

"Nutmeg? *Non!* Only cinnamon."

"Hmm."

Sébastien picked up the bottle and rolled it back and forth between his fingers. As I observed him, I wondered if he'd noticed it was slightly different from the others. When he placed it back in the rack, I tried to read him, but the lack of expression on his face didn't reveal anything significant. I wasn't expecting a sudden onslaught of torment or shame, but a little something would have been nice. What I *did* conclude, however, was that he was either very good at hiding illicit crimes or he was innocent. Either way, I couldn't tell by looking at him.

"Do you think this bottle has something to do with the one found in the library?" he asked.

"I'm not sure," I said, making my way out of the kitchen. "But it does seem odd having two identical vials…doesn't it?"

THE CONVERSATION OVER dinner had been enlightening. The fact that I could simultaneously have a discussion with one person while listening intently to another was something I valued as a skill.

While Elenor chatted about her time working as a forensic technician (with great detail), I observed the tension growing between Madeline and Jason. After a few minutes of pouting, Madeline engaged in a conversation with Truman. And what I overhead was curious.

"So, Truman," said Madeline, "what do you do?"

"Why do you ask?"

"No reason…just making conversation. Why, is it some big secret or something?"

Truman sighed. "No."

"Then tell me. What do you do?"

Truman looked to his left and right as if someone could be listening, which was funny because I *was* listening.

"Contracts," he said under his breath.

"That's kinda cryptic. What kind of contracts? Security? Sales? Government? Spill it, Truman."

"It's none of your business, Madeline."

"I get it. You're on a secret mission, aren't you?"

"What are you talking about?"

"I can keep a secret, you know."

Truman stared down at his soup without saying a word.

"You don't have to tell me why you're here...I think I know."

"You don't know anything," he said in a low, angry growl.

"It's fine," said Madeline, who seemed unfazed.

I took a big spoonful of *bœuf bourguignon* and nodded in agreement while Elenor continued to speak. I was trying to be inconspicuous. Until now, my eavesdropping skills had been disastrous, but I hoped this time would be different.

Madeline scraped her spoon down the inside of her bowl, making sure to get every last drop. "Actually," she said, "I have a secret, too."

"And what's that, exactly?"

"I saw Mr. Whitmore, you know."

I nearly choked on my stew.

"Really? Where?" Truman zeroed in on her like a lion about to pounce.

After Madeline wiped her mouth with her napkin, she took a tube of lipgloss from her pocket and applied several coats. "He came to the house to see Jason," she said, resuming another glide across her lips. "He's been working for him for the past few days, but like Harrison, he hadn't met him face-to-face either...just wrote emails back and forth. Weird, eh?"

"Why did he come to your house?"

"I'm not sure...didn't hear their conversation. But he handed him a big yellow envelope. I haven't got a clue what was inside, though."

"How do you know it was even Mr. Whitmore?"

"Well, I'm not totally sure it was him, but he was old...like really old...sixty? Maybe sixty-five? He had white hair and was dressed in a business suit. By the time I got downstairs, he was gone, and when I looked out the window, a black limousine was pulling out of the driveway."

"What did Jason say?"

"When I asked who was at the door, he told me he was some telemarketer trying to sell us a new internet provider. But I obviously knew he was lying. What telemarketer comes to the door in a limousine? Right?"

"Why did you guys even come this weekend anyway?"

"Because Jason was supposed to meet Mr. Whitmore here."

"And did he?"

"No. For all we know, he's stuck in a snow drift somewhere and can't get to the lodge."

"Huh," said Truman, stroking his chin.

"You seem quite interested in Mr. Whitmore," said Madeline. "Is that who your contract is with?"

Truman wiped his mouth, sipped some water, and left the dining room without answering Madeline's question.

I stared at my stew, hoping I successfully infiltrated the secret conversation without detection. The fact that Truman might also have a connection to Mr. Whitmore made my head spin. Was it more than a coincidence that they were all here this weekend? I was beginning to think it wasn't.

AFTER DINNER, I DECIDED to get some fresh air, and a walk in the icy air was bound to give me some clarity. I abandoned the shoveled pathway and trudged my way up the hill. My phone still had no bars, and I wondered how far I'd go before getting reception. *At least the flashlight still works,* I thought, thankfully.

After popping another two Advil, I labored through the fresh, white snow, observing scattered animal tracks—most likely elk or deer—leading the way to the road. I was relieved they weren't made by something more ferocious.

The view was stunning, and besides an owl hooting off in the distance, it was serenely quiet. So quiet that it gave me time to think about the suspects:

Sébastien was spotted entering through the mystery door after stating he had only left the kitchen for a smoke break. And, when I showed him the empty vial in the kitchen, he didn't seem to notice that it was different from the others, or at least he didn't let on that it was different.

Harrison had found both bodies and was keeping secrets about the lodge from the rest of the staff.

Victoria was scared to death her secret would be exposed.

Sam was in the library at the time of the murder, while Elenor was found in the kitchen holding the empty vial of nutmeg.

Jason and Madeline had secrets of their own (no wonder their marriage was in trouble).

And Gretchen—whose major downfall was being hated by everyone at the lodge—seemed not to want anyone snooping around her room.

Rebecca might have discovered Victoria's affair with Caffrey, and Truman implied that he also may have had mysterious dealings with Mr. Whitmore.

But none of them (except for maybe Rebecca) had a motive to kill Caffrey. And to make matters even more complicated, I couldn't come up with a plausible explanation for why anyone would want Henry dead. As far as I knew, no one even knew who he was.

I was getting so lost in my thoughts I didn't realize I'd been swallowed up by total darkness. The forest was no place to find yourself alone—especially at night. Since my phone wasn't giving me a decent signal, I figured I'd better start back before I couldn't find my way out.

When I finally reached the parking lot, I spotted Quinn standing on the steps, arms folded and shivering like a leaf. She must have noticed me because she began waving her arms over her head like an aerobics instructor.

"What are you doing out here with no coat on," I yelled. "You're going to freeze!"

"I'm waiting for you," she yelled back.

I lumbered up the stairs and pushed her back toward the lobby. "I'm sure you could have waited for me inside."

"I couldn't wait to tell you."

"Tell me what?"

"You'll never guess what just turned up?"

"What?"

"The murder weapon."

48

It was the chef in the library with the pool cue!

I KICKED OFF my boots and dropped my coat on the floor, anxious to hear what had transpired while I was out for a walk. The den was already filled with the usual suspects, now staring at the pool cue strategically placed in the fire.

"Who noticed it?" I asked.

"I did," said Truman.

The red stripe on the shaft caught my eye, glistening between the flames like a beacon. It was murder weapon, alright, but who put it there?

"Who was the last one to stoke the fire?"

"Me, of course," said Harrison. "I *have* been the only one to do so for the past few days. But I can assure you, it was not there when I last tended to the fire."

"So," said Madeline, "the killer just happened to put that long, shiny stick in the fire without anyone noticing? How is that even possible?"

"When did you last check the fire?" I asked.

"Just after dinner. And if I'm not mistaken, I believe Sam can vouch for me," Harrison said with pleading eyes.

"I think I can," said Sam. "He was doing something with the fire when I came in to retrieve my glasses from the coffee table. I realized I must have left them here. I took them off to rest my eyes before dinner."

"Can you even see without your glasses?" Truman asked.

"Don't get me wrong, I'm definitely required to wear them if I'm behind the wheel of a car, but I can fumble my way across the room without them."

"But if you weren't wearing your glasses," said Gretchen, "how could you even see that the pool cue wasn't in the fire?" Gretchen asked.

"I can't be sure either way whether it was there or not."

Harrison seemed to deflate. "Well, I certainly can. I have never played pool in my life; therefore, I would have no reason to touch that stick, much less put it into the fire."

"Unless you killed Caffrey," said Madeline.

"Which I most certainly did not!"

"So you say."

"Okay," said Jason, "if not Harrison...then who?"

The room went silent enough to hear an audible sigh. It was Elenor.

"What is it, dear?" Sam urged.

"Oh, heavens! I don't want to get anyone in trouble."

"The fact is," said Quinn, "someone's already in trouble. If you know something, you need to tell us."

Elenor dropped her head. "I think I may know who put it in there."

"Who was it?" said everyone in unison.

"It was Sébastien. I can't say it was the pool stick, but I saw him put something in the fire."

Sébastien wasn't in the den to defend himself, and I could see why he didn't like hanging out there. Could he have killed Caffrey? He had the opportunity.

"We need to go find him!" demanded Madeline.

"I knew it was him," said Gretchen. "I could see the hate in his eyes when Caffrey confronted him about the soup."

"It's one thing to be caught red-handed," I said, "but Elenor isn't even sure what he put in the fire. You can't honestly think that questioning him about his menu choice would be reason enough to kill him, do you?"

Gretchen shrugged. "I've heard of flimsier motives."

"Yes," agreed Sam, "but we can't go around accusing him of murder before we confront him."

"We should wait for the police to get here before we talk to him," said Truman. "There's knives in there…probably already figured out that we're on to him."

"I say we go in there fast and furious," said Jason. "He won't see us coming."

"Hold on a minute," I said. "If he really is the killer, we don't need him feeling threatened. Maybe if one or two of us approached him in a nice calm manner."

Jason laughed. "What do you suggest we do? Talk to him over a nice cup of tea? He killed two people; he's dangerous!"

"Let me go talk to him," said Victoria. "I know him, and I can't believe he's even capable of such a thing."

"I think that's a good idea," I agreed, "he might be more receptive to you."

"Well, she can't go in there alone," said Harrison.

"I'll go with her," I said, "Harrison, you should come, too. You've known him for a long time. *Is* he capable of murder?"

"I would be shocked, to say the least."

I realized Rebecca must have been in the kitchen with Sébastien. She didn't socialize much and always seemed to be in the kitchen doing something. *Did she suspect she was working alongside a killer?* Someone had to warn her.

"Alright," I said, "Harrison, Victoria, and I will talk to the chef and make sure Rebecca is alright. The rest of you stay within earshot of our conversation in case something goes wrong."

WHEN WE APPROACHED the kitchen from the dining room, we heard the *clanging* of pots and pans. Sébastien and Rebecca were like busy beavers: scraping leftovers into containers, emptying clean dishes from the dishwasher, wiping down countertops, and mopping floors, all while preparing our decadent evening snack.

Sébastien didn't look like a guilty person. In fact, if anything, he appeared downright blissful. While he moved from the dishwasher to the refrigerator, whistling some little ditty, his mustache fluttered off his lip.

"Everything alright in here?" I said, trying to feel the vibe in the room.

"*Oui, c'est fantastique!*" said the chef. He grabbed a container of strawberries from the top shelf of the refrigerator. "Why do you ask?"

"Maybe you should sit down, Sébastien," said Harrison. "We need to talk."

Sébastien and Rebecca looked at the three of us standing before them, and the chef continued to be unreadable.

"What's this all about?" Rebecca asked, removing dinner plates from the dishwasher.

"We found the murder weapon!" Victoria blurted out.

The plates nearly slipped from Rebecca's hand as she tried to place them in the cupboard. "What? You found the murder weapon? Where? Who—"

"Do you want to tell her, Sébastien?" I said.

Now, he looked guilty.

He set the strawberries in the sink and wandered to a stool on the far side of the kitchen, plopping down as if he had lost the use of his muscles. Before he spoke, he set his gaze on Victoria.

"*Oui*, I put the stick in the fire."

"Sébastien!" Victoria cried. "You killed Caffrey?"

At that moment, the guilt on Sébastien's face changed to confusion. He shook his head, blood draining from his cheeks. He was visibly shaken.

"Answer the question, Chef," said Harrison.

"*Non*," he answered, still fixated on Victoria. "I thought you did it."

49

It was the chef...wait! The maid?

AT THIS POINT, the rest of the group barged into the kitchen. And although the kitchen was marvelously large, it was not large enough to accommodate a throng of interlopers eager to watch the drama unfold.

"Maybe we should take this into the dining room," I said.

As I led the way, questions flooded my mind. *Did Victoria kill Caffrey? And if so, why did Sébastien have the pool cue? Did she kill Henry, too?*

We sat around the table, patiently waiting for Victoria to speak. If anything, I thought this would be the perfect time to admit to the affair I assumed she was hiding.

"No," Victoria began. "How could you possibly think I could kill Caffrey?" Her eyes pleaded with Sébastien. "And before you even ask, no! I didn't kill Henry either. I didn't even know him."

He looked confused. Why did he think he had to cover for her? His behavior suggested as much. He and Harrison were like overprotective uncles.

"So," I said, "did you remove the murder weapon from the library?"

Sébastien wiped his face with a towel. The interrogation had begun, and he was now in the hot seat. "You don't understand," he said, "Victoria is like a daughter to me. I couldn't bear to see anything happen to her."

"But why did you think Victoria was the killer?" asked Madeline.

The chef again peered at Victoria through watered eyes but said nothing.

"Sooner or later, you're going to have to talk, chef," said Sam. "I think you better start now."

"It's okay, Sébastien," said Victoria. "This is all going to come out anyway." She pulled herself away from the table and began pacing the room. Perhaps it was for an easy escape.

"I know why he thought I might have killed Caffrey," said Victoria. Her sigh was deep and shaky. "When Caffrey first came to the lodge six months ago, we became quick friends. And no! We were *not* having an affair. Did we share secrets? Yes. But we never crossed the line because I knew he was seeing Rebecca. But, I did share something with him that I didn't share with Rebecca."

Rebecca's glare was like a laser beam. "What was that?"

"Well...I—I've been diagnosed with kleptomania."

"That's the stealing thing, right?" said Gretchen.

"Well, yes. I take things that don't belong to me, but I can't help it." She took a breath before continuing. "I've been known to slip an item into my pocket while cleaning the rooms, and sometimes I don't realize it until the end of the day."

"Seriously?" barked Gretchen. "You're stealing from us?"

"Well, I *had* been doing extremely well. I hadn't taken anything in such a long time. But seeing the pink suitcase in your room…it must have triggered something."

"What did you take?"

"I—I don't know if I took anything from your room." She shrugged. "But I did take something from Quinn—which I've already confessed to."

"What about the rest of us," said Madeline. "Were you snooping in our rooms? Did you steal from us too?"

"No!" she said emphatically; then she began to waver. "I don't think so…but it's possible."

"Well, my dear," said Eleanor, "that doesn't sound like a good reason to kill Caffrey."

"Of course, it isn't! If anything, I was carrying a much bigger secret, something that I assumed no one else knew."

Rebecca scoffed. "What secret could you be keeping that I don't know about?"

"I'm not saying you don't know, considering you were dating him."

"What is it?" said Jason.

"Caffrey made me promise not to say a word. He said his life could be in danger if anyone found out."

"Oh, for goodness sake," Madeline said, "tell us already!"

Harrison grabbed her hand. "Whatever it is, Victoria, I'm sure it can't be that bad."

"Besides," Quinn said, "Caffrey's dead. It doesn't matter if you tell his secret."

"True, but I'm afraid you might jump to conclusions if I tell you."

Victoria turned to Harrison, pursed her lips together, and mouthed, "I'm sorry."

"Heavens!" said Harrison. "What is it?"

"Caffrey was Mr. Whitmore's son."

50

Plot twist

I WAS WIRED. The last thing I needed was another cup of coffee, which had a soothing effect when dealing with things of this nature. However, I suspected the display of rainbow macarons lying before me would not help much with my insomnia. Nonetheless, I was first at the plate.

As I nibbled on a coral-colored cookie, I wondered why we had only just learned of Caffrey's last name. How did it not come up in conversation? Perhaps it was because of his *first* name. Like Bono or Drake, Caffrey was unique. It didn't occur to me he even *had* a last name.

But this only stirred up more questions. Questions that needed answering.

I studied Harrison's reaction, which seemed to imply deception of some kind. "Did you know Caffrey was Mr. Whitmore's son, Harrison?"

He threw up his hands in defense. "I just found out a couple of days ago, I can assure you."

"When, exactly, did you find out?" asked Gretchen.

"It was just before you all arrived. Thursday. Yes, I believe it was Thursday, but I didn't feel the need to inform everyone. It didn't seem relevant."

"Not relevant?" said Jason, standing to his feet. "Even after his death?"

Harrison didn't answer.

"Did the rest of the staff know about your conversation with Mr. Whitmore...about taking over the lodge?"

"What do you mean, taking over?" said Sébastien.

"Well...I...um—"

"Take your time, Harrison," said Rebecca, "I'm interested in the answer."

"Right—yes, of course. We *did* have a conversation, but it was through emails only. There was a possibility I was to inherit the lodge. Mr. Whitmore was supposed to join us this weekend; I assumed to make the announcement."

I wondered if much of this "conversation" was fact or just wishful thinking. "Did Mr. Whitmore say he was passing the lodge down to you?"

"Well, not in those words, exactly. But he did imply he was looking for someone reliable, competent, and knowledgeable of the day-to-day. Naturally, I assumed it was me to whom he was referring. Whom else would he be talking about? At that point, I was unaware that he even *had* a son, let alone an heir to take over when he was gone."

"It must have made you quite angry," I said, "when you discovered Caffrey was not only Mr. Whitmore's son but here to take over. After all, you were the one who kept this place running for the past twenty-two years, not Caffrey."

"I was perturbed. At first. But if you're insinuating I killed Caffrey over sour grapes, then you, I'm afraid, are quite mistaken."

"But it was you," said Sam, "who found the body. You had the motive, the means, *and* the opportunity. Give us a reason why we should believe you had nothing to do with the murder?"

"Because I can prove I had no motive to kill Caffrey."

"This should be good," Gretchen said, leaning back in her chair.

"No one knew I had spoken to Caffrey before his…"—he cleared his throat—"untimely death. It was when he stumbled out of the dining room yesterday. He looked quite ill, perhaps even a bit out of sorts."

"You mean drunk."

He grimaced. "Yes, Madeline, quite. It seemed he was rather intoxicated, and I asked him if he was alright. He mumbled something under his breath that I couldn't make out. Then he repeated it."

"What did he say," asked Quinn.

"His words were garbled, 'My father wants me to meet someone,' or something to that effect. I asked him who his father was. He said, 'Whitmore.' I asked him if he was here for the lodge."

"And?" said Elenor. "What did he say?"

"He laughed."

"Hmm," said Truman. "It's interesting to me that you kept this juicy bit out of your account on your whereabouts after the murder.

Harrison nodded. "I realize I probably should have told you all this before now. But I knew you would think I had killed Caffrey, which, in fact, I did not."

"It still doesn't *prove* anything," said Quinn. "The fact that you learned Mr. Whitmore was Caffrey's father only days before his death gives you the best motive."

"Exactly," I said. "You realized that all the hard work you put into the lodge over the past twenty-two years was in vain. Caffrey would be boss now, and you couldn't handle that."

"No!" shouted Harrison. "I took Caffrey upstairs to his room and gave him some water."

"If he had no intention of running the lodge," said Sam, "why was he even here?"

"I don't know; I can't answer that question. But the strange thing is he uttered something else."

I leaned my elbows on the table, wondering where this would lead. "What did he say?"

"He said, 'They're trying to kill me.'"

"Again, Harrison," said Jason, "this would have been good to know."

"Who was trying to kill him?" said Elenor.

"I haven't the foggiest."

"You sure he said they and not he…or she?"

"I'm positive."

"Assuming you're telling the truth," I said, "this doesn't explain why anyone would want to kill Henry? What does he have to do with anything?"

"I don't know," said Harrison, rubbing his chin with his thumb and index finger. "But I must admit, it's quite the vexed question."

51

Too much caffeine

SPENDING THE BETTER part of the evening discussing motives, theories, and alibis had me thinking we were close to finding the killer; at least some riveting information had come to light.

The most intriguing news was not Sébastien removing the pool cue from the crime scene to protect Victoria—although that was a bit of a jaw-dropper. No. The part that had us all talking late into the night was unearthing the relationship between Caffrey and Mr. Whitmore. It was notably a clear-cut motive, as far as Harrison was concerned.

On the other hand, Victoria quashed the affair rumor. But that didn't absolve Rebecca; she still could have suspected an affair, which meant she still had a motive.

I crawled into bed, knowing a good night's sleep was out of the question. I lay there, wondering how the next day would play out in my mind and if the killer was thinking the same thing. Were they worried time was running out? Did they fear we were close to foiling their plan?

What if the killer barged through the door, assuming I had found a clue that would solve the murder? A troubling thought, I know. I sat up, pressing my fingers against the throb of my head. Overthinking was not at all productive.

Quinn had propped herself against the headboard, her book sprawled over her chest like a blanket. She seemed to be immersed in just as much thought as I was. "Can't sleep either, huh?"

"Not one bit," she said. "I thought once we found the murder weapon, we'd have our killer."

"I know. You'd think it'd be an open-and-shut case. What about Harrison? He could have done it."

Quinn laced her fingers behind her head and stared at the ceiling. "True. But he pleaded his case so adamantly that I almost felt sorry for him. Almost."

"We know he can act; he may have just given us the performance of a lifetime. There are too many things that don't add up. For starters, if Caffrey wasn't here to take over the lodge, why not tell Harrison? Why keep him in the dark for so long?"

"I know. And why keep his last name a secret?"

"And why would the killer mislead us into believing he and Henry were poisoned with nutmeg when they were clearly poisoned with something else?"

"Exactly," added Quinn. "What about all the guests who seem to have a connection to Mr. Whitmore? Maybe they're all in it together somehow."

I laughed. "Sure, and Elenor is the ringleader."

"Ha! Somehow, I can't picture her barking out orders...but stranger things have happened—especially here at the lodge."

I let the clues percolate before having another thought. "What if…"

"What if what?" said Quinn, swinging her legs over the side of the bed.

"What if we're looking at this thing all wrong."

"What do you mean?"

"What if the intended target wasn't Caffrey at all…or Henry?"

"Okay."

I threw off the covers and leaped out of bed. I loved it when a clear thought surfaced. Maybe it was the coffee or the exuberant amounts of sugar I'd ingested over the last couple of days. Still, the adrenaline coursing through my veins was enough to kick my brain into overdrive. "Okay, so we know that, according to Harrison, the only reason Caffrey was still at the lodge was because he was supposed to meet someone."

"I'm with you so far."

"That would mean it's someone here now…either a guest or one of the staff members."

"You're losing me, Scarlet. Of course, it's someone here. I think we've at least established that much."

"Stay with me," I said, pacing the room.

"Okay, but I think you may need to cut down on the coffee."

I pointed my finger at her in all seriousness. "You're probably right, but it's working for me and not against me right now."

"Continue."

"Don't you think it's odd that Mr. Whitmore was planning a trip to the lodge on this particular weekend? As far as we know, he hasn't been to the lodge in the last twenty-two years.

So why now? Why, after all this time, would he decide to come to the mountains during a snowstorm?"

"I don't know."

"You know what I think?"

Quinn just stared at me, so I continued.

"I think that Jason was right. Maybe someone here at the lodge was out to get Mr. Whitmore. They somehow found out he was preparing a trip to the lodge and figured it was the best place to kill him. I suspect Caffrey stumbled onto something he wasn't supposed to. It would make sense if the killer, or killers, knew Caffrey was on to them; naturally, they would have to kill him. That would explain why Caffrey seemed a little off when I first met him. He might have already known about the killer before the tour or, at least, suspected trouble."

"So, all we gotta do now is figure out who that is...which we've been trying to do for the past two days."

"Maybe I'll have another talk with Jason in the morning and see if he can tell me anything new."

"I like the theory," said Quinn. "However, there's a couple of things wrong with it."

"Like what?"

"Why isn't Mr. Whitmore here, and what does Henry have to do with it?"

I was coming down from my high, and I felt disgusted with myself for eating so poorly. I knew my body was telling me to smarten up and get some rest. "How about we sleep on it," I said. "Maybe something will come to us in a dream."

52

In the right place at the right time

I MUST HAVE fallen asleep sometime after two. However, something startled me into a sitting position before my body could descend into a deep slumber. It took me a minute to recall where I was, but once the cool air swept across my face and my eyes adjusted to the darkness, I knew exactly where I was.

Quinn was sleeping like a baby, and the thought of nudging her—just a little—tumbled through my mind. But what kind of friend would I be if I disturbed her from such a peaceful state? I decided to let her sleep; I could snoop on my own.

I sensed the angry roar in my stomach and suspected that was the reason I was awake. Convincing myself a covert investigation required some kind of snack, I grabbed my hoodie from the end of the bed and slid into a pair of slippers.

Abandoning the safety of my room, I padded down the hall toward the stairs. Again, I lowered myself to the top, hoping for a silent descent.

When I reached the bottom, I heard noises coming from the kitchen. I wondered who else was experiencing the midnight pangs of the munchies. I infiltrated the dining room, about to push through the swinging doors, but heard voices spilling through the crack.

"You said this was going to be easy," said a voice.

"Well, it was supposed to be," whispered another. "But you're the one who overreacted with that pool cue, so now our plans have changed."

"That's because you didn't use enough."

"How was I supposed to know it wouldn't kill him?"

"And what about Henry? He wasn't part of the plan."

"It'll be fine. Just stay calm."

"How can you be so sure? Scarlet's nosy, and she will figure something out sooner or later."

"And by the time she does, we'll be long gone."

"What'd ya mean?"

"Don't worry, I've got a plan…you just need to be patient. And don't say anything that will screw this up for us. We've been planning this too long, and I intend to see it through. Soon enough, we'll have enough money to retire on an island far away from this place. So keep it together."

"Fine. Let's go!"

I quickly moved away from the door and crouched down on the other side of the bar. Hoping they weren't in the mood for a hot toddy, I sat there until I heard them leave.

So, there were two killers.

How was this going to play out, I wondered. It was tempting to follow them, but I was scared I'd get caught. I could still figure out who the killers were while leaving the apprehending to someone else. Obviously, the murder didn't quite go according to plan, which was perfect—at least for me. It meant the killers already made a mistake; if they could make one, they were bound to make another.

I waited for another minute before peeking my head over the bar. Once the coast was clear, my first instinct was to make a beeline back to the room, but I knew my stomach wouldn't allow for a restful night until something substantial fed it. I rummaged through the kitchen like a raccoon in a dumpster and settled on a banana smothered in peanut butter.

When my hunger was adequately dealt with, I skirted back to my room and mulled over the conversation I had just witnessed. It would have been nice to chat about theories with Quinn, but since she was out like a light, I'd have to wait until morning.

53

The killer has escaped!
Sunday

IT WAS A SHORT night but a productive one. And it took everything within me not to cannonball onto Quinn's bed. According to my watch, it was only seven o'clock, but patience had never been my strong suit. The fact I had considered every possible scenario of who could be the killers for most of the night—while Quinn slept like a baby—made me anxious to start the day. And watching her sleep (like she was some kind of expert) irritated me.

She began to stir, so I excitedly hovered over her like a hummingbird. "Finally!" I mumbled. Now was my chance to wake her before she launched another REM cycle. I shook her, expecting an immediate response. "You awake?"

But when she moaned and pulled the covers over her head, I threw all niceties out the window. "Quinn!" I shouted. "Get up! I know who killed Caffrey."

She whipped the blankets off her face and sat up like a Jack-in-the-Box. "Wha—what do you mean?" Deep, red lines circled her cheeks, and her hair stood straight off her head like she'd hit a wall head-on—it was not a good look.

"Looks like you slept well," I said, laced with a heavy dose of envy.

"I *was* sleeping well."

"Come on! Get up!"

She rubbed her eyes and begrudgingly threw her legs over the side of the bed, letting them dangle as she stretched. "You're already dressed? Did you even sleep?"

I went into the bathroom and turned on the hot water in the shower. "No. Too wired to sleep, but I'll fill you in once you're ready."

"Ready for what, exactly?"

I grabbed a towel off the rack and threw it across the room, impressively connecting with Quinn's head. "We have a big day ahead of us. We're going to catch a killer."

YESTERDAY, WHEN I stepped into the hallway, it was steeped in sugary goodness; however, the only thing that tingled my senses today was the blueberry waffle body wash permeating Quinn's freshly showered skin. Not only were no heavenly aromas wafting from the kitchen, but it was eerily quiet.

Too quiet.

"Maybe it's just a continental breakfast this morning," I said, hoping it wasn't so.

Quinn pulled her phone from her back pocket. "It's almost eight...you think everyone slept in?"

"Doubt it...but something's up."

We hustled down the stairs, and I noticed the fire in the den wasn't burning with its usual flare. "It feels extra warm in here this morning."

"Actually," said Quinn, "the floor upstairs wasn't as cold either."

"The power must be back on."

"I wonder if the phones are back up and running, too?"

"Let's go check, but first, let's see what's for breakfast…I'm starving."

Quinn laughed. "What else is new?"

My stomach was venting again, and I was beginning to think a worm had taken up residency inside my body. I would have to deal with that disturbing thought later. First, I had to deal with a deserted dining room.

"Where is everybody?"

"No clue," said Quinn, pushing into the kitchen.

I saw what looked like an attempt at breakfast. Bowls were out, eggs cracked, coffee perked, and the fruit had been sliced and arranged on a decorative plate. But the kitchen was void of people. *Where did they go?*

At the same time, we heard a commotion rising from somewhere outside. We ran back to the dining room to look out the window. Everyone was embroiled in a passionate dispute. "Wonder what that's all about?"

"I say we go find out!" said Quinn.

We grabbed our coats and boots and labored up the hill to see an agitated crowd huddled around the big rock. "What's going on?" I asked.

"The killer has just escaped," said Truman, pointing his finger out over the snow.

"What do you mean escaped…who?"

Madeline was as frantic as usual. "It was Harrison—I knew he was the killer. He just hopped on a snowmobile and took off down the road without saying a word."

"We heard him starting it up and ran out here to see where he was going," said Gretchen. "No sooner did we get outside, he escaped through that path over there and onto the road."

"A snowmobile," I said, "where did that come from?"

"I don't know," said Jason, "but wherever it was, it seemed to be waiting for Harrison."

"Interesting." I reflected on the conversation I overheard the night before. It was all starting to make sense. I just needed to keep everyone calm. "It looks like the power is back on. Has anyone checked the phones to see if they are working?"

"No," said Sam.

"We should go back inside," said Madeline. "Maybe we can finally call someone to get us out of here."

"What about Harrison?" Gretchen said, waving her hand toward the road. "We can't just let him get away."

"We'll deal with him later," said Sam. "At least now we know who the killer is."

"Come on," I said. "Let's go! Maybe the police are on the way."

"PHONES ARE STILL DOWN," I said, returning to the den.

"Well, that just sucks!" Madeline said, slumping further into her mood.

I threw a couple of logs on the fire since Harrison wasn't there to do it. Immediately, a dense smoke billowed off the wood, causing my eyes to water and stirring up an irritating tickle in my throat. I assumed the logs must have been damp because sparks were flying everywhere.

"I can't believe there was a snowmobile here this whole time," said Jason, oblivious to the fact I was struggling to keep the smoke at bay. "We could have used it to go get help. Although, it makes sense why Harrison didn't say anything."

"Whose is it anyway?" Sam asked.

"To be honest," said Victoria, "I didn't know there was one out there. I have no idea where it came from."

"It wasn't there when we did the tour," said Elenor. "Or at least I didn't see it."

"That's because Caffrey didn't take us up to the rock; it was probably hiding in the trees."

I appeased the angry fire with a few strategic pokes before joining Quinn on the sofa, as far away from the fire as possible. The group had already launched into deep conversation, debating whether Harrison could even be *capable* of getting away with murder. And while I tried to keep my attention on theories spouting from one person to the next, something distracted me.

Up until this point, I wasn't entirely convinced. But at that precise moment, it all became crystal clear.

I know who both killers are!

But the unraveling would have to wait.

Out of the blue, the roar from a snowmobile racing down the parking lot interrupted our earnest deliberation into an eery silence.

Quietly, we listened.

A few seconds later, the door swung open, bringing a state of befuddlement.

"Harrison!" yelled Madeline, leaping to her feet.

A familiar scene unfolded. Harrison waddled to the entrance of the den. His face was red as an apple, and his breath labored like an old jalopy struggling to start. He removed his hat and held up his hand. "I know you must be wondering where I ran off to in such a panic, but I finally got word from Mr. Whitmore. He managed to make it halfway up the mountain but, as I suspected, got his limousine wedged in a ditch."

"Why didn't you tell us about the snowmobile?" Jason said.

"I didn't even know about it. But this morning, while gathering firewood, I saw the shimmer through the trees. Naturally, I was curious and trekked up there to see what it was. Of course, I planned on apprising you of the discovery at breakfast, but when I read the email from Mr. Whitmore, I thought it best to use the snowmobile for the rescue."

"So where did it come from?" Truman asked.

"I haven't the foggiest. But what luck! I wouldn't have made it down the road without it."

"Well," said Sam, "did you find him?"

And then, it happened.

Harrison stepped aside, allowing a tall, white-haired man wearing a long, black trench coat to enter the den. He flicked snow from his shoulders with a gloved hand like some notorious villain from a mystery novel and awaited his introduction.

"Everyone," said Harrison, "meet Mr. Whitmore."

54

The plot thickens!

I HAD MORE confidence in believing that Mr. Whitmore was a figment of a few overactive imaginations than considering him an actual live person.

But there he was.

Before this moment, no one at the lodge had ever met him face to face. But he was there, standing before us like a fictional character coming to life.

"Thomas!"

Okay. Apparently, someone *had* met Mr. Whitmore before.

Collectively, we turned our heads in time to see the blood drain from Gretchen's face. "I—I didn't think you were coming."

"No," he said, shaking his coat to rid the snow. "I don't suppose you did."

"You know Mr. Whitmore?" asked Jason.

"Of course she does. I'm Thomas Whitmore, the owner of Mystery Ridge Lodge." He walked across the hardwood, leaving slushy puddles everywhere. "And this is my beautiful wife."

Okay, what?

You could have heard the rumble in my stomach, probably because we were all shocked into silence (not to mention I hadn't eaten breakfast yet).

"I thought you said you were separated," said Elenor. "Isn't that why you came to the lodge?"

"Yes—yes, of course...I—"

"Separated?" Thomas uttered a thunderous laugh. "Is that what you told them? I think you may have omitted a few crucial details, don't you think, my dear?"

"Thomas, you don't understand—"

"Oh, I understand more than you think I do."

"Is anyone else as confused as I am?" Madeline fell onto the sofa and crossed her arms.

Gretchen slid from Mr. Whitmore's grasp, securing a seat next to Madeline. She rubbed her eyes with both fists but still managed to send an icy glare his way.

"Well," said Thomas, "I guess you've all had quite the eventful weekend. Harrison filled me in. And I'm sure, by now, you're all aware that Caffrey was my son."

"I'm so sorry for your loss," I said, not knowing what else to say. The rest of the guests followed my lead with their condolences.

"Thank you. I was devastated when Harrison broke the news, but not surprised."

That's an odd thing to say after hearing your son's been murdered.

"On my travels to the lodge on Friday evening, the snow became too thick to continue up the mountain. My driver decided it was best to take a hotel; we would try again when the roads cleared."

"Where is your driver?" Sam asked.

Thomas chuckled. "I'm afraid he's still back at the hotel. I let him sleep while I attempted the trek this morning alone. I would have taken him along for his brute strength had I known I'd get myself stuck. I'm not as young as I used to be. I've called him, and he's aware of the situation."

"Maybe he'll come with the police," Madeline murmured.

"Anyway, I was made aware of Caffrey's passing that evening. I—"

"How could you have possibly heard about the murder?" Gretchen's eyes were red from rubbing them so hard, and she was still reeling from the fact that Thomas had made it to the lodge."

"I had arranged for someone to keep me apprised of everything that happened."

"Like a mole? Who?" Gretchen barked.

My first thought was Jason. After all, he told me that Mr. Whitmore had hired him. But when Truman slid to the edge of his seat, I was confused.

"It was me," said Truman.

"Yes," said Thomas, "Mr. Gladstone has been very helpful these past few days."

"How were you even able to communicate with Mr. Whitmore?" I asked. "The phones were down, and our cell phones weren't getting any service…were you emailing him?"

"Actually, the phones *were* working."

"That's absurd," said Harrison. "If they were, don't you think we would have rung the police?"

"We could have if you hadn't disconnected all the phones."

"Wait! What?" Madeline got up and ran to the phone in the lobby. "The wire thingy is still in the wall." She picked up the receiver. "But there's still nothing."

"That's because the landline was disabled from the box outside."

Elenor looked at Harrison like a disappointed mother. "Why would you prevent us from calling the police?"

Harrison took a sheepish step back. "I can explain."

"You better," said Madeline, "the police could have made arrangements a couple of days ago to get us out of here. What were you thinking?"

"I—I understand how upset you all must be. But I was only thinking about the lodge. I didn't want the police coming back here to find Victoria's plunder in the shed. They've already been out here once." He turned to Thomas, his cheeks as red as ever. "Oh, Mr. Whitmore…I'm sorry you had to find out this way."

"Nonsense, Harrison. I'm aware of everything that goes on in the lodge. I've been aware of Miss Hale's disorder for years. I was confident that you would protect her. And I was correct, wasn't I? It seems you went to great lengths to shield her from the police. I knew I hired the right man for this job." He smiled and gave an approving nod to Harrison.

"How did you know about the phones, Truman?" asked Sam.

"It was my business to know. I have kept a close eye on all of you. When we all went up to change out of our costumes, I noticed Harrison heading downstairs with a screwdriver, but not before I made a call to Mr. Whitmore. There was no answer, but I left a message, apprising him of what happened.

I quietly followed Harrison outside through the laundry room. It didn't take a genius to know what he was up to. When I ran upstairs to my room, my suspicions were confirmed. There was no dial tone when I picked up the receiver."

"I knew he was up to something," I whispered to Quinn.

"But you decided to play along," said Jason. "Why?"

"Because I asked him to," said Mr. Whitmore. "I figured since I couldn't make it to the lodge, the killer would be stuck here too."

"But we still don't know who that is," said Elenor.

I weighed out the tension in the room and concluded it was as good a time as any to begin the unraveling. Butterflies rushed through my stomach as I zeroed in on my target. "I think I can shed some light on who that might be."

"By all means," said Mr. Whitmore, waving his hand to give me the floor."

I smiled and glanced at Gretchen, who had pulled out a small bottle of Visine from her sweater pocket. "It must be quite an inconvenience to have winter allergies."

She scowled at me, placing a few drops in each eye. "It is. I can usually tolerate a fire or two, but something in the wood here is causing my eyes to burn."

"When you first arrived and stood in front of the fire, your eyes were quite red; later, when you came down for the meet and greet, they were fine."

"What's your point?" She screwed on the cap and placed the bottle back in her pocket.

This was it—the answer to everyone's question. I was about to reveal the killer. Sure, I was used to delivering satisfying conclusions on paper in the privacy of my own home, where I could step away from my laptop for a few hours before returning to edit. But now, I had to lay out my thought process in the presence of people I've only known for three days—not to mention call out a cold-blooded killer.

I took a deep breath. *Well, here goes nothing.*

"Is that what you used to poison Caffrey?"

Again, silence fell over the room.

"What are you talking about, Scarlet?" She took out the bottle again and shook it. A clear liquid swooshed near the top of the lid. "It's full. I'm pretty sure you can't kill someone with a few drops of Visine."

"Well," said Elenor, "you could have brought two bottles."

"If you must know, I only brought one."

"That's because you filled up a spice bottle with Visine before coming to the lodge."

Gretchen leaped to her feet.

"Ridiculous! What purpose would that have served? Why put Visine into a spice bottle?"

"Because pouring eye drops into a thermos full of coffee would seem a little too suspicious, but shaking a little spice into Caffrey's thermos, like, say...nutmeg? Not so much. Especially because we all smelled nutmeg wafting from the steam in his coffee."

"That's absurd, Scarlet. Caffrey must have added the nutmeg himself."

"I'm sure he did. I smelled nutmeg on his breath when we first arrived. And you knew that; that's why you *chose* the nutmeg bottle. Because you wanted everyone to think he was poisoned with nutmeg. But you dosed Caffrey's thermos with Visine before we left the lodge, perhaps during the meet and greet; that's why he was acting so strange on the tour."

"But," I said, pacing the floor and holding up my index finger. "Panic set in when Caffrey hadn't succumbed to the poison. You realized he needed a much bigger dose. You returned to your room to get the vial and to fill it with more Visine, only to find it had vanished."

At this point, I directed my comment to Victoria. "I assume you took the vial from Gretchen's room?"

She shrugged. "I found it in my pocket and decided to leave it on the counter in the kitchen. I didn't even realize there was no room in the spice rack. I'm so sorry I didn't say anything."

"It's okay, Victoria."

I was on a roll and didn't want to lose momentum, so I continued. "You began to panic, Gretchen. You had to quickly craft another scheme, so you took the nutmeg bottle from the kitchen that belonged with the set in the spice rack. Your plan could still work.

"You have quite the imagination, don't you, Scarlet? I didn't murder Caffrey. I've never even been to this lodge before. Besides, Caffrey was killed with a pool cue. What do spices have to do with anything? How would I even know Caffrey liked nutmeg in his coffee?

"You wouldn't," said Quinn. "But your partner would. Isn't that right, Rebecca?"

I could see the malice in her eyes when Rebecca turned to face me. It was over, and she knew it.

"Rebecca?" Sébastien said with a gasp. "It was you...but why?"

"I had nothing to do with Caffrey's death," Rebecca insisted.

"I think you did," I said rather confidently. "You also had the means, motive, *and* opportunity. When I learned that you and Caffrey were dating, I immediately moved you to the top of the list for motive. I mean, it's the first person you look at in a murder, right? The girlfriend? And, of course, you had the means. You've worked in the kitchen for the last few months, getting to know Sébastien's habits, like when he takes his break. But I couldn't figure out how you managed to leave the kitchen, kill Caffrey, and make it back without being noticed."

"Exactly," said Rebecca. "I told you after I finished in the kitchen, I went to my room to lie down because I had a headache."

"And you did," I said, placing my hands in my pockets. "We already know that after Gretchen left the dining room after lunch, she returned to the kitchen for a glass of water—or so she said. I believe she was there to run through the plan with you. Somehow, she convinced Caffrey to meet her in the library at two O'clock…which was pretty convenient, huh? Considering that was the same time Sébastien took his break. It gave you twenty minutes to head down to the basement through the secret door in the kitchen, come up through the library to join Gretchen."

"Once Caffrey got there, maybe the plan was to distract him while Gretchen doused his thermos. But something went wrong, didn't it? Caffrey must have realized what she was attempting to do and tried to wrestle the vial out of her hand. That's when you picked up the pool cue and hit him in the head."

I could almost hear Gretchen seething. *Was she trying to intimidate me?* Well, it wasn't going to work this time. I continued.

"Sometime later, after we had discovered the body, you must have realized you had dropped the bottle and went back to the library to search for it. I'm sure you were relieved it was still there, and you figured you could grab it and return it to the kitchen with no one the wiser. The only problem was you hadn't counted on the chef replacing the old spice bottles with new ones which weren't engraved."

"Okay, so let me get this straight," said Jason. "After Gretchen got her glass of water, she went to the library to kill Caffrey?"

"Not exactly," said Quinn. "She *did* go to her room, but only because she had to wait for the sedative to work."

"Sedative?"

"Yes," I said. "Everyone knew I was to meet Gretchen in the library at two. Before leaving the dining room, Rebecca gave me a top-up of coffee, which I believe is how she drugged me. They wanted to frame me for the murder. Sam didn't see me when he came into the library to search for Truman because I was fast asleep on that comfortable sofa."

"But why?" asked Elenor. "How do you even know each other?"

Gretchen refused to talk, clenching her arms tighter with every accusation.

"I think I can answer that one," said Mr. Whitmore.

I had almost forgotten about Mr. Whitmore. He must have been flabbergasted by all that unraveling. But not as much as I was by what he said next.

"Gretchen and Rebecca are sisters. And not only that," he said, "Gretchen attempted to murder me as well."

55

She's unraveling

"THOMAS…PLEASE! You don't understand."

"Oh, sweetheart, I understand completely. But I regret failing to cripple your spiteful actions before it compelled you to murder my sons."

I was confused. "Sons?"

Mr. Whitmore closed his eyes and expelled air with a forceful sigh. "Yes. Both Caffrey and Henry were my sons."

"Gosh!" said Elenor. "This must be devastating news."

"Yes," he said, wiping the moisture from his eyes. "I knew you wanted to get your hands on my money, Gretchen; I've been on to for a while. When we married five years ago, I gave you the impression I had no children. You probably figured since that was the case, you'd be first in line to inherit my estate after I died. Unfortunately, I became estranged from my sons shortly after their mother died, and the burden I carried grieved me enough to keep that part of my life from you. But I ensured, early on, that if anything were to happen to me, my entire fortune would go to my boys. Though we hadn't spoken in nearly ten years, I knew I owed them that much.

"But six months ago, Caffrey reached out to me, saying he wanted to make amends; he was tired of living with the anger he harbored toward me. My sons never wanted to be a part of the family business."

Quinn leaned in and whispered in my ear. "I wonder how shady this family business is."

"Shh," I whispered back.

"I gotta question," said Madeline, raising her hand. "How did you know Henry was here?"

"I didn't know that Henry was actually at the lodge until Harrison informed me on the way here. But Truman has been my eyes and ears for the past ten years. He kept track of my boys, so I knew where he lived. In fact, I hired him soon after my first wife passed away."

"So, he knew who Caffrey was?" Sam asked.

"Yes," Mr. Whitmore said, acknowledging Truman with a nod. "He kept an eye out for them, but they were unaware of who he was. They wanted no part of me, but I couldn't just walk away from them. I had to know they were safe. That's why I hired Truman."

Quinn bumped my elbow. "That's why he was being so evasive."

"Shh," I hissed again, "this is getting good."

"So why do you need me?" Jason said. His arms were folded across his chest, accentuating his massive bulk.

"I beg your pardon?"

"Why did you hire me if you already had Truman here investigating for you?"

"Truman is kind of a Jack of all trades. He's been on my payroll for years. I trust him."

"So he's your bodyguard?" said Sam.

"Not exactly. That's the reason why I hired you, Jason. This weekend was going to be a trial run to see if you had what it took to be head of my security."

"You didn't say anything about heading up your security."

"I wanted to see how you would do before I offered you the position."

"Well," said Madeline, "did he get the job?"

Thomas sighed. "The weekend didn't exactly turn out the way I expected. I thought there was time to make it to the lodge before anyone could get hurt. Unfortunately, I didn't account for the weather."

The story was unfolding like one of my bizarre dreams; it made sense up to a point, but there were still some things that didn't add up. "Why didn't you tell us what was going on, Truman? If anything, we might have been able to stop Gretchen from killing Henry."

I couldn't even wait for his answer before returning to Gretchen. "I can understand how you found out that Caffrey was Mr. Whitmore's son…because he reached out to him. But how did you know that Henry was a Whitmore?"

Gretchen was in a trance, ignoring evidence that her perfect plan had been foiled. The mistakes she'd miscalculated aired in front of her as though she were on trial.

"I'm afraid I might have been to blame for that one," said Truman.

"What do you mean?"

"When Henry arrived at the lodge, I knew I had to warn him. I didn't know whether or not Gretchen was aware of who he was, and I couldn't take any chances. I confronted him outside as we took turns shoveling out our cars. He didn't seem surprised to learn I worked for Mr. Whitmore "

"Why didn't he tell us that Caffrey was his brother?" Sam asked.

"Because he knew he could be next. He said it's why he cut ties with his father in the first place; his business dealings had a way of inviting trouble into his life. I told him I would do my best to keep him safe. Unfortunately…"

"What makes you think you're to blame?" Quinn asked.

"Because when I turned to give the shovel to Sam, Rebecca was standing behind me. I sensed she overheard our conversation, and when she beelined it to Gretchen, it only boosted my suspicions.

Rebecca's demeanor hadn't changed much the entire weekend. She was hard to read. "I heard no such thing," was her only comment.

"Why couldn't you reach Mr. Whitmore?" I asked.

"Well," said Mr. Whitmore, "that brings me to why I couldn't make it to the lodge on Friday. The last thing I remember was kissing Gretchen goodbye on Friday morning. I could still see her smug smile as she walked through the door. The next thing I remember is waking up on the kitchen floor several hours later. I must have passed out. I'm guessing, my sweet Gretchen, that you tried to poison my morning coffee?" He patted her knee. "Thought I was dead, didn't you?"

Gretchen jumped up, with much more hysteria this time. "This is crazy! I don't have to listen to this garbage anymore. There's a get-away vehicle out there, and I intend to use it."

Rebecca stood up as well. "I'm right behind you. Let's get out of here."

There was no way I was going to sit there and let Gretchen and Rebecca get away with murder. Our plan was to smoke out a killer, and that's what I did—literally.

"You're not going anywhere. In fact, you'll sit there and wait for the police to arrive."

"That's where you're wrong, Nancy Drew. I've had just about enough of your meddling. If it weren't for you sticking your nose where it didn't belong, *you'd* be the one accused of murder...not me."

I left the comfort and safety of the loveseat and advanced toward Gretchen. I wasn't exactly sure what to do once I reached her, but I was invincible. Like I had just uncovered the biggest mystery of all time and was about to apprehend the killer...like a detective.

But, as with all best-laid plans, there was a scenario I hadn't thought through.

"Scarlet, what are you doing?"

I didn't even feel the tug on my sweater from Quinn trying to hold me back.

I was focused. Determine. Fixated on my goal.

Then it happened.

The thing I didn't see coming.

In that brief moment, when I felt like I could take on the world, Gretchen reached for the poker and swung.

56

It was a what?

THE AIR WAS nauseatingly clean, and I could no longer feel the warmth of the fire on my skin. I attempted to move but discovered I'd been tucked into a stiff, white sheet, wreaking of caustic bleach and hand sanitizer. What happened to the soft Egyptian cotton that wrapped me in the sweet floral scent of lavender?

I opened my eyes, unprepared to see the rustic charm of the lodge replaced with a white canvas of nothingness. I freed myself from the sterile linens and, once again, tried to sit up; my attempt was greeted with a wave of queasiness and a sharp pain. I raised my hand, splaying my fingers across a thick bandage wrapped tightly around my head. *Gretchen must have really walloped me.*

"You're awake!"

I turned toward the voice, my eyes still adjusting to the fluorescent lights in the room.

Quinn placed her hand on my arm and repeated herself. "You're awake!"

"I'm a little groggy…and my head is killing me."

"It's no wonder. You took a *beating* to the head. We didn't think you were going to make it."

"Really?"

"Of course! We've been worried sick. Dominic is out getting coffee; he should be back soon. He's been beside himself."

"So you were finally able to reach him?"

"What are you talking about? Yes. I called him right after the accident."

"Ha! I wouldn't call it an accident. More like attempted murder. Did she get away?"

"Did who get away?"

My eyes focused enough to see a bandage over Quinn's face, and her arm was in a sling. "Did *she* do that to you?"

"Scarlet, are you okay? Who are you—"

"Scarlet! Thank heavens you're awake. Are you alright?"

"Dominic," I said as he kissed me on the forehead, "I'm sorry I left without saying goodbye."

"Babe, don't worry about that. I'm just glad you're alright."

"Where is everybody else? Were they allowed to go home? Did the police come?"

"I think she might have a concussion," said Quinn. "She's been talking kinda weird."

"Well? Did the police get there in time?"

"You mean, did the police come to the scene?"

"Yeah…to the lodge."

"What lodge, Scarlet? What are you talking about?"

"I see you're awake and talking," said a doctor entering the room. "That's a good sign."

"I'm just confused. No one will tell me how I got here or if the police arrested Gretchen."

"I see," said the doctor.

"She's been talking about police and a lodge," said Quinn. "I'm not sure that's such a great sign."

"I'm sorry, babe, but who's Gretchen?"

"She killed Caffrey."

"Caffrey?" Dominic laughed. "I think maybe we've been watching too many episodes of *White Collar*."

"No—it's not funny. Gretchen put Visine in his thermos, and when that didn't work, she killed him with a pool cue. Or maybe it was Rebecca—I don't know, but they were in on it together."

"Oh dear," said the doctor. "You may have hit your head harder than we thought."

"What do you mean, hit my head? Gretchen hit me with a fireplace poker. I was trying to stop her from getting away. Isn't that what happened to you, Quinn? Did Gretchen hit you with the poker, too?"

"Oh, Scarlet. Don't you remember? We were in a car accident. We hit a moose."

"No—I mean, yes, I remember that. But we only grazed him. Henry saw the whole thing."

"Henry?"

"Yes! His big truck helped get your car out of the ditch. He came to the lodge and—and Gretchen killed him too."

"No, Scarlet! We got in a terrible accident. The moose totaled the car, and you hit the windshield so hard I was sure you were—"

"That can't be," I said, frustrated they weren't listening. We made it. The moose made it, too. You were fine, and I—I did hit my head, but I was sure we were okay. We made it to the lodge, and Harrison was there. Victoria stole your Angora sweater, and there was a secret tunnel and—

"Okay, okay," said the doctor, "maybe we should let you sleep a little longer. He nodded to a nearby nurse. "This should help you relax a bit."

"Thank you, Dr. Whitmore," said Dominic.

"Whitmore!" I yelled. "Did you say, Whitmore? You were there too, except you didn't look like you. You own the lodge and—and Gretchen is your wife and Caffrey's your son… and…Henry is too. Nutmeg…there was nutmeg…but…that's not what killed Ca…"

"She's asleep. It's probably best we let her be for a bit. She has quite the active imagination, doesn't she?"

"She's a mystery writer," said Dominic. "She's always loved a good mystery."

"Yes," said Quinn, "but she's having trouble coming up with the ending to her latest novel."

"Well, it sounds like she's been hanging out on the pages of one of her books. She'll be as good as new with a little rest."

"Thanks again, doc."

"Maybe you two should try and get some sleep as well. I suspect Scarlet won't wake up until morning."

I WOKE TO the sweet aroma of baked goods and freshly brewed coffee. My mouth salivated as I watched cream cheese frosting slide off a cinnamon bun sitting on a plate beside my bed.

I slowly rolled to my back, thrilled that Quinn and Dominic were still there and so close to my bed that they were almost on top of me.

"Hey, you feeling any better?" Dominic grabbed my hand and squeezed.

The events from the previous day were fuzzy, but I recalled being quite upset that no one would take me seriously. I rubbed my head and flinched. "I think so," I said, not entirely convinced.

"You were saying some pretty crazy stuff yesterday," said Quinn.

"I was, wasn't I? You know, it still seems so real. I must have dreamed it. You know how my dreams are in the best of times."

Dominic chuckled. "Oh, I'm aware."

I looked into his big, brown eyes and touched his face. "I'm pretty sure you were in my dream, too."

"Oh, really?"

"Yeah, I—I think you were Caffrey."

He laughed. "Oh! You killed me off in your dream, huh?"

"Not only that," I said, laughing with him, "I think a few people from Mahogany Falls made it in there as well."

"Not surprised there," said Quinn. "You serve coffee to them every single day."

"You would have been so proud, Quinn. I had spunk and confidence and even took the lead on the investigation."

"Now, I know you were dreaming."

"And you know what? I kinda liked it. Not sure I'm ready to channel the Scarlet from my dreams, but I have made one decision."

"What's that?"

"I'm not ending the Chase Ridgeway series. He makes me happy; I think he makes my readers happy, too."

"That's awesome! I'm sure Joan will be pleased."

"I guess the question is," said Dominic, wiping frosting from my chin, "do you have an ending to your book?"

Finally, I propped myself to a sitting position and took another bite from my cinnamon bun. And after washing it down with the best-tasting coffee I'd had in three days, I smiled.

"Pass me my laptop."

57

The Chase

An assault of snow and ice peppered his face as Chase gained momentum down the mountain. It was a quick descent and one he was too old for.

How did he even get here? For years, the only goal was to bring his wife's killer to justice, hoping there'd come a day when he'd let his guard down. Now, finally, a mistake that had Chase reuniting with Richard Wells in a setting he'd never thought possible. Who could have imagined he'd bump into him while on vacation? Whatever the reason, this was his chance.

But he had to catch him first.

Carefully, he moved his hand, adjusting the axe just so. With the other hand, he reached out, tickling the back of Well's jacket with the tips of his gloves.

With one last push, he lunged.

But then, a rock struck the tip of his axe, ripping it from his hand and triggering an impetuous downward plunge.

Engulfed in a deluge of snow, he continued the descent, flopping down the mountain like a fish. He heard the snap of a bone and desperately tried to gain control of his flailing limbs. The pain was sharp and excruciating but not as unbearable as realizing he'd missed his opportunity. All he could do now was surrender to his wounded body.

A few curious bystanders ran to his rescue when he collided headfirst into a snowbank, ending his pursuit abruptly. Helpless, he gazed upon Wells, climbing onto the back of a snowmobile that curiously awaited him.

Physically and mentally exhausted, Chase dropped his head in the snow. "It's not over!" he said softly, trying to push air past his dry, crackled lungs. "I won't stop…until you're behind bars."

Utterly dejected, Chase watched through heavy eyelids as the snowmobile disappeared into the sunset.

ACKNOWLEDGMENTS

Thank you for reading *The Game of Murder*. I hope you enjoyed accompanying Scarlet and Quinn on their murder mystery adventure just as much as I have.

I would especially like to thank a few special people. Patti, your constructive feedback when reading a *very* rough draft of this book. I Love your passion. Never change!

Lois, thank you for your kind words and being such a supportive and faithful friend. The world is a better place with you in it.

And, of course, I want to thank my family (Jeremy, Logan, MacKenzie, and Chloe) for allowing me to spend countless hours immersed in a world of mystery and murder. Your encouragement compelled me to do something I didn't think was possible. Love you guys!

And for the many others who have supported me along the way...thank you!

HAPPY READING!

Sign up to get the latest news on upcoming mysteries!

https://bio.site/KLeeBrown

Then follow me on social

https://www.facebook.com/profile.php?id=100088714272847

https://instagram.com/k.leebrown_author